# THE THIRTY-ONE DOORS

# THE THIRTY-ONE DOORS

## KATE HULME

CORONET

First published in Great Britain in 2022 by Coronet
An Imprint of Hodder & Stoughton
An Hachette UK company

1

A CIP catalogue record for this title is available from the British Library

Hardback ISBN 978 1 529 34401 1
Trade Paperback ISBN 978 1 529 34402 8
eBook ISBN 978 1 529 34404 2

Typeset in Fournier MT Std by Manipal Technologies Limited

Printed and bound in Great Britain by Clays Ltd, Elcograf S.p.A.

Hodder & Stoughton policy is to use papers that are natural, renewable and recyclable products and made from wood grown in sustainable forests. The logging and manufacturing processes are expected to conform to the environmental regulations of the country of origin.

Hodder & Stoughton Ltd
Carmelite House
50 Victoria Embankment
London EC4Y 0DZ

www.hodder.co.uk

For Dad

# CHAPTER ONE

## THE POLICE STATION

12 December 1924

T he sky had been clouded over since Tuesday, the telephones had been quiet all day and the front page warned of the coming ice storm. Detective Sergeant Frank Glover put down his newspaper and rubbed his eyes. Quality journalism had gone to the dogs. Even the decent papers were leading with sensationalist editorial now – *Blue Bloodbath*, a headline read. *Manchester's aristocracy running scared in wake of blue-blood killing spree.*

The light outside the village police station window had dimmed to a navy blue; another half hour and you wouldn't be able to see your hand in front of your face. Back in Manchester the street-lamps would be blazing and the pavements busy with feet hurrying between work and theatres, home and restaurants. Buses would be ambling past as cabs were hailed; umbrellas would be nudging each other as voices thrummed the cold air.

But here the air was quiet and still. He could hear Betsy typing and muttering under her breath, and somewhere a fox screamed; but that was it. The glass baubles on a small, feather-branched tree in the corner caught the light as they span slowly. The walls closed in. He could feel his usually sharp mind softening in this place. Months on and he still bristled at being removed from a danger that he considered to be his job to face.

'I'll be off shortly, Betsy,' he said, picking up his coat and pulling the arms the right way in. He checked the pocket for his keys. 'Time you finished up here too.'

'Cycling,' she said, 'on a night like this?' She raised a matronly eyebrow. Women of her age always seemed to want to mother him. He didn't overly mind.

'I'll be fine, he smiled. 'It's only a five-minute ride.'

'As you wish,' she said. 'Take care, mind. It's going to snow – I can feel it.' She picked up another sheet of paper and rolled it into her typewriter carriage.

'Snow won't kill me,' he smiled. 'Finish that tomorrow, why don't you? Don't you have a home to go to?'

'Don't *you* have a home to go to? I like working when it's peaceful. I get a lot more done when you lot aren't making a racket.' Still, she pulled the page back out and settled the cover over her typewriter.

A sudden shrill cry split the air, making them both jump, then Betsy laughed and pointed at the telephone receiver rattling in its cradle. She picked it up.

'Gothbury police station,' she said. She rolled her eyes at Frank.

Frank picked up a crisp apple from a bowl on her desk and bit into it, shifting his weight from foot to foot. A lost cat, no doubt. Village life was for bell ringers and door tappers, not for people like him. He had to find a way back to Manchester's hustle and bustle – who was better placed than him to track down the rest of the blighters? If you hid away every time you jailed one of them, they were winning.

Frank had grown up in Manchester's city streets. They were full of opportunities for trouble, especially for a troubled young boy with fire in his eyes. An adolescence spent running riot and picking fights could easily have led to a life of gangs and crime, but instead he'd taken a different path and gone in for policing.

Same behaviour, different context. Being wrapped in cotton wool was not his style – he was more than capable of keeping his wits about him. He'd not been fooled yet.

Frowning, Betsy held the receiver out to him and moved to put her coat on.

'Detective Sergeant Glover,' he said, still crunching on the apple.

There were a couple of clicks on the line. He cradled the handset under his chin so he could wind his scarf around his neck. 'Glover,' he repeated, getting ready to put the telephone receiver down and head home. Betsy waved and shut the station's front door behind her. He could see her through the window walking up the dark street to her cottage, a small figure, bent slightly over and looking uncharacteristically vulnerable on her own in the dark street.

A crackle and he heard a woman's voice. She sounded young, though the fizz and static of the line muffled it. 'Is that—?' she said, her voice breaking up. 'Come at once!'

'You need to give us a reason, ma'am,' he said. 'I'm not the butler.'

'Come,' she said again. 'Please!' The line was so bad he could barely hear her.

He sensed a genuine edge to her voice. 'What's all this then?'

'Just come.' The line crackled. 'Scarpside—', another shriek of crackles. 'Please.' And the line went dead. He stared at the receiver for a second, as if he was expecting to see the woman's face appear in ghostly form, and then he replaced it.

He unlocked the small, iron safe under Betsy's desk and took out the station revolver. He checked it was loaded and the safety catch was on and put it in his inside jacket pocket where it sat, heavy and cold, against his chest. He pocketed his notebook and pencil, sighed under his breath and headed out into the night, locking the station door behind him.

It was rather beautiful here at night, if you liked that sort of thing – the wide expanses of moorland surrounding the small village, the night sky dimmed by the evening fog. He turned down the lane and cycled through the village towards the Red Lion, Gothbury's only public house. Not a soul out on a December night; and why would there be? The pub was dimly lit, a single lamp over the door barely illuminating the scuffed painted sign above.

He leaned his bicycle against the stone wall and opened the door. Inside, the yellow light glowed and the place was alive with laughter. He could smell beer, sawdust and smoke. By the bar, as he'd expected, were Marsh and Riley.

'Glover!' Marsh shouted across the crowded room. They both looked to be on at least their second ale.

'What are you looking for, the train to Manchester?' added Riley.

'If it's here, I'll take it,' said Frank. 'Listen—'

'An ale for the man,' said Marsh to the barman.

'No, I can't stop,' said Frank quickly. 'Listen. Scarpside – where's that? We've had a call, sounds like there's a bit of bother there.'

'That's the big house,' said Marsh. 'You know – the one on the hill.'

'On the cliff edge, you mean?' It loomed suddenly in his mind – black, perched high, somehow lonely and aloof. He should have known from the name. It looked as menacing as it sounded and it was a good stretch from the village.

'A cliff? It's a mere bump, Glover,' Marsh laughed. 'An ale, please,' he repeated to the barman, who reached up for a glass. 'He'll have—'

'No.' Frank tapped his foot impatiently. 'Not for me. Nor for you, in fact. You'll be wanting to down those sharpish if you're coming up there with me.'

Marsh and Riley both laughed. 'Not bloody likely,' said Riley.

'Quite right. I'm not going all that way in this weather unless someone's been murdered in their beds,' added Marsh. 'In fact, make that two someones – it looks like snow.'

'It's parky out there, Glover,' said Riley, sipping his ale comfortably without so much as glancing at the window. 'We'll stick here, thank you very much.'

'Don't you worry, though,' said Marsh. 'We'll come and rescue you if it's blazing with gunfire.' They both laughed.

Frank was getting nowhere. Camaraderie was not something he had inspired in his fellow Gothbury policemen so far. 'Right, I'll have a look on my own, then. I'll call in on Betsy when I'm done. You know the drill.'

'Yes, yes, no word and we'll be there to rescue you . . .'

'. . . from the old manor's ghost,' said Riley, winking at Marsh.

'Don't say we didn't warn you,' called Marsh after him. 'I'll have his,' he added to the barman as Frank walked away with his lips pressed together and jaw tight.

He pulled the door shut behind him and stepped into stark and bitter silence. It felt as though the temperature outside had dropped, even in just the past few minutes. The sky was an ominous yellow, the narrow lane empty.

He cycled down the main street and towards the hill road where the mansion house stood, perched like a black rook on a branch, looking down onto the edges of the village and the wind-tangled moor. His nose was ice, his fingers were numb in his wet woollen gloves and the cold air was frost in his lungs. He cycled hard, the wind against him.

After a while the dimly lit streets, their white-washed cottages standing shoulder to shoulder, gave way to emptier roads, just the occasional farmhouse or crofter's dwelling marking his way on the wet, black road. The icy air rasped his mouth and muffled his ears. Now he could see the edges of the moors in the distance and, between their dark expanses and him, she stood – tall, and watchful. He stopped to rub the warmth back into his hands, keeping his eyes on the monumental frame and the bright, sightless eyes in the distance. He ploughed on, and after fifteen minutes or so pulled up to a sudden stop and quickly dismounted.

'What in hell's name?' he muttered to himself.

He was at the foot of a steep drop. There was a wind-beaten, deserted wooden platform at the bottom of the slope, its grain sooted by years of dirt; chickweed and nettles nibbling at its edges. A sort of cherry red train or tram carriage sat there, empty, looped to the top of the steep incline by a thick cable. The train's sloping roof met a wood-panelled body, with three doors that opened on to what looked to be a fairly rough space with wooden benches. He looked for a porter's lodge or stationmaster's room, but the tiny station was unmanned. So this was where the posh folks got on? The image of guests in their best with their maids and valets sitting on these cold benches didn't sit right, somehow. Perhaps they saved the big welcome for when you were inside.

The slope rose steeply in front of him: not quite vertical, but near enough. He looked up, straining to see a path through to the top. The thick wire cable that would carry the carriage up the hillside looped its way up, but he could see nothing else but wet rubble, rain-mottled moss and huddling staghorn ferns. Towards the pine trees at the top, the ground levelled out and what might be – must be – statues stood sentinel in the gardens outside the house. The ground floor windows were blazing with light. A distant plume of music snaked its way down the hillside towards him. A gramophone was wailing out some popular jazz. The notes spiralled out of the house and into the cold air, taking him back to his short, sweet time with her. Her soft smile, her guarded grey eyes. She always smelled of lilacs. From taking her statement to urging her first to lie low and then to get out of the city felt like long months of his life, but you could count it in weeks; days even.

Frank thought of his small, comfortable cottage back in the village. He could have been stretching out on the rug by now, some music on the gramophone, a whisky by his side. But the urgency in the girl's voice on the telephone, that hint of frenzy, had told him to come here – that he was needed.

He strained to see the path to the top. There had to be a way up – they'd got up there, after all, whoever it was burning all that gas. He edged closer to the rock face, his face wrinkling in concentration. He was a fair climber in good weather, though this was far from good weather. He weighed it up. It wasn't really a cliff face, more an extremely steep, rugged hill. Perfectly doable. Perhaps as he climbed, the way would become clear – a winding path just out of sight, a road not visible from this angle. He tucked his bicycle out of reach of the bad weather in a sheltered spot by the hillside.

And then he saw it. Neat, black-painted capital letters on a wooden board, next to a bell pull.

*RING FOR FUNICULAR*

Well, he'd seen it all now. He pulled the bell – a curious thing shaped like a howling face. He yanked it again and stepped back to look up the hill for signs of a coming train. Nothing. The pine trees on the upper stretches of the slope whispered in the gathering wind. His face and hands were ice cold. His thoughts flitted to the warm pub, the cold ale, the cheery voices, then back to the chill, the wind, the stretch above him; the work to be done.

Back to the bell. He gave it another tug. And then another for luck.

To hell with it, he'd climb. But just as he was assessing the slippery rock face for the clearest route up, a tinny answering bell sounded twice.

The sky had deepened to black now and, other than the lit-up windows of the house, the only light was from the full moon. A bright star next to it – Polaris, the North Star, he knew that from his old man. The night was quiet, as all nights were around here. He heard an owl twit and another reply with a twoo. It was starting to snow.

After a moment's hesitation, he got into the waiting carriage and felt it start to tug upwards, away from the sleepy village and towards the towering house.

# CHAPTER TWO

## THE LIBRARY

The carriage moved haltingly upwards, black stacked rocks slipping by beneath it. The windows rattled and the wind found a way in, pressing cold fingers onto his cheeks. The great house leaned over him.

Around halfway up the track a carriage passed him coming down, empty but for a few rough sacks. It sailed on, driverless, towards the road back to the cheery lights of the village and, for a brief second, Frank envied it. His own carriage juddered on upwards, past rough crags and damp ferns. He looked down – the road was far away, the distant village another world.

Soon the carriage slowed to a halt just below the precipice lip. He dropped lightly onto the platform – a close copy of the one at the bottom of the slope. A stack of sand bags sat by the platform edge; they'd be the weights to carry the carriage down the slope, pulling its twin up as it descended. His feet rang in the snowy air as he strode across the platform and down the steps to the hill face.

He was standing in a sparsely wooded area among the pines he'd seen from the road. The trees stood in straight lines, reaching thirty or forty feet into the dark sky, protecting him from the snow and muffling any sounds from the house. He could hear rustlings of small creatures in the undergrowth. His heavy boots were loud in the still air, crushing the pine needles and releasing their sweet resin scent.

Just then a figure appeared in the darkness.

Frank stopped dead. The figure didn't move. Heart quickening, he took a step forward. His blood sang in his ears. It was too tall to be a man: too still, surely? Was it staring at him, daring him to move first? Could it be a bear? But that wasn't possible.

Then his shoulders dropped. It was some sort of topiary creature. He stepped on more quickly, but he could still feel the tree-bear's eyes on him. Around the next corner another creature loomed – a wolf howling at the moon. In the distance he could make out what looked like the shape of a horse. The creatures circled the place, guarding the grand house from the bleak moors and distant village. He saw a shape, now, that was rather more like the figure of a man and though his pulse raced, his mind quietened it – just another strange leaf-carved creature or statue. As he turned away, it seemed that the creature moved away down the slope, but Frank had always been good at controlling his nerves and he walked on. A bell chimed eight times in the cold air.

With some relief, he left the dark of the trees and crunched onto gravel. He strained to see up and into the house. Every window on the ground floor was lit, spilling out brash light. The house had a handsome but reticent face, the imposing relic of a gentler century. Though the windows at ground level were wide and many paned, somehow they looked as secretive as the smaller attic ones. He listened intently but could hear no voices and there was no music now.

It was a few steps up to the deep porch. He had to bend his head slightly to get into the cold ante-room. A bronze dog's head stared, dead-eyed, at him from the gnarled surface of the heavy wooden door. The metal of the creature's head was surprisingly warm on the cold night. He slammed it down against the wood and waited for the sound of footsteps.

Nothing.

He knocked again. The echoing thump of metal against wood. The chill silence of the garden. The moon's cool gleam. His icy feet. The smog of his cold breath.

Nothing.

He glanced instinctively over his shoulder at the strange animals surrounding the house, reminded suddenly of playing Grandmother's Footsteps on the street as a child. He almost thought he could hear the crunch of foot on gravel, but he looked over his shoulder and there was no one. He knocked again, hard, and pushed at the door.

To his surprise, it gave way under his slight pressure and he pushed it open slowly, peering around to try and make his presence known. But the large, wood-panelled hallway was empty. All the wall sconces were lit, puddling light onto the dark stone floor. Portraits of a severe-looking aristocratic couple in high-necked, old-fashioned clothes glared at Frank from the dark walls. He waited for a butler or a maid to appear, but no one came. A small beetle of discomfort burrowed its way into his gut. Where was the butler? Where was the girl who'd telephoned?

The soft crunch of a footstep or falling branch faded to nothing; sound carried strangely by the moors, he knew that. He'd like to be out of here and on his way home soon, before the roads were impassable in the snow.

He took another step into the hall, looking for a door to a dining room or a morning room, the sound of voices or dancing feet, a glint of glass catching the light. But the place was deserted. The panic in that young woman's voice still sounded in his mind. His ears and eyes were keenly focused.

They'd be drunk and arguing, some woman trying to stop her brother from falling out with an old school friend while someone else quietly emptied the last of the whisky into a champagne glass. All that was needed would be the firm voice of a stranger, an official encouraging them to calm down and move along. There must be another route down the rock face for vehicles – he'd look for it on his way out. That footstep again. Or was it? He listened, intent, but the sound had gone.

'Hello there!' he called again. 'It's the police!' His footsteps scuffed the stone floor. His heart was beating faster.

Suddenly something inhuman rushed at him, a mass of black movement and wild cries. He bent down, covered his head and backed up against the wall. It surged at him and he pressed himself into the cold stone, feeling it billow past and flee down the dark corridor. He was shaking. And, like a trick of the light, the mass separated into wings, claws and beaks. Surely not . . . But he was right – crows: a regular murder of them. He looked for the open door or window they'd flown through; the sign, perhaps, of a rapid and unplanned departure. There was a scratch on his cheek – he rubbed it with his finger and felt blood.

'Anyone there?' he called again. His voice echoed around. He looked through the first doorway he found and saw an empty room with curtains fluttering wildly at an open garden door – no doubt where the crows had come from. It looked like some kind of formal sitting room, high-backed chairs gathered in one corner, pedestals displaying ornamental vases and marble busts against a wall. He looked through the open door into the empty garden, scanned the room for dropped belongings or furniture nudged out of place. When and why had someone left here in a hurry? Had the half movement in the dark grounds he'd dismissed as a figment of his imagination actually been a person fleeing?

The crows were flapping around the hallway, their feathers beating in panic. He strode down the corridor to let them out, scanning, as he went, for sight or sound of the girl or the house staff. He opened the heavy front door and the birds streamed out into the night, cawing at the moon.

'Hello in there?' he called again to the empty hallway. 'It's the police.' The silence gathered around him.

At last he heard real footsteps behind him, steady ones, running towards him. A voice called 'Je—,' then stopped short. He turned, fist instinctively clenched, heart pounding. A maid was running down the corridor, strands of her blonde hair slipping out of place beneath her white cap; the girl who'd called the station.

'Who are you? Are you the police?' she said, a little out of breath. She was frowning.

'Yes, miss,' he said. 'I'm Detective Sergeant Frank Glover. Could you tell me what the trouble is?'

'They've all gone,' she said. 'It doesn't make sense. They've *disappeared*.' There was a slight catch in her voice. He looked at her closely. 'And now Jessop's disappeared too,' she added.

'Who's gone?'

'Everyone,' she said, at his elbow now. 'It's not possible, is it? People don't just disappear. Where can they be?' The tremor of emotion was still there, rasping the edges of her words. 'Me and Jessop were looking for them and then he disappeared too.'

'Slow down, miss,' he said. 'Take a breath or two.'

She passed her hands down her apron, took a deep breath, lifted her chin as if to say that she could calm herself without his help. 'They disappeared into thin air,' she said, her cheeks pale, her eyes fixed on his. 'They were here and then they . . . *weren't*. And now you're here,' she added. 'How do I know you're the police? You could be anyone.'

He took his warrant card from his inside pocket and handed it to her. 'Detective Sergeant Frank Glover,' she read. 'It says Manchester constabulary. So what are you doing here in Gothbury?'

'I'm stationed in the village at the moment,' he said, putting the card back in his pocket. 'Now, tell me what happened here tonight.'

'They were here,' she said, rubbing the back of her neck irritably, 'and then they weren't here. That's it. That's everything. We served the entrées and cleared. A little while later we came in with the fish and they'd all vanished. Lord and Lady Forester – everyone. Everything was as we left it in the dining room, glasses on the table, candles burning, except that all the guests had vanished. We were about to search for them properly when Jessop disappeared as well, and that's when I really got scared.'

He looked behind him to the silent entrance, over her shoulder towards the end of the empty hall. 'Alright, then. I think I'll need some more details. Let's start with who you mean by *everyone*. The rest of the family? The staff?'

'Our guests.' She followed his gaze towards the end of the corridor. 'They're not there,' she said. 'That's the first place we looked.' Her lips were set in a straight line.

'Right. So, there was a party here tonight. How many guests?'

'Just a dinner party. Ten place settings.' She took a slow breath in and seemed to settle herself with some effort. 'The large party is the summer party,' she added. 'The Christmas one is more intimate.' She was carefully spoken, though her short vowels and the soft edges to her words suggested a local upbringing. 'More private,' she added.

'They'll be somewhere in the house, then, surely? Why the panic?'

'But there's no sight or sound of them. There was no reason for even one of them to leave between courses, never mind for all of them, without word or warning, to vanish in that manner. If they needed something, they'd have called us. Lady Forester is very particular about her dinners. She wouldn't do this.' She frowned and bit her lip, eyes wide. 'And why would Jessop just up and vanish too?'

'Right then. Take me to the dining room and let's have a look. But first why don't you tell me your name and who you are?'

She tucked a stray curl of hair behind her ear and nodded. 'I'm Dottie, Dottie Howarth. I'm Lady's Maid here at the house.'

'Lady's Maid, you say?' Yet there was a tiny spot of gravy on her pristine apron. 'Pleased to meet you. Could you lead me to the dining room please, Dottie?' He was alert for the sound of low-ered voices, muted footsteps, creaking floorboards, but the surface of the deep silence was unspoilt.

'This way, sir,' she said, and she led him away from the entrance hall, past the ivy-decked wood panels and towards an intricately panelled double door at the end of the corridor. Their footsteps were loud on the stone floor and the tall walls of the grand house reached over them, curving to meet at the ceiling.

'How long have you worked here with the family?' Their feet beat in time.

'Eight years. I started when I was fourteen, as a housemaid at first.'

'And who are the family?'

She turned to him, astonished. 'The Baron and Baroness Scarp-side!' she said, waiting for his look of recognition.

'Their names?'

'Lord and Lady Forester. Here we are, sir.' She stood at a heavy oak double door, one hand on its knot-swirled surface, looking back at him questioningly.

'Open it, then,' he said. 'Let's have a look.'

She turned, one palm on each door, and pushed with the flat of her hands. Slowly the crack widened to a slice and opened on a brightly lit but empty dining room. For a second Dottie stood there, silhouetted by lamp light, arms stretched out to either side, then she stepped to the left and stood with her hands tucked by her back. The large, oval table was set with linen and china, crystal and silver and the wall behind was painted with a wood-land scene, the dark branches gleaming with small, bright eyes. Holly, ivy and a bauble-studded wreath hung on the fireplace. The chairs were pushed back from the table, glasses half full, napkins unfolded. The large windows were uncovered, looking out across the snow-speckled gravel.

Frank looked around quickly, instinctively seeking the out of place, the unnoticed and the unseen. There were ten seats at the table, one at each end and four to either side. The chair to the right of the head of the table was pushed further back than the rest and at more of an angle. There were three wine glasses on the table. One had fallen, spilling a trickle of pale liquid onto the rug. Candles spluttered in the centre of the table, shivering in the draft from the opened door. A brightly patterned shawl lay on the back of one chair. Name cards sat by most place settings; one place had a small pile of two or three cards gathered together. A gramophone in the corner, its needle still in the final groove, was the source of the haunting music he'd heard from the road. Frank carefully picked up the arm and replaced it beneath the brass trumpet.

'Interesting,' he said. 'The gramophone was still playing when I arrived.' He was calculating – with a gramophone record taking around three to five minutes to play each side out, that meant that only a short time before he'd arrived at the bottom of the rock face, someone had been in the room to put the music on. 'The staff were preparing service when you noticed the guests were missing, you say?'

'Yes,' she said, 'that's right – just now.' He glanced at his watch – the call to the station had been an hour ago.

'I see. And why are you serving? That's not normally the job of a Lady's Maid. Where are the others – the kitchen and serving staff?' The room smelled of pine, beeswax, red wine and perfume. The candles had burned down perhaps an inch. The plates were, as she'd said, cleared.

'It was me and Jessop tonight. The maids, cook and footmen, all of them, they were sent away. I'm always in charge of the kitchen at the private parties. I do the sauces, keep the food warm, that sort of thing.' She moved to the table and reached for the fallen wine glass.

'Leave everything as it is, please,' he said quickly. 'Where have you looked for them?'

'We were just going to look in the garden room – that's where they normally retire for after-dinner drinks. Jessop was right behind me. Then I looked round and he'd clean disappeared! I was scared out of my wits. I ran back to the dining room to see if he was there, then went to look in the butler's room, and that's when I heard the front door. I thought it must be him but it was you.' She looked around anxiously. 'It's horrible. I feel as though they are about to leap out at us. Where *is* he?'

'And what's through there?' He pointed at a half-open door on the other side of the room.

'That's the library. The gentlemen sometimes retire there for their cigars and brandy.'

'And you've looked in there, I presume?'

'We could tell it was empty.' She glanced nervously at the library door. 'You think they'd be hiding unseen in there, silent, the ten of them, while we talked? We haven't heard a sound.' She looked over his shoulder towards the corridor, winding a lock of hair around her finger. 'Oh, where's Jessop?'

'Alright then, let's have a look.' Frank stepped carefully across the dining room. Of the three wine glasses that remained on the table, one was empty, one half full and one had tumbled over, spilling its contents. The empty glass had a red lipstick mark on it. Had seven of the party taken their glasses with them, going some-where where they expected to carry on drinking? There were two dull red marks on the rug between the table and the library door, the larger one the furthest from the table. He bent down and had a look. It was not candlewax, though the candles on the table hap-pened to be a deep red.

She was right behind him. 'What's that?' she said, a tremor in her voice.

'Not to worry,' he said, and stood up. 'Ten people dining, you said? Can you tell me who they are? Tell me a bit about them.'

'Lord and Lady Forester – the Baron and Baroness – of course. Their daughter, Mrs Radcliffe, she could be a star of the screen, she's such a beauty. She's a widow – the War took her husband. Prince Rudolph, he's Lithuanian royalty. Mr Gray and his wife – you'll know her name.' She paused. 'She's very well known – Anna Gray. She's American, you know.'

'Anna Gray. It does ring a bell,' he said. 'An American singer, isn't she? Carry on.' He stood at the door scanning the library methodically, left to right. The walls were lined floor to ceiling with books. There were tall windows on two sides, all shut, but the open curtains offering glimpses of the circling topiary animals. A reading table with six chairs around it was in the centre of the room, easy chairs by two of the tall windows. At the far end of the room was a desk, spot-lit by a green lamp. He stepped over the threshold, Dottie close behind him.

'Miss Fox, the fashion designer – she's so clever,' Dottie continued. 'A bit frightening to some, maybe, but I . . .' She paused, staring into the middle distance for a second, then carried on. 'Professor Webber – he's a great friend of the family. An inventor, you know. The Dowager Lady Abbott – she's a very old friend of Lord and Lady Forester. And Mr Bell, the American tycoon . . .' She stopped. 'What is it?'

They both saw it at the same time. Dottie gasped and let out a high shriek. She stepped back towards the dining room door, holding her hand to her mouth.

'Sit down,' he said, directing her to the easy chair that faced away from the dark pool, 'and watch the door,' more to keep her occupied than anything. 'Don't go anywhere.'

'Jessop,' she said, hand over her mouth still. 'Is it Jessop?'

'Sit down for now,' he said.

He crouched down, sniffing. Yes, it had that queasy, metallic tang. There was a lot of it, and it looked recently spilt. A deep puddle of it by the bookshelves and a splatter by the desk.

He walked round the room slowly, taking in every detail, his mind fixing on each and storing it away, occasionally flicking back to Dottie then onwards. The chairs at the library table were pulled in neatly. He tried one of the windows. Locked. No key in them. No drops of blood near the windows, just the two in the dining room. The house was silent but for the rattle of the windows. He could hear his own blood thumping in his ears. There should be a riot of noise. Staff and guests rushing around, the doctor summoned, a gravely injured person lying near the blood or carefully taken elsewhere. But there was nothing.

He glanced at Dottie again, sitting bolt upright on the edge of the chair, her pale profile unmoving. She was staring at the door back into the dining room, her hands trembling. If she was the sort to attack someone and draw half or more of their blood, then she was a good actress.

'I'll need to know exactly where you've been in the house,' he said. His mind was drawing together all of the strands: ten missing guests and a missing butler; a violent incident; a gravely injured, or perhaps dead, person removed without trace; absent staff; small indications in the dining room that all was not well with the group when they left it. And on top of all that, the house would be remote even in the best of weathers, never mind with a winter storm closing in.

There was a blotter on the desk. Next to it, a piece of paper had seven names written in a sweeping hand with deep indigo ink. *Lady Abbott, Prince Rudolph, John and Anna Gray, Cecilia Fox, Cleveland Bell, Leon Webber*. He folded the paper in two and slipped it into his inside pocket.

She was staring at the blood again, seemingly hypnotised by it. 'It's blood,' she said slowly. 'It's a person's *blood*. They must be dead, mustn't they, to have lost so much?'

'Perhaps. Perhaps not. A person can lose a lot of blood and recover.' His mind was yanked back to the scene in Little Ireland just a few months ago – the streets of Hulme, his old stamping ground, just a beat away. 'Nothing is certain yet,' he added, though his own money would be on this poor soul not having long unless a surgeon could see to them. He paused for a moment before continuing. 'So, there are seven guests and our three hosts. But what about the staff?'

'Yes,' she said blankly. Then, 'Jessop's the butler.' She looked up at Frank, a fresh urgency in her eyes. 'We've got to find Jessop. What if he's been taken?' She stood up. 'What if it's his blood?' Her eyes were wide with fear. 'His nerves aren't good. Maybe he's hurt or trapped somewhere.'

He nodded. 'We've seen enough here for now,' he said. 'Let's find this Jessop, then.'

'Are you just leaving . . . it there?' She didn't look at the blood.

'For now,' he said. His expression was grave. 'Maybe he went back to the kitchen or the pantry – let's take a look.'

'This way,' Dottie said, standing more upright now they were out of sight of the blood.

'Perhaps he'll be with the rest of the staff,' he said, intending to soothe her.

She gave a high, slightly giddy laugh. 'I told you. There *is* no one else,' she said.

And then the lights flickered and went out. They were alone in the pitch-black hall. Frank could hear Dottie's quick breathing, but everything else was silence.

# CHAPTER THREE

## THE KITCHEN

**F**rank felt his hand going to Dottie's arm, as much to reassure himself that she hadn't disappeared into thin air as anything. But there she was, flesh and blood. He could feel the warmth of her skin through the thin, black cotton. The dark seemed to amplify every sound. The clank of a pipe, the scratching of a mouse, the wail of the wind outside. Frank thought of his bicycle at the bottom of the scarp edge – his route back to warmth, light and normality.

'Don't worry, Sergeant, the electricity should come back on in a moment,' Dottie said, a note of hesitation in her voice.

They stood there together in the darkness. He felt that they were on stage, waiting for the house lights to come on and show them the audience. And then the wall lights flickered back on – so it was electricity, not gas that must be lit by hand.

He blinked in the sudden light. 'Electricity?' he said. 'All the way out here?'

She nodded, her expression lifting. 'We've got everything,' she said. 'All the latest inventions – the Baron is keen to be modern. We've had electricity since I've been here, longer even.' They stepped through the double doors into the hall, the electric wall lights fizzing softly as they passed them. There was a small, wooden, disembodied head next to a door to their right – a gargoyle or monster of some kind, like the one at the bottom of the hill, glazed by many years of touch.

Dottie pushed open the door. Behind it was the familiar comfort of a warm kitchen. A man sat motionless at the table in the centre of the room, in front of a long bureau covered with dishes of all shapes and sizes. A small, slight woman stood with her back to them, talking quietly into his ear. As Frank and Dottie stepped in, she retreated to the fireside to pile logs into the burner. The man had thinning, red hair and was wearing the short jacket and white tie of a butler. He was leaning forward, head in hands, not moving. Then he came to life and lifted his head from his hands. His face was flushed and there were beads of sweat on his forehead.

'Jessop!' said Dottie. 'You're here! I've been so worried about you – you disappeared. Where did you go like that?'

'No need to worry,' he said, in a thick voice. He stared at Frank. 'And who are you?' His voice was high and a little sing-song – a slight Welsh accent, perhaps.

'I'm Detective Sergeant Frank Glover. And you're Mr Jessop, is that right?'

'Jessop will do,' the man said.

'Jessop. Where are your guests and your staff?'

'They're not my guests. They're guests of the house, of the Baroness. And I don't—'

'We don't know,' said Dottie, her voice trembling. 'Where have you been, Jessop? I searched and searched for you. There's blood,' she added, her face crumbling again. 'A *lake* of it. Whose is it? Oh, I can't . . . Who did it? We need to get away from here.'

'It's a shock,' said Frank firmly, 'but I'm sure we can get to the bottom of it. The guests had sufficient wherewithal to make off with their wine glasses, after all. Now, Jessop, can you tell me what you know?'

'Like she said, they just went and vanished. Just like that. One minute they were there, the next . . .' He snapped his fingers.

'Poof,' he said, his eyes slightly glazed, as if he were thinking of something else entirely.

Standing in the large, warm kitchen Frank had a sudden image of how it should look in the middle of a fashionable party – bustling with staff, crackling with heat, heady with smells and activity and voices. But all he could hear was the drip of a tap and the wind harrying the windows. The space left by the ten missing people felt vast.

Suddenly, the room filled with a monstrous, rumbling crash. The three of them stared at each other, aghast. Dottie's face was white. Jessop swallowed hard. The huge thuds and reverberations continued for a while and then stopped. What was left behind was an unearthly silence.

'What was that?' Dottie said. She was gripping the side of the table. Jessop didn't move or speak. 'It sounded like it came from outside.'

Jessop shook his head slowly. 'The clock tower,' he said. 'It's not finished, there's a good deal of loose masonry. Stones may have fallen.'

'Right,' said Frank. 'I need to go and have a look. You both stay here. Where's the girl who was just in here? Call her and ask her to stay in here with you.'

'That was just our kitchen maid,' said Dottie. 'She'll be in the scullery.'

'Call her in to wait here with you,' he repeated. 'I'll be back as soon as I can.'


Frank shut the kitchen door behind him. The hallway lights shuddered briefly but stayed on. As he turned to go, he felt the prickle of eyes on his back and heard a soft footstep. Heart jumping, he turned quickly but of course there was nothing there – his mind playing tricks.

He slammed the heavy front door behind him. The snow was cold on his cheeks and he was glad to have those watchful eyes off his back and take a breath of clean air. The snow was falling lightly but steadily. He felt observed from all sides — from the bright eyes of the house and the dark shadows of the woods. He heard a twig snap as though it had been trodden on. He looked around quickly. Nothing.

There was no sign of fallen stonework. He strained to look up at the clock tower Jessop had mentioned, and he could see it there, still intact. The clock face showed the time as a little before nine. The low stone balcony surrounding the clock was unfinished on one side, its rough-hewn edges showing, but there was no indication that any of the slim, pale grey stones had been dislodged. He walked the perimeter of the house, the gravel crunching under foot, loud in the chill silence. His feet left shallow indents in the snow. He could see nothing out of place.

He fiddled with a warm stone in his pocket and his fingers were unwillingly transported back to the smooth skin on the inside of Mary's arm, her hand lifting her dark hair off the nape of her neck, her fingers drumming impatiently on a table as he talked her through the implications of what she'd done: of her courage. 'We're here to protect you,' he'd said. 'We'll make sure they don't find you.' How swiftly his feelings had spiralled, the need to protect her fighting the desire to keep her close. He pictured her, a few days later, swirling her gin in her glass, the lamp light giving her skin a golden sheen. She'd taken his hand and given him that smile and all was right with the world. But that was the last time he'd seen her. The very next day he'd been bundled off to this godforsaken village. And that was that.

The wind was bitter and the clouds were yellow with snow-bloat. His hair blew about his face and his eyes watered with the cold. He had reached the edge of the gravel. Just through the pine trees the sandstone archway of the station was half-hidden among the shrubs and scrub where the slope dropped steeply to the village road below. He'd make for that and take a closer look.

As the clock chimed nine, he picked his way through the thorns and nettles towards the platform, hands plunged deep in his pockets, head down against the wind. Once he'd reached it, the wall sheltered him from the onslaught of wind and snow. He climbed the steps – but the carriage he'd taken was gone, stopping him in his tracks for a second and making his heart thrum. He walked across the empty platform – not so much as a box or a bag on it – to look down towards the road. He could see the tracks plunging vertiginously through the dark trees and shrubland. The wind moaned querulously, plucking his coat from his back then setting it back down again as if it was trying to chafe at his nerves.

Though there was a single track leading down in front of him, it split into two just outside the small station. A thick wire cable led down the hillside and another cable led back up. If the carriage had gone (and if it had, who had taken it?) then why was its twin not back at the top where it should be? He decided to follow the cable and climb down. The crash had been vast – he'd see the cause of it soon enough.

He sat on the edge of the platform, the stone cold and wet beneath him, holding the thick, twisted wire. He'd use it to grip on to as he dropped down to the forest floor beneath and then as a guide on the way down – a climbing rope, effectively. But the wire was slack in his hands, not taut as he'd expect. Already the horror was rising in him.

He put his damp gloves back on and hauled himself down to the ground below the station, scraping the back of his thigh painfully through his damp trousers on the way. Not to worry, the cable could still guide him. It must be broken somewhere, so it makes a hopeless climbing rope, but it would take the most direct path, so he'd follow it. The floor was thick with pine needles, dead leaves, grey twigs, stinging nettles, thorny shrubs. Beneath them, insects would be worming and burrowing into the hard ground. He could smell the sickly resin perfume of the pine and a deeper, woodier smell. Beneath it the urgent stench of some dead animal. His feet were cold.

He worked his way down as quickly as he could, step by careful step. The cable was thick, a good three inches in diameter. Here and there it was still silver, but most of it had faded to a dull charcoal. It looked strong enough to lift a carriage or two. Above and behind him he could feel the house looking silently down.

It was steep here, between the sandstone platform and the long drop to the road, and slippery, but the thicker pine needles in the higher, forested parts of the slope helped his grip. Before long he'd left the cover of trees and here the way was rockier and more treacherous. Moss covered part of the rocks, but it had been transformed to a slick slime by the rain and then the snow. The crags were wet, covered by snow in places and unpredictable – changing from rough to smooth, from jagged to slippery without warning. Ahead of him, perhaps halfway between him and the road below, was a small brick building. Due to the steepness of the slope between them, he was looking down on its wet, terracotta-tiled roof – it looked small from this sharp angle, a gingerbread cottage to fatten Hansel and Gretel. Had part of it fallen down, or some machinery inside it exploded?

A stream followed the same route down the crag face as he did – at the bottom it would join the stream that ran through the village. Here it was studded with man-made contraptions – he counted two water wheels as he climbed down and, looking back, he thought he could see another in the distance up beyond the big house. The water was fast over the rocky bed and would be cold, perhaps starting to freeze over. A steep drop – you wouldn't want to fall in there and be dashed to the bottom, breaking like a fresh egg on the rocks below. He scanned the water for smashed machinery but it flowed icily clear down to the bottom.

He made his way slowly and painstakingly down the slope, away from the small, sandstone station and towards the ginger-bread house. Near the halfway point he turned to look back at Scarpside. She – for he thought of the house as a she now – stood tall and indifferent, face turned to the moonlight, eyes blazing with cold fury.

He turned back to the cable and continued to climb down, snow numbing his cold hands and cheeks, wind like a death rattle in his ears.

# CHAPTER FOUR

## THE POWER HOUSE

The snow was getting heavier now, patting his arms and cheeks like tiny hands that wanted to be noticed. Frank was almost at the building – closer up, it looked like a shed or a workshop, but why would you want one of those halfway up a rock face? If it were a part of the mechanics of the train or water works, something in it may offer a clue to the crash.

He slid precariously down the last few steep feet before picking his way sideways to the building. There was just one window, blackened by dirt or coat dust from the main house's chimneys. Six glass panes were criss-crossed by wood painted the colour of old teeth – blistered and pock marked, the paint would scrape off easily with a thumbnail. The brick of the walls was newer than the house bricks; they still had a slight factory brashness to their orange, though the mortar was starting to crater in places.

He rubbed at the black dirt on the window pane with a cold thumb, leaving a frown behind in the greasy dirt, but he could see very little in there by the dim glow of the moon so he pushed at the wooden door. In the low light a vast engine was cranking with slow, inhuman effort. Frank felt as though he was inside a machine. Rods and pistons moved and turned, groaned and creaked. At the far end of the room there was a hefty metal cupboard – a little like a bank safe – with all manner of dials, gauges and tarnished brass levers. A huge pipe connected it to the engine and then disappeared into the ground. The room was sparse and dusty, but the equipment, whatever it was, looked clean – polished, even – and there were no signs of a disturbance. He scanned the room quickly, thinking of Dottie and Jessop holed up in the kitchen with the maid. Out again and back to the climb. The wind fussed at the birch and pine trees and he braced himself for a difficult, cold clamber down.

The scarp was black, streaked with white snow. His mind kept going back to Dottie and Jessop and the shy scullery maid, terrified and shaken in the house above him. Were there strange hands trying the kitchen door handle, pushing against the wood of the door, creeping round the back of the house to look for windows to break?

The cable was slippery now in the heavier snow and grating under his gloved hands. The wind seemed to whistle through his ears and into the centre of his brain. Now he'd got past the powerhouse, Frank could make out the red carriage sitting halfway between it and the lonely road below. The cable Frank had followed down hung off the back of it, slack as a broken arm. Frank suddenly felt sick. It wasn't right. The carriage was off the tracks – some way to the left of them, in fact – and it was smack against a large crag. The front of it looked wrong, too close to the rock for the dimensions to work.

Frank picked his way across the precarious rocks with quick and steady feet, his pulse tapping a fast beat.

Frank slipped and had to grab at the wet rock to stop himself falling. His gloved hands snatched snow and slimy moss before his knee hit the rough ground hard. He swore and pushed himself up again. His knees were wet now, uncomfortable in the cold wind. He leaned into the red-painted wood and made his way carefully around to one of the doors, stepping sideways and feeling his way. It was getting harder to see more than a few inches in front of his face, but he could now see that the front of the carriage was crumpled up like an old tin can. What was that pushed against the window at the front? It looked like some sort of sack, filled with something heavy. It would be the weighted sandbags, of course, that he'd seen on the platform edge when he arrived – the weight that carried the carriage down. But who had taken it? Had they run off down the hillside after the carriage had crashed?

He took another step, and another. Another. His gloves were dark against the chipped red paint. Another sideways step.

Then he recoiled in disgust and disbelief.

It wasn't a sandbag. That was a jacket – a dress uniform. Hair. Could it be hair? It looked too lumpy, too wet.

Another step closer. This time he had to stop and steady himself. He looked away, closing his eyes, horror prickling his mind like hot mustard.

He took slow steps now, speaking quietly under his breath to reassure and comfort himself. It's fine. Just another step. Don't mind it, just look for a second then look away.

Now he was level with the foremost of the three doors. It was smashed up, looking like a badly drawn door with its angles going in all the wrong directions. The whole front of the carriage was concertinaed up against the rock. There was splintered wood all around him on the wet rocks. And that thing at the front. That pile of meat.

He looked again. One arm lifted above what would have been a head, as if it were waving. A knee raised. It was a mannequin caught in an improbable posture forever. Hand over his mouth, he looked more closely – a uniform with gold and blue medals, with colourful braiding and a bright sash. This must be the Prince Rudolph from the guest list – he recalled an image of him in the same dress uniform in the newspaper just a few days ago.

The face – what once was a face – was pressed against the smashed glass, which was pressed against the rock, which was pressed against stony earth. A peach thrown against a brick wall. You couldn't even see that it had once had features. That this mess of blood and old muscle had once smiled, once lied, once hoped.

He turned around and was sick over the wet rocks.

And again.

He sighed, head still down, and wiped his mouth with the back of his hand. His fingers were cold, his breath was hot, his mouth tasted rough.

With the train now broken and the rock face rapidly icing up and treacherous, they were trapped up there. He could see his bicycle at the bottom of the rocks from here – he just had to get there and get on and start pedalling and soon he'd be moving fast away from this place, towards friendly faces and voices and lights. In another half hour or less the road would be impassable. But, sighing, he turned back towards the house and began the climb back up.

He could never remember this part of the climb later. He had no memory of how steep or easy the rocks were. Of how they felt beneath his cold hands. It was like the hours after he had been told that his mother had died, twenty-odd years ago now, when he was just a boy; you couldn't even say the minutes and seconds were gone, because they had never really existed for him.

Some of his colleagues loved the murder cases, especially the hard to solve ones, seeing it as a problem to untangle, an opportunity to use their grey matter. Not so for him, though he was good at them and he was well aware that this was the sort of thing that got you promoted. He felt each death as a horrifying mystery. That the so-vivid life that animated the flesh could just disappear – to where? He was not a religious man so he could not rely on some eternal ever after. Where did the dance in a foot, the joke in the corner of a mouth, the soft kiss goodnight while you slept go? Twenty years ago as a boy he'd searched the world for those precise things, and he did it again with every death he encountered, though his mind shied swiftly away from his own grief, which the skin had grown over. Maybe that was why he was good at it, but it held no pleasure for him.

It had been a spring morning when the policeman had come to the door. He now knew that the hat under the arm told it all, though he hadn't known that then.

*Your dad in, sonny?*

They were in the kitchen for hours. Frank had been able to play with his truck uninterrupted – move it over obstacles, create a ramp, use the chair as a mountain with a steep, perilous edge, drive it in and out of the curtains, toss boulders in its way.

'She's gone,' was all his dad said when he eventually came out. 'She's gone. She's left us.'

Frank thought she'd moved away to another town. She'd surely come and get him though, her best boy, the best boy in the whole wide world? He packed a bag and put it in the corner of his room, hidden by the side of the bed, and waited for the doorbell. But she didn't come that day, or the next. His grandma came instead – his heart had near stopped when he heard the door, and then crashed in bitter disappointment when he saw her white hair and small mouth. 'You'll need me now your ma's dead,' she said. 'She's not dead,' he shouted and he ran to his room and stayed there. He heard his grandma tell his dad to leave him, he needed to cry it out.

He didn't remember anything much of that spring or that summer, but by autumn he'd come back to himself – come back a different boy. He unpacked the bag and put it away where he couldn't see it and be reminded of his own stupidity. It wasn't pos-sible to untangle it. Her body had gone; but that was only part of her. Where had her laugh gone, her talent at watercolours, her voice, her giggly whisper, her mad energy for solving the world's problems, the gleam in her eyes that told of love and restlessness and excitement all at once? She'd read all of those books – hundreds of them. The books remained, but what about the words that had gone into her head? And then the books went too, taken out in cardboard boxes by his dad and heaved away to who knows where. Once, maybe a year on, Sylvia, a neighbour, told him he had his mother's laugh and he was so angry he had to run up to his bedroom and punch the bed and, when that didn't hurt enough, the wall. He didn't want her laugh. It was no good to him without her.

But he had learned to keep all that away in a locked cupboard that he didn't open. Someone, he didn't know who, occasionally opened the cupboard at night and let out a tendril that found its way into his dreams – flowers crushed by trucks, her in a maze just out of sight, a train to catch urgently that he just missed – but it was always safely locked away again by morning.

One foot in front of another. His lips were numb and the snow buzzed around his ears, slapping him in the face, teasing his hair, trying to push him back to the house on the hill. He thought of Jessop's bare head, of Dottie's warm arm – he thought of that most deeply human of qualities, hope – and he continued pulling his way up the icy slope, more quickly now.

Somehow the way back was easier than the way down. He felt for the rocks and pulled himself up steadily. The snow covered most of the rocks now, leaving just the occasional patch of black, but it hadn't yet frozen over. It was difficult, but not impossible by any means. His thin boots slipped here and there but there were tricks to it – look for foot placements; once you have set your foot keep it still; hold your heel low; that sort of thing. In just a few minutes it would be a different story – you could already feel the snow thickening under foot, settling over ice and compacting on it.

The physical exertion of the climb cleared his mind. He liked the feeling of his body being worked, of having to focus just on the next thing. It had perhaps saved him in his younger years, climbing, when he was in the long hinterland between his mother going and adulthood coming; and later, after the War, when his mind was dislocated by the horrors he had seen, and by the horrors he had done. And it saved him now. He climbed away from the warmth of lit windows and tended vegetable patches and village gossip, away from a cup of tea by the fire and a laugh at a sentence that didn't need to be finished and a warm cheek on a soft pillowcase, away from light and normality and up towards that angry house sitting alone on a heap of slick, black rocks.

Before long he was back near the top, looking up on to the pine-needle-coated floor. This time he'd approached from a slightly different angle and he could see the house side-on through the trees. There she stood, blank faced, staring straight ahead. Now his eyes had got used to the dark he could see her sentries too, the leaf carved animals and birds staring out at him and circling the house. For a second he thought he saw the wolf move – just a twitch of a leg, a small adjustment of posture – but of course, it was a trick of the mind and of the light.

But then, in a heartbeat, the world swung on its axis again. He was standing next to the station platform at the top of the crag, staring at the cable – on the way down, of course, he hadn't seen it from this angle, facing, as he had been, the foot of the hill not up towards the house. The cable was unhooked from its housing, lying slack on the rocky floor. Footprints led away from the cable back towards the house. He had a closer look – small for a man's, large for a woman's, no pattern on the sole. A sturdy, practical shoe, though he didn't think it was a boot. These prints had been left since he arrived – since the snow had started to settle. Someone in the house had sent Prince Rudolph to his death then gone back inside.

Not for the first time that night, he was afraid. He was here for the foreseeable, trapped with whoever had done these crimes and still wandered around unseen.

With an effort he walked the last few yards and pulled himself up over the brink and back into the strange, resin-scented world. He looked around him and picked up the sturdiest stick he could find, testing it in his hand a couple of times before he left the cover of the trees, leaving a trail of black prints in the snow. Something looked different, wrong. What was it? The eyes – windows, he quickly corrected himself – they'd been lit up brightly before and now they were almost dark, glowing gently in the night like a cat's eyes snagged on a torch's beam. Something had changed since he had left.

He walked to the house quickly now he was on level ground, then began to run. He pushed open the front door, racing straight through the empty entrance hall to the dimly lit corridor. He was alert for any movement or sudden sound. His eyes adjusted to the dim light quickly and darted back and forth, looking for trouble. All was silent. The portraits glared at him, the grotesque heads on the servants' bells still leered. He dropped the stick.

He quickly glanced ahead towards the dining room, but it looked as he'd left it, except that its lights were now switched off. He could see the plates on the table, the half-empty wine glasses ready to be filled, the forks picked up and abandoned, the napkins that had been dabbed on the corner of a mouth and replaced. It was as though the guests were all still there and watching him, unseen. Every open door he passed revealed an unlit room that he was certain had been lit just half an hour ago.

He reached the butler's room, ran the last few steps to the kitchen. He tried the door but it didn't open. He rattled it, fearful and frustrated. Nothing.

'Dottie,' he said, his voice echoing strangely in the deep silence, sounding like it belonged to somebody else. He raised it. 'Dottie! Jessop.' What was her name, the maid? 'Dottie!'

Out of the corner of his eye he saw something move and, still trying to turn the door handle, he looked round, back towards the front door. Probably the wind blowing a curtain. But his heart leapt in his chest.

A tall figure in black was drifting towards him, a trail of insubstantial black matter behind it. Its face was pale and deathly, its stare fixed. Its eyes were black rimmed. Despite himself, he gave a sharp gasp.

# CHAPTER FIVE

# THE BUTLER'S PANTRY

The figure slid steadily down the hall, staring at him intently. Frank took a step back and tried the kitchen door again. It didn't budge.

Then he heard footsteps inside and the door fell open. Dottie tumbled out and was followed, more slowly, by Jessop. Dottie stood at Frank's side and stared at the figure in the hallway. Frank's heart was thumping. He could feel Jessop behind them, stock still, breathing heavily. The figure drifted closer.

Then, 'Miss Fox!' Dottie called.

'And who is this?' said the figure, suddenly sounding more earthly than ghostly.

'Miss Fox, this is Detective Sergeant Frank Glover,' said Jessop. Frank did not hold out a hand.

'How d'you do?' she said. 'Thank you for coming.' She was next to him now, a tall reed of a woman in a black cocktail dress with a sweeping train that trailed gossamer veils and fringes. She had dark, bobbed hair and a shaky half-smile on her face. 'Whatever was that infernal crash?' she added. There was a small, circular, bronze-coloured pin badge on her shoulder, holding her train in place.

'We heard it too!' said Dottie. 'We were terrified.'

'God only knows what's happening here tonight,' Miss Fox said. 'This lot are peculiar enough at the best of times, but we don't normally end up in hiding.' There was a wideness to her eyes that belied the sharp confidence of her words.

'Which lot?' Frank said sharply.

'Our little party. The Penny Club, we call ourselves.'

'Where are—' Frank began.

'I'm glad to see you, Miss Fox,' interrupted Dottie. 'I've been so worried, but here you are, unharmed. Where are the others?'

'We're in the billiards room,' said Miss Fox. 'We thought we'd feel safe there.' She laughed mirthlessly. 'No such luck, though.' There was a falsely bright note in her voice.

'All of your party?' said Frank.

'No, I'm afraid we're not all accounted for. Where's Prince Rudolph? Is he in there?' She strained to see over their shoulders into the kitchen. 'And Professor Webber and Mrs Gray?' She let out a trembling sigh and rubbed at the edge of her eye with the heel of a hand. 'We've wasted so much time arguing.'

'We haven't seen Prince Rudolph,' said Jessop. 'He's not been this way. Nor the other gentleman and lady.'

Frank's mind caught on the horrible mess in the carriage. 'Prince Rudolph,' he said slowly.

'Yes. The man who came to get you,' Miss Fox said impatiently. 'Now can we get out of this damned corridor and move somewhere that feels a little safer?'

Frank took a deep breath. 'I'm afraid your little train, the funicular, I suppose it is, has crashed,' he said. 'Crashed, I mean to say – I'm sorry to say – with Prince Rudolph on it.' He left the silence unfilled for a second or two, so its meaning could settle. Miss Fox put her hand to her mouth, Dottie gasped a quiet *oh*, and Jessop pressed his lips together and put his hands behind his back, as if awaiting orders. *The ice*, he muttered.

'Who are you with, Miss Fox?' said Frank.

'Nearly everyone,' she said, 'but we haven't seen Professor Webber or Mrs Gray since dinner and the Dowager Lady Abbott seems to have popped out—'

'Popped out?' Frank repeated, incredulous.

'. . . perhaps to find Mr Bell, who also disappeared a while ago when he went to send the funicular. Is he with you?' She looked over Dottie's shoulder into the kitchen again. 'Is *she*?' She grimaced. 'Oh, dear God. Rudolph,' she added. 'How very dreadful.'

Frank shook his head. 'Everyone is upstairs, you say – in hiding?'

'Wouldn't you be?' Miss Fox's eyebrows darted up. 'But once we were up there, there was a great deal of fuss and bother about what we should do. Should we go and search, should we barricade the door . . . You've heard of this blue-blood killer, I suppose, Sergeant Glover? Do you suppose it's . . .' Her words trailed off. 'Upstairs they're all saying it must be him.' Her hand shook slightly as she brushed some hair off her cheek.

'Let's not jump to any conclusions,' said Frank. 'Are they safe up there, would you say? For now?'

'Not all,' she said. 'As I said, we're missing a few. Professor Webber, Mr Bell, Mrs Gray . . .'

'Right,' said Frank. 'I'll need to have a word with the three of you – four of you,' he corrected himself sharply. 'Where's your kitchen girl? I told you to stay with her.'

'She'll be in the scullery,' said Dottie. 'Or the pantry.'

'Fetch her. We'll go somewhere and get some facts straight.'

'I feel watched here.' Miss Fox glanced over her shoulder. 'And I need a stiff drink.'

'This house,' said Jessop darkly. 'It doesn't want us here. It sees our sins and it wants revenge.'

'Whatever do you mean?' Frank said.

Jessop's eyes flashed. 'Everyone knows about it,' he said. 'The girl's in the pantry,' he added.

Frank's toe tapped impatiently on the cold floor. 'Let's go,' he said. 'Where's the pantry?'

'This way,' said Jessop. He took a few steps down the corridor back towards the entrance and opened a door.

Jessop and Dottie seemed to communicate without talking, the way people who work closely together do. She closed the door quickly behind them as he pulled out three hoop-backed wooden chairs at a circular table by the window. Miss Fox and Frank followed, past the butler's sink, a cloth neatly folded over the taps, and tall shelves stacked with softly gleaming silver and glassware. Frank nodded at the three of them to be seated.

'Where . . .' he began, but then a slight figure emerged from a door in the corner of the room. There were shelves stacked with jars and flour bags and bottles behind her.

'There you are,' said Dottie. 'Sergeant Glover, this is—'

'Mary,' he said.

'Mary,' said Dottie, then, 'how do you—'

'Mary,' Frank said again. She hadn't said a word. Her grey eyes were a still but clouded pool. Her face was pale. He reached for her then quickly put his hand in his pocket. 'What are you doing here?' His heart was thumping.

She reached up and adjusted her collar then nodded at Jessop, as if seeking permission to speak. 'I'm housemaid here at Scarpside House,' she said. 'I've had the position a month or thereabouts.' She hesitated. 'It's good to see you're well in yourself,' she added, smiling at Frank then glancing at Dottie and blushing.

'Well, this is mysterious, Mary. However do you know our sergeant?' Miss Fox's smile was shaky, and she glanced over her shoulder as she spoke.

'Well, I . . .'

'We knew one another in Manchester,' Frank said quickly. 'A distant family connection. A second cousin twice removed, something of that sort. Only met at a family do a year or so ago – you know how it is.' He didn't meet Mary's eyes as he said it.

'That's right,' Mary said. She smoothed her apron down, not meeting his eyes.

'Well, I never,' said Miss Fox. 'Small world. Could you fetch a bottle of brandy, Mary? It's been rather a night.'

Frank's heart was still lurching with the sight of her. The pleasure of seeing her alive – alive and well! – the shock of seeing her face without warning. He stole a glance at her departing back, but she was moving quickly towards the larder. He wondered if, meeting her here for the first time, he'd have had any inkling the courage she'd shown in coming forward, her steeliness in leaving everything she knew behind to retreat to the other side of the city, or her quiet resolution when he'd told her he was leaving, for now, and that she should too. Would he see the strength or just a quiet kitchen maid on her second or third position?

He coughed. 'Miss Fox,' he said. Her face was pale, her dark hair a smooth frame around it. Her features and posture brought to mind marble sculptures or the figureheads of ships. 'Can you tell me what happened here tonight?' Frank pulled out a chair, scraping it on the stone floor, and sat opposite her. Out of the corner of his eye he saw Mary emerge from the larder with a bottle. He forced his eyes away from her. His heart was thumping.

'That brandy, Jessop, if you wouldn't mind,' Miss Fox said.

Jessop poured out a large glass with trembling hands. Then he reached for a second and third glass and poured out an inch of brown liquid into each. He half turned to look at Frank and raised an eyebrow. 'And for the constable?' he said.

'Sergeant. And no, thank you. Miss Fox – you were about to tell me why you're all here tonight.'

Miss Fox leaned forward in her seat and took a sip. 'It's our Christmas soirée tonight, Sergeant Glover. We do it every year – our charming little celebration of survival in the face of adversity.'

'We?'

'The Penny Club – find a penny, you know the saying. Anyway, we were not long into our meal when we discovered, or Lord Forester discovered, I should say, a rather nasty little note.'

Dottie and Jessop looked up quickly. 'Note?' Frank said sharply. Mary sat down on a chair by the wall, her hands in her lap. She didn't look at Frank. So, she had left the city – the thought kept drumming through his mind – so she had left, she had left. He stole a glance at her sweet face, flushed with life.

'Yes,' said Miss Fox, 'a rather creepy little affair. Words cut out from some magazine or catalogue. It read something along the lines of *the unlucky will die here tonight*. I don't remember the precise wording. We called Professor Webber in – only he wasn't there.' She hesitated, seemed to shudder then swallow. 'A huge pool of—'

'Blood!' said Dottie. 'We saw it too! Oh, horrible. It must be his, but who—'

'Well, that's just the point,' said Miss Fox. 'No one could have – we were all in the dining room, except Mrs Gray who'd left by the dining room door to freshen up. By this point we were terribly spooked, as you can imagine, so we made haste to the billiards room.'

'You didn't look for the missing parties – Professor Webber, Mrs Gray . . .?'

'We were in rather a hurry to get somewhere safe. The dining room and library are surrounded by windows on all sides – anyone could burst in – and are right on this main corridor. We looked in the Grays' room, of course, but nothing.'

'Why didn't you just leave?'

She laughed. 'How would we all escape, exactly? We tried the phone line, but it was down, of course. Prince Rudolph gallantly offered to go and get you, which seemed an excellent solution. And here you are. But how did he manage to alert you before his . . . accident?'

'He didn't,' Frank said shortly. 'Thank you, Miss Fox.' She nodded and took a long sip of her drink, drumming her slim fingers on the smooth surface of the table and glancing nervously at the window behind her. Mary sat, quiet and still.

'Where are all the rest of the staff? I can't believe that a large house like this runs with only a butler, a kitchen maid,' he didn't look at her, 'and a lady's maid.' Frank's eyes were on Jessop.

'There are no *rest of the staff* tonight,' Jessop said. 'It's just us. The Penny night is a private party. The baron doesn't like a lot of staff getting in his way. And then, what with the storm coming, they went off a little earlier than they would have. They went with all the guests' maids and valets after afternoon tea was served, so as not to get stuck here.'

'On a night when your Lord and Ladyship would want everything to run smoothly?'

'The food was all prepared,' said Dottie. 'It was just a matter of serving it – I always do the finishing touches when it's a club night. They don't want village tittle-tattle; you know what maids can be like.' She worried at a loose shard of skin on the side of her thumb. 'Anyway, ten isn't so much, really. There were eight of us, growing up.'

'How long were you gone from the dining room, between clearing the entrée and announcing the next course?'

Jessop drummed a finger on the table once, twice. 'Twenty minutes,' he said.

'That's rather precise.'

'We clear twenty minutes before serving the next course.'

Dottie leaned forward in the chair next to him. There were a couple of beads of sweat on her pale forehead and her skin had a waxy quality. He spotted a jug of water and some glasses by the white ceramic sink and pushed his chair back from the table.

'And while you were in the kitchen – did you hear anything unusual? See anything unusual?' He poured some water as he spoke and handed Dottie a glass. She took a long drink.

'No. We heard nothing strange, saw no one. All was . . . as usual,' said Jessop.

'No one especially drunk or disorderly?' He glanced at Miss Fox, but she didn't react.

Jessop laughed. 'Probably,' he said. 'I said the same as usual, didn't I?'

'So, you heard nothing strange, saw nothing strange. Heard no one coming down the corridor . . .' Frank's back was to the half-open door. He glanced over his shoulder.

'No.' He saw Dottie's eyes flit to Jessop. Mary sat, stock still, hands in her lap, not looking at anyone. Frank stood up, looked in the pantry behind her, and closed the door firmly. He sat back down, glancing at her, took his pistol from his pocket and placed it on his lap.

'The kitchen door was open or shut?' he said.

'I don't know,' Jessop shrugged, his arms folded.

'Open,' said Dottie. 'It's always open during serving when the guests are seated at the dining table and we're going back and forth.' She sat up straighter. 'It's closed the rest of the evening, of course.'

'No one passed?'

'We'd have told you if they had,' said Jessop.

'How about a back way out? Where is the tradesman's entrance?' The kitchen windows were like black glass. The wind knocked against them steadily and brutishly.

'Just next to the butler's room,' said Dottie, gesturing to their right.

'And that will be where all the carriages are, I suppose? The back of the house?'

Jessop looked pleased. 'One might think that,' he said, 'but no. Scarpside is a very unusual, a very *special* house. Our guests are collected from the train station or drive to the bottom of our hill. Then they all arrive at the house itself by our little train. They enjoy the experience.'

'Jolly good fun,' said Miss Fox, without feeling.

'If rather inconvenient.' Frank observed.

Miss Fox furrowed her brow. 'Speaking of the train,' she said. 'How exactly did you come to know of our plight, sergeant, if Prince Rudolph didn't reach you?'

'Someone, one of your party, I assume, telephoned the police station and asked us to attend.' He paused, thinking for a moment. 'The telephone line is faulty now, you say?'

Miss Fox nodded, 'Afraid so,' she said.

'I'll try it myself. Where can I—'

'The butler's room,' said Jessop. 'I'll show you.'

Frank shook his head and stood up. 'Just direct me,' he said. 'Keep the door shut, please.' He glanced involuntarily at Mary, who didn't look up. 'Keep everyone safe.'

'The room after the kitchen and before the dining room,' said Jessop. 'Mind the step.' He held the door open, and Frank followed his outstretched arm back into the empty hallway. The lights flickered for a second or two again but stayed on.

Frank shut the door behind him. He heard the thin trail of a sound just ended – some music or a bell – but it had gone. Alone in the empty hall, he resisted the urge to keep looking behind him, back towards the grand but desolate entrance. His footsteps were loud on the stone floor. Shadows gathered in corners. The walls watched.

He walked past the kitchen and looked in. The room was near empty, the serving table still laden with dishes of uneaten food.

The butler's room was pristine. A fob of keys hung on a hook by the door and a single, iron bed was pushed against the wall. It was neatly made and looked remote as an oil painting. It was hard to imagine an impression of a body on it, the warmth of skin inside it.

Two jackets hung on the iron mantelpiece beneath a photograph in a plain frame, a screwdriver and a box of matches. He looked at the picture – a woman in the old-fashioned clothes of the previous century, or perhaps the beginning of this one, holding a small baby. She was standing next to a younger man in labourer's clothes.

In the far corner, over a desk, was a strange affair – a cupboard with a series of tiny, numbered doors set into it and two wires leading from the bottom. A red light was flashing above one of the strange little doors – number fourteen. Frank moved to have a closer look. Each door was perhaps two inches high by one across, numbers stamped on the front in black ink – one to thirty-one. Frank opened one small wooden door. Inside was a small, round socket. It must be a telephone exchange. He closed it again.

There was a pencil and an ink pen, a small, black-bound note-book and a neat stack of cream writing paper on the desk next to a telephone. He would call the Red Lion and Riley and Marsh would just have to . . . well, the way up was impassable by now, but they could organise help.

He unhooked the receiver and pressed the button once, twice – nothing. He swore under his breath. He pressed the button again, then again, a small bubble of panic rising in his chest. He tried the button one last time, then replaced the handset. His chest compressed with the claustrophobia of it all. They were trapped here until morning at the earliest.

Plenty of times in his personal life he'd been accused of being a mite too impetuous, but at work he liked to gather information and let it ripen. He enjoyed the feeling of clicking through files in his brain, pushing them one way or the other, thinking things through. He stood for a second or two in the stark, quiet room, listening to the trees shivering outside in the dark.

A strange absence of servants, which, despite the justification, didn't quite add up. According to the remaining servants it had all happened just minutes before his arrival – and the crackling gramophone told the same story. Yet the station had been telephoned a good hour earlier. And there were more problems and inconsistencies; little details that were part of a bigger picture than Dottie and Jessop were sharing.

He strode back to the pantry. Miss Fox, Mary, Dottie and Jessop were exactly where he'd left them, but Miss Fox's glass was empty, and Dottie and Jessop had made good headway with the other two glasses. Though they had been mute when he left, now they were talking quickly to each other, looking around the room, their faces half-fevered. Mary sat quietly in the corner, her hands folded on her lap. Frank's heart leapt towards her – after all she'd been through in the summer, she must be terrified. She didn't look up as he came in.

'I'm afraid the line's dead,' Frank said.

'Eh?' said Jessop. 'Dead? Who's dead?'

'The telephone line. It's gone – as Miss Fox said.'

'That will be the storm,' said Dottie. 'The telephone works on wires, you know, and if they get blown about by the wind, they can get dislodged. Then the sound can't travel – the connection is broken.' She said it slowly but not unkindly.

'I see,' said Frank. 'Now let's find the others, shall we?' He thought of the long corridors, the creaking boards, the dark corners, a fragile mind that had already witnessed too much. 'We won't need Mary,' he said. 'She can wait in here. There's a lock on the door.'

Mary nodded; he could sense her nervous relief. 'Keep yourself quiet and ring the bell if you need us,' he said. 'Get her a blanket and a cushion or two, would you, Jessop? Miss Fox? Dottie, are you ready? Jessop, the keys?'

The four of them walked in mute procession past the shelves of silver and glass, their gleam dulled by the low light. The house was completely silent. Frank's thoughts snaked to Mary, safe and comfortable in the pantry, then moved on to the work to be done.

# CHAPTER SIX

## THE BILLIARDS ROOM

They stood in the empty corridor, the lamps throwing shadows onto the cold floor. 'Could you take me to the billiards room?' said Frank. He looked at Jessop and tilted his head towards the pantry door. Jessop took the set of keys from his pocket.

'Certainly,' said Miss Fox. 'This way.' And she sloped elegantly back towards the entrance hall, black chiffon trailing behind her like a wicked afterthought. Only her quick looks to either side and folded arms betrayed her unease.

'Come along,' said Frank to Dottie and Jessop, and they followed her along the corridor and up the stairs. Frank threw a look behind him into the dark corridor as they left. But behind them, all was still.

The billiards room wasn't reached from the main upstairs corridor, but instead had to be approached by a circuitous route, through a room hung with paintings and across a grand drawing room. They went through a short, empty corridor overlooking the snow-topped pine trees and finally into a dimly lit room in the furthest corner of the house.

'It's me!' called Miss Fox. 'Let me in! I have our policeman, and Dottie and Jessop.'

Frank heard furniture being scraped across the floor and the door opened. A man, perhaps in his fifties, stood there, a small bureau shoved hastily against the wall next to him. He had dark hair, a slightly red face and he filled his dinner jacket comfortably. On his lapel was the same circular bronze pin that was on Miss Fox's shoulder; it looked like a penny.

'Lord Forester,' Jessop said with studied enunciation. 'This is Detective Sergeant Glover, a police officer from the local constabulary.'

Lord Forester held out a hand. 'How do you do, Sergeant Glover? Very glad to have you here.'

Frank shook his hand. 'Good evening, sir,' he said. He quickly scanned the room. Huddled in the far corner were two men and two women, sitting on the floor with their backs to the wall. A billiards table was in the centre of the room and easy chairs were gathered around a round table in the near corner. A sofa sat under a painting of a woman dressed in black, an unhappy grimace on her face. 'Could you tell me who else is here and accounted for?' He took his notebook from his inside pocket.

The older of the two women in the corner stepped forward. The younger man and woman sat hunched over, barely glancing at the newcomers before bending their heads back down.

'Lady Forester,' Jessop said, 'Sergeant Glover.'

'How do you do?' she said. Her smooth hair was the same grey as her dress. Her face was like stone, though there was a glint of buried fire in her eyes. 'Thank you for coming, Sergeant – terribly good of you. This is my daughter, Mrs Radcliffe.' The young woman in the corner frowned. 'And you may have heard of Mr Gray here. He's a member of Parliament, a member of the Conservative and Unionist party.' The man gave a tight smile. 'Dottie, Jessop,' Lady Forester nodded, 'we're glad to see you. We tried to telephone the butler's room, but we got no answer.' She, too, had a small penny pinned to her dress. Her voice was loud but unusually unvaried, like someone who was used to giving orders and not having to repeat them.

'We were in the kitchen,' said Dottie. 'Oh, Lady Forester, I am glad to see you all alive! I've been scared out of my wits. Some terrible things have happened here tonight. Where is Mrs Gray? She doesn't like to be alone.'

'Yes, indeed. Do you know where the rest of your party is?' cut in Frank.

'Got separated in the chaos, I'm afraid,' said Lord Forester. 'I expect they're hiding out elsewhere too.'

Mr Gray stood up. He was a tall man. His face was pale, his eyes were wild and his ruffled hair sat oddly with his well-tailored jacket. There was a small penny badge on his lapel. 'We haven't seen Mr Bell; he went to send the train,' he said. 'Have you seen him? American chap, in his mid-thirties. Brown hair. My wife hasn't been seen since entrées, when she left the table to freshen up. Nor has our friend Professor Webber. And Lady Abbott came up here with us but has since . . . vanished,' he shrugged with a heavy sigh. 'We didn't see her go. I suppose that the call for the train was you. Thank you for coming. I think it's time we all got to safety. Where's Prince Rudolph? Let's get our coats and go.'

'Could I interject?' said Lady Forester. 'While Mr Gray is correct to say that Professor Webber is not with us now, it is not true that we haven't seen him since dinner. My husband saw him when we came up here earlier.'

Frank looked to Lord Forester, who threw his wife an irritated glance. 'I can speak for myself, Sophia,' he said. 'Yes,' he nodded at Frank. 'I called out to him, but he didn't come and we were in no mood to hang around. I assumed he'd found his own hiding place, perhaps in one of the bedrooms.'

Frank looked at his list of guests. 'And . . . the Dowager Lady Abbott?' he said. 'When did she go?' Mrs Radcliffe twirled a lock of brown hair around her finger, eyes wide. No one spoke. Lady Forester let out a long breath and Lord Forester tutted. Frank folded the guest list in two. 'I hear you found a note. Can I see it?'

'Yes,' said Lady Forester. 'That's—'

'—correct,' interrupted Lord Forester. 'I imagine you'll have seen those signs of . . . ah . . . a struggle in the library?' He reached into his pocket and handed Frank a piece of paper, folded in four.

Frank opened it quickly. Words and phrases from articles, or perhaps advertisements, had been glued on to read,

*Coming soon! Death will meet with the lucky tonight.*

Silently, he refolded it and put it in his pocket.

'We imagine,' said Lord Forester, 'that it's the blue-blood killer, or what have you. You'll have read about his killing spree. We're sitting ducks up here, of course. Why this idiot wife of mine thought to install us in a house perched on a rock, I shall never know. She may as well have handed this blue-blooded devil a gun.' He shot Lady Forester a look, which she did not return. Her expression didn't change.

'Two deaths is not a spree,' said Frank firmly. 'Don't believe everything you read in the newspapers. Now it is extremely important that everyone remains—'

'I don't want to remain anywhere,' said Mrs Radcliffe in a wavering voice, eyes wide. 'We need to get out of here. Mummy, tell him.' She gathered her brown hair into her hands and released it again. Her red dress draped over her knees and flowed to the floor. She started to cry.

'Quiet, Florence,' Lady Forester said.

'Let's go, I said,' said Mr Gray. 'When Parliament hears about this mess . . .'

Frank held up his hand. 'The train's broken. There's no safe way down to the road with the ice storm high. We will all have to stay here until the weather clears and help comes.'

'The train's broken!' repeated Mr Gray. 'For Christ's sake, we're trapped. And Prince Rudolph, was he . . .'

Frank nodded grimly. 'I'm afraid so.'

'Rudolph's dead,' said Miss Fox flatly. 'And there's that horrid lake of blood in the library – it's not his, so whose is it?'

'My God,' said Lord Forester. 'Who would dare kill a royal?' They all stood in the centre of the room, a couple of feet from Frank, the queasy yellow lamplight splashed across their faces.

'Minor *European* royalty, but yes, still very shocking,' said Lady Forester, head tilted a little to one side, face unreadable. 'Poor Rudolph,' she added.

'I'm not sure why you're all assuming it was foul play,' said Frank, giving her a sharp look. 'It appears to me that the train, the funicular, had crashed.'

'Another horrible accident,' said Jessop. 'My Lady, another horrible accident. The house doesn't like us being here. It's tripping us up, sending the train off the rails.' He was moving his hands together repeatedly, as if he was washing them under hot water.

The wind rattled the windows violently, shaking them as if it would have the life out of them, then there was a splintering crash. Mrs Radcliffe screamed and Frank heard Jessop and Dottie gasp behind him. 'Christ!' said Mr Gray. The wind wailed through the broken glass, snow pouring into the warm room, the chiming on the hour of the clock tower suddenly loud.

Everyone stared at the window. The snow was dusting onto the thick, green carpet. 'For heaven's sake, do something!' said Lord Forester. Jessop mutely walked to the window, picking up shards of glass as a flurry of snow iced his shoulders.

Mrs Radcliffe ran to the door. Frank quickly barred her way. 'You're safer in here,' he said. She tried to push past him, but he stood firm.

'Florence,' said Lady Forester. 'Please.'

'And what exactly do you intend to do, Sergeant Glover?' Mr Gray said. He had a low, steady voice and the politician's way of gripping your gaze a little too tightly.

'The most important thing at the moment is that you all stay put. I'll gather the missing guests and you can wait here till help arrives.' The wind whistled through the broken window. Frank pulled his coat together.

Miss Fox lit a cigarette and held it to her lips, shivering in her black dress. 'We're back to the same conundrum we've been stuck on for hours. To search out there for our friends or to barricade ourselves in here where we feel safe? I was always on the side of searching. I'll come with you, Sergeant Glover. Anyone else game?' She stood at the door, holding it open. The black train of her dress lifted in the icy breeze.

'Me – I'll come. I know the house best,' Dottie said quickly. No one else spoke.

'No one move,' Frank said, and he followed Miss Fox out of the room, Dottie close behind. 'Be careful, Cecelia!' Florence called. The door shut behind them and they were alone in the corridor. Another grotesque wooden head leered at them from the wall and gusts of snow tapped at the window like trapped birds in a cage.

In the drawing room beyond, a floorboard creaked and then there was silence.

# CHAPTER SEVEN

## THE ELECTRICAL ROOM

'Right,' said Frank. 'When Mr Bell went to send the funicular, where did he go exactly?'

'You'd think, just here,' said Miss Fox, pointing at the door to their right. 'This is the electrics room. But it was hours ago.'

All three of them glanced at the door. No one moved towards it.

'This is the only place he could do it from? The only control room?'

Dottie shook her head. 'You can do it from the butler's room too,' she said. 'It's more often Jessop that works it. Or from the station at the top.' She glanced nervously at the door to the electrics room and then to the drawing room door. 'Sometimes the electrics fail, though, up here. It's not used as often. He may have tried here, then gone downstairs.'

The silence shouted that none of them had seen him downstairs. Frank nodded. 'Let's check here first, then,' he said, keeping his voice neutral.

He pushed open the door. The wall facing them was chequered with an elaborate grid of metal boxes, support rods, cables, levers and gauges. The lights were flickering and the whole room buzzed, as though they were in the centre of an enormous swarm of bees. Behind him, he heard Dottie take a sharp intake of breath that she held in her mouth for some long seconds before releasing it as a quiet moan. 'Oh, God,' Miss Fox said quietly. 'Oh, God, no – not Cleveland.'

Lying on the floor, one hand clutching the air in a tight claw, was a man in evening dress. Frank looked at him and quickly looked away. He may have been handsome once – perhaps as recently as an hour or two ago but now his face was contorted into a silent scream. His skin was red and blistered and something about his eyes was wrong, as if a dot of ink had spread on blotting paper. He lay next to, in line with, the grid of metal boxes. There was a small amount of blood around the fingers of his clawed hand. His legs were together, and his other hand was at his side. The same penny badge was pinned neatly to his lapel.

'It's Mr Bell,' said Miss Fox quietly. 'Oh, Cleveland.'

'It's awful.' Dottie's face was white.

'How could he be so stupid?' said Miss Fox. 'It must have short-circuited when he pulled the lever for your train.'

'Stupid?' Was there a way to leave this life that wasn't grossly undignified or was Frank's perspective sullied by all the horrors he had seen?

'So stupid as to die.' The phrase sat sadly in the empty air of the close room. The three of them stood there, wordless, for a few breaths. Mr Bell's body lay silent, its chest horrible in its stillness.

Dottie breathed out slowly. 'What happened?' she said quietly. 'Was he electrocuted?'

'It looks as though—' said Miss Fox.

'It's not quite as simple as that, I'd say,' said Frank. 'How long was he gone?'

'He went not long after we hid up here,' said Miss Fox. 'It would have been around eight o'clock.' Her gaze snagged on the form on the floor then moved away.

'And no one thought to look for him?'

Dottie looked at Miss Fox with interest, waiting for her answer.

'There was a great deal of disagreement on that matter,' was all she said, but she rolled her eyes and sighed heavily.

'I'd have gone!' Dottie burst out.

'I know you would.' Miss Fox placed a hand on her arm. 'You're a brave girl and a good one. More than I can say for all of those in—'

Frank gave her a quick look. She met his eye. 'Don't worry, Sergeant,' she said lightly. 'I wouldn't do anything so shabby as to do away with them, much as some of them might deserve it.'

'You can go back to the billiards room,' he said. 'But please let me inform the others about this latest . . . incident.'

Miss Fox nodded, eyes averted from the strange and sad sight that had once been Mr Bell. The door clicked shut behind her. Frank heard the billiards room door open, gasp out voices and shut with a soft thud. There was silence again.

Then Mr Bell's clutching hand twitched violently. The arm rose briefly into the air and fell back down again. Dottie gasped. Frank froze. A shudder and the arm went still. He could hear Dottie swallow.

'He's alive,' said Dottie. 'He's not dead, he's alive.' But she moved away from the form on the floor, not towards it, shrinking back towards the wall. Frank bent down and placed a finger and thumb to either side of the wrist. The neck. And the other wrist. The strange feel of flesh without spirit. It was like wood. The window rattled wildly and stopped dead.

'Nothing,' he said. 'He's gone. Spasms can occur for a short time after death.' He said it to himself as much as to her. 'It can happen,' he repeated. His own breath was quick and fast now. His heart felt like it was pushing a river through his veins.

Dottie was against the far wall. 'But it's been hours, surely,' she said quietly. 'He's been dead for about two hours. It must be that long, or where was he all that time?' Frank gave her a sharp look and nodded. 'Do people always remember right?' she added. 'Time can do funny things when you're shocked or scared. Maybe Miss Fox thought it was eight o'clock when he went but it wasn't as long ago. Or why would it,' she looked again at the prone form, 'why would it still be . . . moving?'

'Yes, that can happen – people can remember wrong or get the order of events not quite right. But it's not all as you'd expect here. Look at the body, if you can bear it. What strikes you?'

'I can bear it,' she said. She stood up a little straighter and leaned forward, looking closely and carefully. 'It's too neat,' she said. 'You wouldn't fall like that.' He nodded. 'And the arm looks wrong,' she said. 'If someone was electrocuted and thrown away from the thing that electrocuted them, the power source, you would expect the hand to be thrown back or to the side, not clawed up like that.'

He nodded again. 'Exactly it,' he said. 'That's exactly it.' They met each other's gaze as the snow pressed damp, cold tongues onto the windowpane.

Frank pushed open the billiards room door. The broken window had been cleared, the snow swept up and a painting leaned against the jagged hole, though the wind was lacing icily through its thin canvas.

Lady Forester sat straight backed on the sofa, expression fixed, eyes like stone. In the low light she looked carved from rock. On the other side of the room Lord Forester sat at the round table, wild-eyed, drumming the smooth surface of the table with his fingers. Mrs Radcliffe was next to him, knees drawn up to her chest, rocking to and fro. Her long, red dress, pinned at the shoulder by the small, bronze brooch, fell onto the floor behind her chair. Mr Gray was looking out of the window and chewing his nails. Jessop stood in the far corner, a tension in the corners of his mouth and across his forehead, his arms behind his back. Miss Fox sat alone on one of the high-backed chairs by the door, staring into space. Though she sat quietly, her chest was rising and falling fast.

Frank coughed to get their attention. Mr Gray said, 'Thank God!' and jumped away from the window. Miss Fox and Lord Forester stood up and Jessop turned to face Frank. Lady Forester, alone, was unmoving.

Frank took a step inside. 'I'm sorry to report,' he said, 'that it seems there has been an unfortunate accident. I'm afraid that Mr Bell has died.' Everyone stared at Frank except Miss Fox, who looked at the floor by her feet. 'There may have been an electrical fault.'

'Christ,' said Mr Gray, stumbling against the billiards table.

'Whatever can you mean?' said Lord Forester. 'Where is he, man?'

'The electrics room,' said Dottie.

Frank nodded, quickly scanning all of their faces.

Mrs Radcliffe started to cry. 'We're all going to die,' she said. And with that her placidity erupted. She ran to the door. Frank quickly moved towards it and held his arms out. Her hands pummelled him, her fingers grasped for the edge of the door. 'Let me out!' she cried.

'Florence!' said Lady Forester. 'Gather yourself!'

'Open the door,' said Lord Forester, his face blooming with emotion. He pulled at Frank's arm. 'Let us out. Do as the girl says!'

'Come back, damn you,' said Mr Gray. 'We all leave or none of us do.' His hair was wild and tears streaked his pale face. He was rubbing his forehead with a shaky hand, pushing his light brown hair back over his head.

'Anyone would think his *wife* was dead,' murmured Lady Forester.

'Try to stay calm,' said Frank, holding steady. 'Mrs Radcliffe, please. Lord Forester.' He raised his voice. 'Quiet now!'

Lord Forester moved back. Mrs Radcliffe straightened up and took a step away from the door. Dottie swallowed and took a deep breath, looking around at the room and then back at him.

'Oh, God,' said Mr Gray, sitting down on the floor and sinking his head to his knees. 'We're being slaughtered, picked off like flies. And we just sit around and fight.' He raised his head. 'This blue-blood killer will take us all one at a time, just as the note said. We're all going to die tonight, aren't we? Where are the others? We need to find them.'

'Such as his wife,' said Lord Forester. 'Christ, man, have a heart.'

'Yes,' Miss Fox agreed. 'We must find Anna – Mrs Gray,' she nodded at Frank. 'And Professor Webber and Lady Abbott. They must all be together somewhere, in another part of the house, hiding out just as we are. We must join forces. We stand more chance that way.'

The faces around Frank seemed petrified, each caught in a single moment of emotion – horror, fear, anger, grief – but which were real; which affected for his benefit? Frank turned the smooth, flat pebble over and over in his pocket, feeling for the small dip in its surface, rubbing it with the side of his thumb.

There was a strange sound, just outside the door; something like a sharp click. Frank's ears strained keenly towards it; what was it? He knew the sound, if only he could place it.

And then the door creaked and very slowly began to open.

'Thank God. Lady Abbott.' At Lady Forester's words, everyone turned to the door. A white-haired woman in a busily patterned shawl walked through the door. She carried herself like a dancer, Frank noted. The woman nodded at the group. She looked inquisitively at Frank. Her eyes were bright and hard as a kestrel's.

'Lady Abbott,' said Jessop dully. 'Sergeant Frank Glover, a police sergeant.'

'Not before time. I suppose the others have filled you in. Have the rest of the club reappeared?' She gave Frank a sharp look. 'You're a policeman, you say – have you found them?'

'How do you do, Lady Abbott. Where have you been all this time?' asked Frank.

She looked at him levelly, an eyebrow raised.

'Can I ask where you've been?' repeated Frank. 'You really shouldn't be wandering—'

'I wasn't *wandering*, young man – quite the opposite,' she interrupted. 'I went to powder my nose and came straight back again. I may seem of *advanced age* to your eyes, but I've not entered the wandering years quite yet. I suggest we all have a glass of something strong to steady our nerves. Jessop, I believe the gentlemen keep a bottle of something in here?' She bent down to open the door of a mahogany dresser and pulled out a decanter of whisky. 'Ah, there's a good red in here too.' She pulled out a second bottle. 'Splendid.'

'You went nowhere else?'

'Of course. Just, very carefully, to my suite and back.' She looked at Frank. 'You will assume that old ladies are fearful, I suppose.'

'Not at all. But I'd hope they would have a little sense.'

She laughed. 'Oh, quite,' she said. 'Quite.'

'Cleveland's dead,' said Mr Gray flatly.

'Dead!' She put her hand to the tip of her nose and then to her chest. 'Oh, was it his poor heart? We all knew his weak heart would fail him in the end, sooner or later . . . Jessop, the wine, please. Quickly. We must steady our nerves. Prince Rudolph has returned, then? Where is he?' She looked around the room. 'And where are Anna and Leon?' She glanced at Frank. 'Mrs Gray and Professor Webber.'

'We can't find them,' said Dottie, 'and Prince Rudolph is dead too.'

'Oh, good Lord, no!' Lady Abbott put a trembling hand to her mouth. 'Prince Rudolph? It can't be. Are you certain? No, you must be mistaken.'

'I'm afraid so,' said Frank.

Lady Abbott shook her head and sat down, spreading her skirts about her. 'Whatever happened?'

'The train,' Jessop said dully. 'My Lady, it must have been faulty.'

'Thank you, Jessop.' She took a long sip of wine. 'You'll be aware, Sergeant, that something dreadful appears to have happened in the library? We found a foul pool of what looks like blood but we have no idea . . . we found no one with it.' She looked him directly in the eyes. 'It must be Mr Bell's, I suppose?'

He gave her a steady look. 'Do you?' he said.

'Enough is enough,' said Miss Fox. 'It's time we found our missing friends. Come along, Dottie.'

'I'd better stay here and look after everyone else,' said Mr Gray. 'I'm the only young man left.'

'Young!' said Lord Forester. 'Hardly.'

'He's a good two decades younger than you,' said Lady Forester flatly.

'We'll search for the missing three and then we'll all camp in here,' said Frank. 'Please, no one leave the room. Now, Miss Fox, Dottie – let's set to work.'

Jessop poured another glass of wine. The oily, deep red stream looked almost black in the lamplight. Frank, Miss Fox and Dottie made their way out of the billiards room and into the dark corridor.

# CHAPTER EIGHT

## THE ROMAN BATHS

The drawing room light was off, though it had been on when they walked through it just minutes ago. Miss Fox flicked a wall switch and, with a click, the wall lights came on. Frank was relieved to be away from the chill of the billiards room. As if hearing his thoughts, Dottie said, 'It's so cold in there. Shouldn't we take them blankets and hot drinks?'

'They'll manage,' said Miss Fox. 'It's more important we find our friends.'

'Yes,' said Frank. 'Agreed. Now, where did you last see Mrs Gray and Professor Webber?'

'At dinner,' said Miss Fox. 'After the entrée, Anna went off to her room. To refresh her lipstick or something, one supposes. Leon, Professor Webber that is, was in the library. I rather suppose that blood is his – who else's can it be?'

Frank nodded.

'It's hard to imagine anyone could move a body without us noticing,' said Dottie. 'There's no other way out of that room. So, either he got up somehow and walked out by himself . . .'

'. . . or the body's still hidden in there and we didn't see it,' agreed Frank. Miss Fox shuddered. 'I suggest we start with the Grays' room,' he continued. 'Let's focus on Mrs Gray first. They may well be together.'

'That's downstairs, though,' objected Dottie. 'It seems unlikely we wouldn't have seen or heard her. Unless . . .' her voice trailed off.

'Come along,' said Frank, hand instinctively checking for the revolver in his breast pocket.

They crossed the dark room in silence.

The downstairs hallway was lit by moonlight on snow. The three of them walked quietly, Frank alert to any movement or sound. Dottie coughed nervously, then held her hand to her mouth. Miss Fox strode on without looking to either side of her but she held her elegant, black shoulders up a little, as if she were expecting a blow.

The pantry door was closed, locked as they'd left it. Frank's mind reached to Mary sitting in there, alone and afraid, but he knew that though she was fragile and nervous she was also capable of courage – and he knew that she was safe. He rested his eyes for a second or two on the closed door then glanced at the other two and kept walking. The kitchen was empty. The door to the dining room loomed at the end of the corridor, shut against the pool of blood they could all see in their mind's eye.

'Here,' said Dottie, gesturing towards the door opposite the butler's room. 'This is the Grays' room.' She didn't reach for the handle.

'Very good,' said Frank. He listened, looked over his shoulder and quietly opened the door. The room was dark and deserted, its bed made. It looked like a empty theatre, performers long gone, with its swags of fabric and jars of ostrich feathers, an exotic scene painted across an entire wall, the clashing oranges and purples and greens.

'Is she there?' Dottie said nervously behind him.

'Anna?' called Miss Fox. 'Are you in there?'

The answer was silence.

Frank closed the door. 'She came here,' he said, 'or, at least, we suspect she did, though we don't know. Then she must have moved on, perhaps startled by something. If she'd gone up the main stairs, you'd have seen her from the kitchen, is that right? Heard her pass at least, I'd have thought.'

'Yes,' agreed Dottie. 'We keep the door open during service on club nights – there's such a small number of guests. It's almost like a family meal, Lady Forester always says. So, we'd have noticed her walking past.'

'And is there any other staircase? One she may have got to unseen?'

'There's a staircase at the back of the house,' said Miss Fox. 'It leads up to the Roman bath.'

'Roman bath?' He almost laughed. This was a strange place and no mistake.

'Yes,' said Miss Fox, 'Scarpside's rather famous for it. I believe it's a copy of one in a great house in Verona.'

'Let's take a look at this bath, then. Which is the most direct route?'

'Through the butler's room. Jessop won't mind.'

Miss Fox glanced back as they shut the door of the butler's room firmly behind them, filing past the bureau and neatly made bed to the back door. Dottie fiddled with the handle of the glass-paned door. And then it was open to the black, snow-swirled night. Frank shivered.

'This door is usually unlocked?'

'I'm not sure,' Dottie said. 'It's really mostly Jessop who'd use it, unless someone else needs to work the telephone exchange in his absence. The tradesman's entrance at the other end of the corridor would certainly be kept unlocked. There are a lot of comings and goings, especially on the day of a party, and I suppose we're a little out of the way for chancers.'

'Till now,' said Miss Fox.

Frank glanced at Dottie in her thin, black dress and Miss Fox in her thinner evening gown. 'You might want to get your coats,' he said. 'It's bitter out.'

'I'll be fine,' Dottie said. 'We'll only be out a short while.'

'You'll catch a chill, Dottie my dear,' said Miss Fox. She walked quickly out to the hallway, opened a door and pulled something deep red out of a forest of coats and boots. 'Here,' she said, hooking it over her arm and pulling out a dark fur with the other hand, 'use this one.'

'But that's—' Dottie objected.

Miss Fox held the oxblood-red coat out towards her. 'Don't fuss,' she said. 'We can't have you dying of cold, can we?' Dottie put it on, rolled the cuffs up once, twice, and tucked her hair behind her ears. Miss Fox shrugged on the fur.

'Lead the way.' Frank gestured towards the back door, the black whirl of snow in front of them, the watchful gloom of the house behind them.

The garden was dark and the snow was falling heavily now. They were standing in a generous courtyard at the back of the house. An arm of the building curled round to their left, and beyond that was the woods. Frank thought he could see another sentry animal among the evergreen trees.

Dottie looked nervously out to the woods, and he followed her gaze. The snowy tops of the trees were moonlight-iced, their tracery branches deep in shadow. Anyone – or anything – could be hiding out there, watching them, waiting for their next move.

He raised his voice to fill the silence. 'Right, where are these stairs, then?'

The house rose around them on three sides, arched walkways offering protection from the worst of the snow. On the fourth side they were fenced in by the pine and silver birch trees. Dottie nodded and started to walk across the snow-dusted courtyard. Miss Fox and Frank followed. Four formal flowerbeds with neatly clipped box hedges formed crisscross patterns. A wheelbarrow was propped by the far wall, snow settling on its iron handles. The cast of the snow-bloated sky stained everything yellow.

'Do you think they're both dead?' Dottie said. The corner of her mouth quivered and her hands were clenched. He heard Miss Fox take a sharp intake of breath.

Frank hesitated, then said, 'Let's not jump to conclusions until we've seen everything. Tell me a bit more about the house. It's strange they keep themselves so isolated.' The soft red of the brick was still just about visible in the dark of the evening. He pulled his coat closer and tucked his scarf more tightly around him.

'It was built for her Ladyship's great-grandmother,' said Miss Fox. 'It's always been a terrific party house. The family's main house with the hunting grounds and so on was always back in Ireland and this was something of an escape – a folly, you might say, on a grand scale. I believe the Lord and Lady Forester still hope to return one day.'

'The village still tells stories of the great parties held here,' said Dottie. 'It's not been the same since the War of course, but before that – the tales they tell! The great staircase was turned into a slide at one party.'

Miss Fox laughed, 'Oh, yes, Dottie's right of course! The guests slid down it in their tuxedoes, picked up a cocktail at the bottom and walked about the gardens with their drinks.'

Dottie nodded. 'And there were masked soirées – they were famous in the village, you know. Every year, invitations would go to villagers by lottery. My mother went once in a dress made from the living room curtains.'

Frank smiled. 'And the living room?'

'Well, we just did without for a while.'

'It's an unusual house, then.'

Dottie nodded. 'It is that, with a funny sort of arrangement. Bedrooms on the ground floor, a grand bathroom on the first. Most of the beds are upstairs, though.'

'The morning room and drawing room are upstairs,' said Miss Fox. 'A little topsy-turvy, you might say. But that's where the best views are, of course.'

'Look,' Dottie said, pointing. A black iron staircase spiralled up the brick wall to a door on the first floor. But that wasn't what she was pointing at. Leading from it were a single set of snowy footprints, already muffled by the falling snow in the more open courtyard. They looked to be a man's, though it was hard to say for sure, and had a clear lined pattern on the sole. The steps led in just one direction – back to the house. Frank was cold in his coat, snow prickling his cheeks.

'Footprints,' said Miss Fox. 'Someone's been out here.' She shivered, pulled her fur close, and looked around her.

'Let's keep on,' said Frank.

'Here,' Dottie said, taking the handrail. 'They'll be slippery. Watch your step.'

'I'll go first,' he said. 'You two follow. Hold on to the rail tightly. Grab my arm if you think you're slipping.'

The snow was getting in his eyes. The stairs were treacherous and the icy handrail slid beneath his fingers. He got to the little platform at the top and waited for Dottie and Miss Fox by the black-painted door. Even just a few feet higher up it felt colder, the wind pulling at his scarf. He looked out across the pine and birch trees and had a sudden longing to fly across them into the snow-speckled sky away from all this. He turned back to the stairs and held out a hand to help Miss Fox and then Dottie.

He turned the handle of the door. It was unlocked.

He began to say, 'would it normally—?' But a burst of hot steam stopped his mouth, pushing him backwards as it raced from the room, fogging their view instantly. 'Careful!' he said quickly. The steam cleared a little and they moved tentatively into the room. He could see straight away that something was wrong.

They were looking into an arsenic-green-tiled chamber. Through the steam he could just make out a large sunken pool in the corner. Steam filled the room, drawing itself up into columns that might hide creeping shadows, waiting eyes, a cold knife held low. Frank's face was damp with the sudden heat and steam on his cold skin. He spotted a heavy-looking bucket on the floor and moved to push it against the open door to keep it ajar. The steam flew like a ghost into the cold air. As it fled, it revealed an arm in sheer, blue chiffon trailing against the side of the bath, the wrist encased in a heavy gold bracelet. His breath caught in his throat. The two women spilled into the room behind him.

'Dottie, Miss Fox,' he said quickly. 'Step outside.' Dottie cried out and moved past him. He instinctively reached out for her. 'No,' he said. 'Stop—'

'Anna,' said Miss Fox dully. 'Oh, my good God.'

'Oh, beautiful Mrs Gray,' said Dottie. And she sat down on the floor and wept.

'Wait on the staircase,' said Frank, trying to get a clear view of the body, but they didn't move.

Miss Fox was standing stock still, staring at the bath. Dottie didn't move from the floor. She pushed at her wet cheeks with the flat of her hands. 'Oh, poor Mrs Gray,' she said. 'Don't leave her in there on her own. She hated being alone.'

The thought of his ma, a lover of conversation who had died alone, swooped at him unbidden, cawing and pecking. To go back and hold her hand in that moment. He batted the thought away.

'Don't be silly,' he snapped at Dottie. 'She can't feel anything now. It doesn't matter.'

'Of course it matters,' Miss Fox said levelly.

The steam was clearing and he could see the woman in the bath better now. She was submerged to the neck, her eyes rolled back in her head. Her skin was mottled purple. The water was clear; there were no bloodstains on her dress, no signs of injury. 'Don't look,' he said. 'Just sit down, both of you.' There was a wooden bench against the wall, beneath a vast, gold-framed, fogged mirror. 'Here, take a seat – see, over there.'

Dottie stood up heavily and sat on the bench, still and quiet, eyes staring, expression changing second by second. Miss Fox sat next to her, leaning back against the sweating walls, and took her pale hand in hers.

The water in the bath was scalding hot – you could cook a fish in it. The horror of the woman's skin, poaching still.

'Is there a switch to turn this thing off?' he said.

Dottie stood up. 'Yes,' she said, her voice catching. 'It's awful. How can she be dead?'

Miss Fox sighed. 'I saw her just a few hours ago.'

'She'd have hated people seeing her like this,' said Dottie. 'Can I cover her up?' Her eyes were pleading.

'In a second. How do we get this damned thing turned off?' There had to be a switch or a lever somewhere. Everything was slick with steam.

74

Suddenly a crash split the air. Dottie, halfway from the bench to the bath, screamed and put her hand to her mouth. Miss Fox gasped under her breath. Frank scanned the room, heart pounding. 'It's just the door,' he said. 'The wind.' Dottie nodded, her cheeks flushed, eyes wide. Miss Fox let out a long sigh and wiped her brow. 'Shall we turn this off?' he said. 'Do you know how?' He coughed to hide the tremor in his voice.

'Yes.' Dottie took a couple of steps, looking behind her at the door, reached down.

'Do it with a cloth,' he interrupted, picking up a flannel from a stack of them.

'It's been turned up, past the safety catch,' she said as she pushed it back. 'See?' There was a red line on the dial and the arrow pointed a significant way past it.

'How?' he said, thinking quickly. 'Could she have done it herself?'

'You can't do it easily. You need a screwdriver. Look.'

'Possible,' he muttered. 'But you'd have to come prepared and know how to do it. And then there's the clothes . . . But why on earth is there a setting for this kind of temperature?'

'To get it hot quick, sir. You know what these folk can be like when they want something in a hurry.' She was still holding the damp cloth, kneeling on the floor. The tendrils of her hair were damp. She glanced at Miss Fox nervously. 'Not all of them,' she added.

Miss Fox laughed, shortly. 'Don't worry, Dottie,' she said. 'I catch your meaning.' Her dark hair was an inky thumbprint on the damp wall.

'Tell me about Mrs Gray,' Frank said. 'She's the American singer, I believe.'

'Yes. She's a singer. She's very famous.' Dottie said, looking proud. 'Was,' she corrected, the corners of her mouth shifting.

'I knew her in America,' Miss Fox said. 'She played all the nightclubs. There was talk of her going to Hollywood at one time, but it never quite happened.'

'She was beautiful enough,' said Dottie.

He gently touched the wrist between finger and thumb, looking for a pulse he knew wouldn't be there. The steam had almost completely cleared now. She lay back in the bath in a wet dress the colour of summer skies, puffed up and foul, chin pointing at the ceiling, eyes open. Her dark hair was wet about her face. Her red lipstick was smudged. He sighed.

He picked up another towel and placed it over her face. 'What are the other ways in and out of here?' Dottie pointed mutely at a door to their left, opposite the door to the winding, metal staircase.

'That goes to . . .?' He reached it in two strides.

'The main suite,' Dottie said quietly. 'Lord and Lady Forester's.'

He turned the handle, still slippery with condensation. Locked. 'We had better get back to the others,' he said. 'Mr Gray should be told.'

'I don't like leaving her.' Dottie followed him slowly to the door.

'You knew her well, Dottie? And you, Miss Fox?'

'She comes to Scarpside a lot, not just for the parties,' Dottie answered. 'Sometimes she'd visit for a few days, sometimes longer, sometimes with her husband, but often alone. When she came by herself, she wouldn't bring a maid and I'd see to her. We'd have chats while I got her dressed and did her hair, and she'd tell me the stories of her life. I think she had a hard time of it, famous and glamorous though she was.'

Miss Fox lit a cigarette. 'She liked Scarpside for the peace, I think,' she said, staring out of the window at the snow.

'She gave me an old dress of hers once,' said Dottie. 'She called it old, at any rate – I wouldn't.'

'Did she seem happy to you, Miss Fox? Content in her marriage and so on?'

'Yes, sometimes.' Miss Fox looked at him, eyes bright. 'Nobody is happy all the time, are they? Life doesn't really work that way.'

'No.' He beckoned them to follow him out of the still warm, damp room.

He heard Dottie's quiet sobs behind him, Miss Fox murmuring to her as her own voice caught in her throat, and he watched the white flakes swirl over the trees. He let the thoughts gather and flurry – they'd sort themselves into shapes soon enough if he let them be. Then Dottie sniffed and said, 'I'm fine now.' Her voice was thick. 'Good girl,' said Miss Fox.

They descended in silence. Frank shivered. The snow was heavier now and the contrast with the heat of the bathroom was stark. Dottie's shoulders looked reassuringly real. She seemed completely, solidly in the world.

They left footprints in the thick snow that had settled in the courtyard, looping back towards the ones they'd made on the way out. Frank had seen a few rotten things in Manchester, but he wouldn't get the image of Anna Gray's face out of his mind for a while. Dottie and Miss Fox's eyes were darting around the unlit courtyard, their shoulders hunched against the wind and snow, and unseen assailants. His ears were strained for footsteps, rustlings, sudden sounds. A dark figure standing motionless at the side of the terrace snagged his thumping heart, then resolved itself into the column of a tree.

In the quiet, dark of the corridor, the three of them walked quickly and in silence. Miss Fox's arms were crossed over her chest, her brow furrowed. There was a howl of wind that was so sudden and violent that, despite himself, Frank started. Dottie wrapped the borrowed coat tightly around her body. 'Are we safe?' she said, so quietly that Frank could hardly hear her. He didn't reply – what could he say?

Miss Fox shivered. 'Where is he?' she said quietly. 'If he's come for us, this blue-blood killer, where is he hiding?'

The brooding silence of the house loomed around them and the three of them walked in mute procession up the corridor to the entrance hall, bearing horrible tidings.

# CHAPTER NINE

## THE INTERVIEWS IN THE BILLIARDS ROOM

Mr Gray was sitting on the floor in the corner, staring straight ahead of him. His shoulders were hunched and there were tear tracks down his pale cheeks. Next to him, Mrs Radcliffe examined her nails, shifting anxiously. Lady Abbott sat on the sofa, observing the room keenly, Lady Forester next to her, face like stone. Lord Forester was pacing around the room. Jessop stood by the door, hands behind his back, eyes blank as smashed windows.

'You're back,' said Lady Forester. 'Thank goodness,' she added dully, almost as though she were speaking lines.

'Any signs of danger?' said Lord Forester.

'Any signs of the others, more to the point,' said Mr Gray. 'Where's Anna?' His head sank back to his knees.

'We should have looked for them hours ago,' Lord Forester said. 'This ridiculous woman insisted we all cower in fear up here, like dogs afraid of a beating!' Lady Forester didn't move or look at him. Her face was flint. Miss Fox gave Lord Forester a cool look.

Mr Gray's head snapped back up. 'For God's sake! Can we not squabble?'

'Leave her alone, Daddy.' Mrs Radcliffe moved to Lady Forester's side. Lady Forester sat, frozen into position. She didn't acknowledge her daughter.

Frank said, looking closely at Mr Gray and then quickly at the rest of the room, 'I'm afraid we have discovered another body. It's—'

'What!' said Lord Forester. 'You can't be—'

'No!' said Lady Abbott. 'No. It can't be.' She sat up straighter, her white hair bright against her patterned shawl, her eyes sharp as pins. 'We're all good people. This doesn't make sense.'

'Yes,' said Frank. 'I—'

'Who, for God's sake?' said Mr Gray. 'Not Anna. Oh, please God, let it not be my Anna.'

'Who'd want to kill us all?' said Mrs Radcliffe. 'We've done nothing wrong!' She looked around the room as if searching for the answer.

'If you'd just let me—'

Lady Forester took Mrs Radcliffe's hand. 'Now, now, Flo, dear. You're safe in here with us.'

'Unless one of us is the killer,' said Miss Fox, 'in which case you're locked in with a murderer. Good luck, everyone!' Her smile was shaky, her chin pushed up high.

'Stay calm, please,' said Frank. 'And I'll explain what I know—'

Miss Fox put a ball down on the green baize and watched it roll gently across the table as she leaned on the cue, her shrewd mouth fighting her nervous eyes. The storm worried at the window and blew gasps of snow in through the broken glass.

'Ridiculous. None of us are killers,' said Lord Forester. 'We're all upstanding citizens. The best of the best.' He pushed his chest out like a cockerel scrabbling for territory in the dust.

'Why has no one but Mr Gray asked who it is?' said Miss Fox. 'Who it is that is dead? Prince Rudolph, Mr Bell, the unaccounted-for-blood, and now this.' She tilted her head to the side and raised her eyebrows. 'Well?'

Mr Gray bent his shoulders and rested his head in his hands. He shut his eyes.

Frank cleared his throat. 'I'm very sorry to tell you – I'm afraid that Mrs Gray has died.' He watched Mr Gray closely and saw a fleeting look cross his face. It looked strangely like relief. And then he put his head back in his hands and his shoulders started to shake. 'Her body was in the Roman bath,' Frank continued. 'I'm not sure of the cause of death at present. I'm sorry for your loss. I realise this is another terrible shock for all of you.'

'Good Lord,' said Lord Forester. 'Something very evil is afoot here.' He looked around the room almost accusingly, his gaze finally settling on Lady Forester. 'Well?'

'Oh, John,' said Mrs Radcliffe, putting an arm around Mr Gray's shoulders. 'Anna was such a beautiful creature.' Mr Gray didn't respond.

'We tempted fate,' said Lady Abbott. 'We all knew that. If not straight away, we know it by now.' She pulled her bright shawl more closely around her and looked around the room, as if to locate her fate as it approached. 'There's no escape,' she added. 'We'll just have to wait.' She laughed, joylessly.

'She's a superstitious old bird,' said Lord Forester, leaning back in his seat and doing up the buttons on his black jacket.

'Don't be rude, Charles,' said Lady Forester. Her face was strained, the deep lines pulled taut across the surface of her forehead, but her expression, as ever, was thunderous and unreadable.

'What the hell does it matter, being rude, when we're to be slaughtered in our beds!' said Lord Forester. 'Where were you all that time you were gone, Lady Abbott? Eh? Where did you go?'

'For God's sake, really Charles?' said Lady Forester, 'At her age? She's just a little old lady.'

'Do you mind?' said Lady Abbott. 'I may be old and of small stature, but I am no lady. At least, only in name. Anyone would think

I was infirm. Have any of you considered that Mr Bell may have seen them both off before dying of his heart attack? He always had a nasty streak, let's not forget. A tendency to be grabbing, greedy.'

Miss Fox sighed. 'Poor Anna. I hope it wasn't awful for her.'

'It was hardly likely to be dandy, was it?' said Lord Forester. 'For God's sake!'

'I imagine there are degrees of awful,' said Miss Fox, 'same as anything else. I hope she didn't suffer too much. I hope she wasn't too frightened, in too much pain.' She stood there, pale and lost in thought.

'You were wandering around yourself, Miss Fox,' said Mr Gray, 'when you came back, eventually, with the officer here. Are all your movements accounted for?' The group was silent for a moment, the wind-rattled windows the only sound. 'Is the door secure?' said Mr Gray. 'They could find us in here. They found the others.'

'Lord Forester? Jessop? Could you barricade the door? I'll need to interview everyone.'

Frank sat for a second or two at the table in the corner. 'Lord Forester,' he said. 'May I speak with you?'

Lord Forester swayed slightly as he walked, like a boat caught in a breeze. Frank wasn't sure if he was drunk. 'You'll want to know about the evening, I suppose,' Lord Forester said, as he pulled out a chair. 'It's our annual soirée. Rather a good bash. Everyone has a spiffing time. Normally, at any rate.' Lord Forester folded his arms and stared at Frank. 'My wife and I started the club.'

'A survivors' club,' called Lady Forester from across the room.

'Sophia, please, I'm speaking – do shut up. Can we go elsewhere, Detective?' Frank shook his head. Lord Forester sighed and lowered his voice. 'It's a club of lucky survivors. You'll have noticed we all wear a penny badge. Some of us survived the Great

War, some altogether different terrible events. There's a certain mindset that allows one to thrive in adversity and come out on top; that's what our little group celebrates. We got away from the war in Ireland, you know. Terrible business. But that was then and here we are now.' He nodded. 'Thriving. Until now, that is.'

'How do you know Professor Webber? And Mr Bell?'

'We know Professor Webber extremely well.' He shifted his eyes to the left, like he'd spotted someone more interesting at a cocktail party. 'We knew him back in Ireland. He's done so much work for us that we consider him a friend now.'

'He updated the house,' called Lady Forester.

Lord Forester's face immediately contorted. 'Sophia, do shut up!' He spoke quietly to Frank. 'An engineer – an inventor you might say. A brilliant mind. A genius. Ahead of his time. Mr Bell is – was, good Lord – an American businessman. If only Lady Abbott hadn't sent him . . .' He lowered his voice. 'Perhaps we could come to an arrangement – you and I go to the village for help while the others remain—'

'And you barricaded the door as soon as you all came up here?'

'Yes, that's right. Well, not straight away – we wasted a good few minutes arguing about what to do for the best at first. Then the decision was made to barricade ourselves in.'

'Thank you, Lord Forester. Perhaps I could talk to your wife now.'

Lord Forester stood up. 'Of course. Bear with her, won't you. She can be a little slow in getting her thoughts organised. Sophia, the detective wants to talk to you. Sophia! Come on, woman. Don't keep him waiting.'

'No hurry, Lady Forester,' said Frank.

'Don't keep him waiting, I said.' The older man lumbered away, shoulders slightly bowed, scratching the back of his head where his brown hair was thinning slightly. He joined the silent party in the corner of the room.

Lady Forester moved across the floor to Frank's table, looking to neither side as she walked. Her grey hair was in place, her plain dress creaseless. She had a firm set to her lips that looked habitual – it seemed to betray a gruff impatience at other people's follies, a habit of not showing uncertainty or emotion. 'I prefer *please be seated* to *have a seat*, don't you?' she said. 'Have a seat suggests I might want to take it as a gift.' She didn't smile.

'Please be seated, Lady Forester.'

'I believe your name is familiar, Sergeant Glover. I'm certain there was a small piece in the *Manchester Guardian* about you a few months ago. Perhaps I am mistaken. Something about a triumph against one of those, what do they call them, gang leaders? I'm rather surprised they named you, that cannot have been—'

Frank cut in quickly. 'Lady Forester, perhaps you can tell me how you know everyone who was here tonight.' He looked up sharply. 'What was that?' A chair had crashed to the floor. Mr Gray jumped to pick it up then stood there, hand on its red velvet back, face drawn and eyes wild. 'Carry on.'

'As Lord Forester said, we got away from Ireland just as things got rather messy. A boat at the dead of night, left everything behind, that kind of thing. There were shots fired across the water at us, would you believe? We didn't even have time to dismiss the servants or collect our valuables. But perhaps it was the making of us. I, for one—'

Lord Forester shouted from the other side of the room. 'Don't tell the man your life history, Sophia! He's here to enquire about missing persons and suspicious deaths, not write your biography.'

'Can you tell me what happened tonight?' Frank's pencil scratched across the rough surface of the page. The skin on his knuckle was bleeding slightly where he had caught it on the rocks.

Her face was curiously bland. 'Of course – to the extent that I know anything at all. We were waiting for our second course. Mrs Gray left to freshen up and Leon – Professor Webber – went to fetch something from the library. Neither returned. We called Professor Webber and had no reply and then we found that awful note. And when we went to the library door to summon him . . . we saw . . .' She hesitated, as if it might be in bad taste to name what she'd seen.

'Some blood,' said Frank. In the corner, Mr Gray was still standing motionless by the red chair. Miss Fox sat by the billiard table, the swirling wine in her heavy, crystal glass catching the lamplight.

'That's correct. But nothing else. No . . . body or such like.' She winced. 'Professor Webber had apparently vanished into thin air. We became terribly alarmed, as you can imagine and made a decision to move to a safer location. Prince Rudolph kindly offered to seek your help. We hoped that help would come swiftly – and, indeed, it did.' She nodded curtly.

'Where did you find the note?'

'Tucked under a silver platter on the serving table.'

'So, one of the servants put it there, one would assume.'

'Anyone could have. We had people coming and going all day, delivering flowers, wine, linen – everyone you'd expect in the run-up to a party.'

He paused, pencil held above the paper. 'Are there any other ways in or out of the library – other than through the dining room, that is?'

'No, there are not, unless one jumps out of the window.' She raised an eyebrow, smoothed down her dark grey skirt.

'I see. And, later, sitting in here, you all heard the bell for your . . . ah . . . train.'

'Yes. In fact, Lady Abbott heard it first. None of us heard a thing. We argued it was rather too quick. But then a minute or two later we did hear the bell.' She gazed at him, eyes steady. 'And now here you are.'

'So, Mr Bell went to answer it.' For this version of events to be accurate, Frank's pulling the bell for the funicular came less than ten minutes after the group had fled the dining room in fear. Meaning the telephone call to the police station, which he'd estimate occurred around forty or forty-five minutes before he reached the foot of the scarp – an hour before he was looking around the dining room with Dottie – preceded any trouble by a good half-hour. It didn't add up.

'Yes, Lady Abbott sent him. There's a lever to call it up just through there, in our little electrics room, though more often it is Jessop who summons it from his room.'

'And when did Lady Abbott leave this room? Before or after Mr Bell?'

'I'm not certain. We didn't see her go. If she was powdering her nose, she can't have been gone more than ten or fifteen minutes, can she?' There was a clattering chime as a wine bottle knocked unsteadily against Mr Gray's glass. His face was ghastly white. A branch rapped at the windowpane and he flinched then went back to pouring his wine with a shaking hand.

'And who telephoned the station?' he said.

'I'm not sure what you mean. No one telephoned the station.'

'Whose blood is it?' He put his pencil down, sat back in his chair and looked at her.

'Isn't that rather your job to find out, Sergeant?'

'I'm interested in what you think.'

'Perhaps Professor Webber's or Mrs Gray's. That is all that makes sense. But I do hope it's perhaps a macabre joke.'

Mr Gray's chair scraped across the floor. 'Isn't it time to stop the pointless chitter chatter?' he said. 'Isn't it time to get us out of here before someone else dies?' Lord Forester stood up, followed, shakily by Mrs Radcliffe.

'Don't be stupid,' said Lord Forester. 'We're trapped here. There's a raging blizzard outside, the phone lines are dead and our only way out is broken. We're trapped here, waiting to be picked off one by one by a rabid killer, for God's sake!'

Mrs Radcliffe started to cry.

'One by one,' said Miss Fox quietly.

'Sit down, please, Lord Forester. Mr Gray,' said Frank, 'I'd like to speak briefly to Lady Abbott.'

Mr Gray flashed him a fierce look before staring at the floor again as if it might betray a dreadful secret.

# CHAPTER TEN

## THE TELEPHONE IN THE BILLIARDS ROOM

Lady Abbott strode over to Frank's table, giving Lady Forester's arm a stroke. 'Well done, Sophia,' she said. 'You're holding it together admirably. Sergeant, how can I be of help? Can I perhaps get you a small glass of something?'

Lady Forester nodded smartly at Frank and walked back to join the group in the corner. Though the other three were drinking steadily, she didn't pick up a glass.

'No, thank you. Do have a . . . be seated.'

She sat down in the chair opposite him, twisting it round slightly so that she could see the door. She plucked the brightly patterned shawl into place over her shoulders and then adjusted it again, smoothed down her bright, white hair.

'Thank you, young man. What a spineless bunch we must seem, hiding in a billiards room. We've all lived through far worse, you know. We're tougher than we look, the lot of us. There's not much that scares me.' Her eyes were bright. They moved around the room from Frank to the group in the corner to the door. 'Poor Mrs Radcliffe and I have a lot in common.' She dropped her voice, 'She survived the *Titanic*, you know. What a brave girl! As for me, another time, another ship, another story. I won't waste your time with it.' She glanced back at the door, adjusted her scarf and leaned forward. 'I'd advise you not to jump to any gruesome conclusion, young man,' she said. 'There have been a series of very unfortunate accidents here tonight. The supposed blood may well turn out to be a bowl of beef gravy. These things are always less alarming than they first seem. It's a terrible shame that Mr Bell's heart . . .' she lowered her voice to a whisper, '. . . but the way he carried on you would never have known it. Didn't want to be pitied. Perhaps he could have been saved if he'd been more honest. You need to keep an eye on these people,' she nodded at the group in the corner. 'See that they don't become hysterical with terror. I'd keep them topped up with the strong stuff, if I were you. I've always been the one to take on the role of house mother, you know.'

'And the note you all found in the dining room,' he said. 'Where do you think that came from?'

'Probably one of the servants,' she said. 'They're all so bitter and resentful these days, don't you find? Or do you think it's this blue-blood murderer we've all been hearing about?' She smiled at him. 'Of course, I'm not blue-blooded; I married into money. So perhaps I'll be safe.'

'Rest assured, I'm doing all that I can to keep you safe.'

'I'm made of stern stuff,' she said. 'I've lived through wars and disasters, young man.'

He weighed her up. Though her toughness was genuine, he sensed she was lying about something. He nodded. 'Thank you, Lady Abbott,' he said. 'That will do for now.'

She smiled, glanced at the door and stood up.

Mrs Radcliffe sat down in the empty seat. Her eyes were wide and long lashed – sweet but somehow empty. Both of her hands shook violently.

'When are you going to get us out of here?' she said. 'We're sitting ducks, waiting to be killed.' Her face was ice white, there were tiny, damp beads on her forehead and her pupils were dilated.

She'd bitten the corner of her lip until it drew blood. Her brown hair had fallen loose from its clasp and she was twisting strands of it between her fingers till they formed tendrils.

'Good evening, Mrs Radcliffe.' He turned a page of his notebook, glancing across the room at the group gathered there in the corner. 'We'll have to wait till help comes,' he said. 'We'll stay together till then.'

She shrugged. 'How will that help? One of them is probably the killer,' she said. Her eyes were red, her cheeks drawn. She looked as though she'd been crying for weeks – months.

On impulse he asked, 'How has it been in the house before tonight? Has everyone been happy?'

She laughed. 'Oh, we are not the happy sort, Sergeant Glover. It was all as usual.'

He looked down at the smooth surface of his notebook, the ash grey marks of his pencil. He drew a line or two, chewed the inside of his lip and looked up again. 'It must be hard getting by on so few staff, your mother and father doing without their personal staff.'

Mrs Radcliffe shrugged. Her fingers tapped at the table incessantly. 'There's normally a lot more than this. The housekeeper, cook and kitchen maids and all the footmen left early because of the storm. Mother and I share Dottie, but she's more mine than mother's. Jessop attends to father. Why don't you stop asking questions, find Professor Webber and get us all out of here?'

'Tell me about your reason for being in the club. What do you call it – the Penny Club?' He watched her closely, his eyes flicking back to the door every few seconds.

She winced. 'That horrid boat. At first it seemed fine. Then the floor began to tilt and our drinks began to slide. The mortal fear, you can't imagine.' She gripped the side of the table with pale fingers, as if it were about to slide across the floor. 'There were fewer places in boats than people who needed them, but women and children were . . . Anyway. There was shouting everywhere, the lights were flicking on and off, everyone was terrified. We all knew the water out there would be freezing. The blind terror. You could see it on everyone's face – sheer desperation, lost hope.

'Have you ever seen an animal led to the slaughter? They know. You can see it in their eyes. It was exactly like that. You start to lose all sense of up and down and left and right, you realise – it's as if you're already under the surface of the water with no idea which direction the ocean floor is, which direction the air is. The panic is like a virus spreading through you, bubbling into your lungs. But, anyway, I found the boat eventually. I got the last place, you understand. But it wasn't pleasant. It wasn't pleasant at all.'

For a second or two they sat, holding each other's gaze.

'I see,' he said, looking away. The finger tapping resumed. 'Professor Webber and Prince Rudolph, Mrs Gray. How would you describe them?'

'Prince Rudolph's a bore. Everyone knows it. Professor Webber's fine, if you enjoy being lectured by a middle-aged man. Are you finished with me?' She moved the back of her hand across the bottom of her nose and wiped the corner of her eye with her finger, then she stood up and went back to the small group, tossing her hair over a shoulder with a shaky hand. The windows rattled as she crossed the carpet. Mr Gray looked up quickly. Lady Forester sat as upright as an oak in a storm.

'I suppose you want to talk to me now?' Mr Gray's face was crumpled and distraught, his eyebrows drawn together. He sat down heavily. There was a small red patch on each cheek.

'How do you do, Mr Gray?' Frank held out a hand. 'Please accept my sympathies.'

Mr Gray moved to pull a glove off. 'We're past the point of platitudes, don't you think?' he snapped, before glancing down at his hands and pulling his glove back on. His hands were shaking. 'I don't want to see her. I don't want to think of her like that.' He gave Frank a pleading look. 'Must I see her?'

'You'll need to later. But you can gather your strength first.' Frank gestured at the seat opposite. 'Forgive the intrusion at this time, but you'll understand I need to question everyone. You're also a member of the Penny Club,' he said, turning his notebook to the next page.

'Not so lucky now, are we?' His voice was clipped, his eyes wild with grief.

'What was your lucky escape, if you don't mind my asking?'

'I do mind your asking, as a matter of fact. But I was in the War. You won't need me to give you the details. It was a nightmare, and I mean that quite literally. The mud, the stench, the smoke, the blood. Like hell. No escape and the sheer mundanity of waiting around for death. Claustrophobia and terror make horrifying bedfellows. I suppose you're too young to have been in the trenches.' Frank merely shook his head, his mind skimming over the horrors of his past with habitual efficiency. 'Well, we all were up against it, of course. Mr Bell and my wife escaped that dreadful bombing in Wall Street – Russian terrorists, you know. And Miss Fox, of course.'

'Yes. You must have been very worried about your wife all this time.' Frank looked at him closely.

Mr Gray sat up straighter, eyes suddenly alive with feeling. 'Worried?' he spat. 'One might rather ask why *you* are not more worried? Why you're not getting us out of here to safety? What sort of bumbling operation is this, exactly? I'm sure Parliament will be glad to hear . . .' He sighed, looked at the table, looked back up. 'She didn't deserve this,' he added more quietly. 'What happened to her?'

'I don't know for certain yet. But I'm afraid it looks like foul play.' He looked back at his notebook and roughly sketched a table with ten place settings, then turned the page. 'How do you think Professor Webber left the library, given that he's not there now?' he said.

'I can't see that he did. No one could see into the library from the dining table so there's no way of knowing what went on in there. It's a mystery. The man suffered from bad nerves, you know. Perhaps he leapt out of the window and ran off. You're the detective, after all.' He folded his arms and stared at Frank.

'Who discovered that Professor Webber wasn't in the library?'

Mr Gray lifted his gloved thumb as if to chew his nail and then put his hand flat on the table. 'I did. I rather assumed he'd picked a book off the shelves and lost his head in it. But he wasn't there, of course. There was nothing there except blood. And believe me, Sergeant, after the War, I've seen enough of that to recognise it.' His lips sneered, but his eyes cowered. He started to cough. 'Where's my damned . . .' and pushed a white-gloved hand into his pocket, swearing under his breath. 'Never mind.' He sat with his hands crossed in front of him.

'And Mr Bell – what happened there?' Frank said. He put his pencil down. 'What do you think happened to him?'

Mr Gray put his head in his hands, showing the fine, light brown hair swept neatly over the top of his head. 'If you don't mind, Sergeant, this is all a little hard to bear in the circumstances. I will, of course, cooperate fully with all your enquiries in good time.' He stood up, not meeting Frank's eyes, and walked slowly across the dimly lit room, his shoulders straight but his back bent.

Just then, a cawing split the air. Frank froze. After a second, he said, 'The telephone.'

'The house line? But we're all here,' said Miss Fox.

It rang again. Frank met Dottie's eyes, then Miss Fox's.

'Someone answer it then, for God's sake!' said Lord Forester.

Jessop made his way to the corner of the room and picked up the receiver as it rang for a third time. His face was white. Everyone watched him.

The room was silent. 'Jessop speaking.' He held the receiver to his ear for a second, two seconds longer, then he turned around.

No one spoke.

'Well?' Lord Forester burst out. 'Who the hell is it? Speak, man, speak!'

'There's no one there,' he said, and he slowly placed the receiver back down.

Frank swallowed. 'No one?' he said. 'You're sure?'

'There was a voice,' Jessop said, 'but it went away and the line went dead. It said . . .' he stared at Frank, '"come and find me."'

# CHAPTER ELEVEN

## THE MORNING ROOM

Frank turned the stone in his pocket, once, twice. 'I need to have a thorough look around,' he said. 'Jessop, would you come with me and stand guard at the top of the main stairs? You can alert me if you see anything unusual. You and I are not the target here,' he added, an attempt to reassure him, 'if this really is the so-called blue-blood killer's work.'

Jessop coughed, swallowed and nodded. Lady Forester stood up. 'No, send Jessop down to the butler's room, would you? He'll be of most use there – he can connect us to different rooms by telephone. I can show you whatever you want to see.'

'You can't send him there,' gasped Miss Fox. 'That's where that horrid call came from.'

'Why do you say that?' said Frank quickly. 'How do you know?'

'Because,' she said, 'it's the only room that has a direct line to the others. To connect the rooms to each other Jessop has to be by the exchange putting plugs in sockets.'

'Anyway, he's far more use standing guard,' said Mr Gray. 'We're sitting ducks in here without someone on guard duty.'

'No, John!' said Lady Abbott. 'Send him to the telephone gubbins. What if we need the officer? Our only way of contacting him is—'

'I hardly think *this* chap will save anyone's life!' said Lord Forester, pointing at Frank.

'Don't worry,' said Miss Fox to Frank with a smart grimace that contradicted the soft nervousness in her eyes, 'we'll scream if we need you.'

'Have some respect,' said Mr Gray. 'People have died. My wife has died. She's dead! You talk like it's just cocktail party chatter. You always were a heartless little—' Miss Fox just laughed.

'Come with me, Dottie, would you?' said Frank. She jumped to her feet. Jessop, jaw clenched and breath quick, followed. Lady Forester strode to the door and waited for Jessop to move the bureau from beneath the handle.

The hallway was dark and the wind battered at the thin window. Frank was acutely aware of Mr Bell's body in the next room, sucked dry of life in an instant.

The drawing room curtains fell strangely, as though there were figures lurking behind them. A pale cloth covered the round table by the window, fluttering in a slight draft. Every now and then the unseen hand of a sudden gust of wind lifted its edges into the air and dropped them back again. The many sofas and chairs had ruffled slipcovers hiding the tops of their sinewy legs. A piano in the far corner had its lid up, as if someone had, just that minute, been playing it.

Frank once again had the uncomfortable feeling between his shoulder blades: the primal sense of being watched. He tried to ignore it until it got so strong that he couldn't resist looking over his shoulder and around the room.

A man in a brown suit stood, pale-faced and insubstantial, looking directly at him. Frank let out an involuntary cry. The man watching him raised his hand to his mouth and stared back at him mockingly.

Then Frank's perception shifted and he looked at the mirror with clear eyes. His own reflection stared back.

'Come along, then,' said Lady Forester.

Resisting the urge to look over his shoulder, Frank followed Lady Forester through the empty room, Dottie and Jessop behind him. A glass bead or two of the chandelier tinkled quietly in the shadows. His took his revolver from his pocket and held it by his side.

The billiards room, drawing room and picture gallery reached out to the side of the grand upper corridor like an outstretched arm. The hallway between the drawing room and the picture gallery – the elbow – looked out onto the tall pine and birch trees that were now black brush marks against the dark sky. The moon was bright. Heavy snow smudged the scene, nudging it away from the real world and into remembered or imagined horror.

'This way,' Lady Forester said, her voice expressionless.

They walked from the landing into the picture gallery, a vaulted room with deep turquoise walls. A Persian rug ran down the centre of the room. It was an opulent space; one that, like the rest of the house, felt fatally flawed: there was a sense that the proportions didn't quite add up. All four walls were hung with paintings. Some were landscapes, some portraits; a couple didn't depict anything from real life at all.

'Quite a collection you have here,' said Frank.

'Thank you. It's not quite of a national standard, but we do like our little pieces. Some are inherited, but we have extended the collection, particularly with the more modern works you see.' She gestured at a particularly ugly, large painting of two figures made up of geometric shapes.

'I'm sure you have exquisite taste,' he said.

'Yes,' she said. 'One has to channel ones energy and spirit into something, or one would go quite mad, don't you think? Life as it is offered is so constrained, so small. Connections, once made, are so eternal as to be a damnation. But this . . . this is such a shocking state of affairs. This house was always such a refuge, and now I feel it is out to get us all. It's been in the family just four generations and it's always been a place of comfort and joy. But now—' Her manner was curious – expressionless and flat, whatever words she was speaking.

Jessop and Dottie moved quietly behind them, their steps in time with one another. Jessop's breathing was fast. Every now and then he coughed.

'Things are never quite as mysterious as they seem,' said Frank.

'That is some comfort. Thank you.' Lady Forester opened the door that led back the way they'd come, back to the balcony overlooking the grand entrance.

'Stand guard here, Jessop, if you would,' said Frank. 'Any sound or sight which bothers you, just shout. Err on the side of caution.'

Jessop nodded. He looked down the stairs and then behind him, and then down the stairs again. 'Very good, sir,' he said. He swallowed hard.

'Be careful,' said Dottie. 'Can you give him something to protect himself with, Sergeant Glover? Have you got a pistol?'

Frank thought for a second, then reached for his pocket.

'No,' said Jessop. 'Not a gun. I don't like guns.'

'It's not the likes of him that are at risk here tonight,' said Lady Forester briskly. 'It's us and our guests who should be worried.'

'Perhaps,' said Frank. 'We won't be long,' he added. Jessop nodded.

Lady Forester stepped on without a backward glance. Dottie looked worried, but she followed. The corridor was quiet as the grave. Jessop stood behind them, statue still; Frank could feel his eyes on his back as he, Lady Forester and Dottie walked away. He heard a slight sound and turned around quickly – it sounded like a very quiet *please* – but Jessop just shook his head wordlessly. Frank turned back and carried on.

There was something about Jessop – something wooden, unreal even. Frank couldn't put his finger on it. Maybe it was the role he was playing in order to do his job well. It seemed as though a skin had formed over the surface of his character and that there was no way to push past it.

Between the plain ones at the top and bottom of the walls a series of finely carved panels depicted what looked like birds – perhaps peacocks. On the ceiling of the hallway a tile mosaic picked out a similar scene in muted colours – browns, oranges and reds. Suddenly Frank realised that they weren't birds – and nor were the carved creatures to his side. They were flying lizards with long, forked tongues.

'Are these all bedrooms, off this corridor?' he said.

'Most of them. The morning room is at the end there.' Their footsteps rang on the hard floor. 'Where would you like to go?'

'I'll try the station again then I'll search the house. Where's your telephone? Jessop can see you back to the billiards room after you've shown me.'

'Why, there's one in almost every room,' she said. 'They all connect to the switchboard in Jessop's room and from there he can connect any room to another. Which would you like to use? Perhaps the morning room would be best, rather than root around in our guests' private things.'

He nodded. 'Dottie can show me,' he said. Dottie kept quiet, hands behind her back, mouth a firm line.

'Not at all,' said Lady Forester. 'This is my house.'

They approached a door on their left.

'One second,' said Frank. Quickly, hand ready, he opened the door and looked inside to find an empty, well-tidied bedroom, peopled by shadows. 'Carry on.'

They passed two more doorways, both opening to unoccupied, dark bedrooms.

Gradually Frank began to pick up on a very slight noise. The corridor wasn't quite dead quiet; there was a distant pat, pat, pat, as if a large cat were wandering unseen. He listened carefully but the steps faded into the shifts of an old house and the sighs of the wind. He stole a glance at Lady Forester, but she looked unruffled. Dottie walked quietly beside them, her face giving nothing away but the set of her shoulders telling a different story.

'Thank goodness my daughter and Lord Forester are safe,' said Lady Forester. 'The thought of anything happening to either of them is beyond contemplation.' Frank nodded. 'Lord Forester is more helpless than you'd think,' she continued. 'He needs coddling. His mother said that to me on our wedding day. "Take care of him," she said, "because he won't look after himself." A mother knows her son, doesn't she? I didn't know what she meant at the time, but now I can see it. It's almost as if he has no backbone at all. As if he's made entirely of...' She paused. 'I don't know. Maybe we just tempted fate. Thinking we were lucky. Celebrating it, even! We were asking to be proved wrong, every one of us.' Neither Frank nor Dottie replied.

They walked down two shallow stairs and into a wider corridor with five doors leading off it. This landing was darker than the last one. That sense of the house breathing slowly in and out was oppressive.

'What rooms are these?' said Frank.

'These are the best suites, other than the eyrie suite upstairs, which we keep for the very best guests – royalty and so on. The green room and the bamboo room are both exquisite in their own right. We put Lady Abbott and Mr Bell in them.'

'Was he one of your most important guests?'

'They are all important, of course. But yes, he is an important man – was! Oh dear, was. A huge name. Very important in the New York set. It's quite a different world in New York to England or Ireland, or even the rest of America, you know. Society there expects to be surprised, thrilled, excited, all at once. Mr Bell excelled at it. He had a talent for making connections, for bringing people together. He was a friend and confidante to all. Of course, he was what they call new money, so he had to try a little harder.' She reached for the door.

'I'll do it,' said Frank quickly, and glancing back over their shoulders he listened at the door for a second and then opened it fast, looking around. He nodded them in. Dottie looked over her shoulder quickly and then followed Lady Forester and Frank in, standing, almost as if to attention, by the door.

The room was lit by a few puddling wall and table lights, the curtains swaying slightly in the breeze. The walls were swirled with green, red and yellow. It was dressed for Christmas, an evergreen tree in the corner decked with candles and red ribbons. A handful of glass decorations hung from the branches. A grinning monkey, a wolf, a yellow-eyed cat hanging by one leg, a mouse, a rabbit. The marble fireplace was hung with holly and ivy. There were tinsel-decked mirrors on three of the walls, two of them in deep alcoves, reflecting the whirling colours back at them infinitely. The room was peopled with games tables and high-backed chairs, all with stiff, animal-like legs. A number of large, snaking plants made the room feel like a hostile jungle; the one by the window swayed slightly in the breeze.

'There's talk of a ghost,' Frank said.

'There's always talk of a ghost in large houses,' Lady Forester said. She walked to the windows and looked out across the gardens. This was the front of the house, but you couldn't see as far as the trees, never mind the road or the village in the distance beyond. Her face was closed. 'You believe in ghosts, do you, Sergeant? I think less of you than I did. I must admit it's long been a story told about the house. But people like stories, don't they? They like stories more than the truth.'

'Perhaps.'

He glanced at his watch. They'd very probably still be in the Red Lion. He lifted the black receiver from its brass hook, hoping to hear an operator's voice – a reminder of the bustling, normal world beyond the snow-fogged windows, snow-glazed pine trees and silent, black slopes.

Nothing.

'It's dead,' he said, trying to keep the dashed hopes out of his voice. He replaced the receiver. There was a small pile of calling cards next to the telephone, a message from Lady Forester written in a thick confident hand, in blue fountain pen, across the top. He caught Dottie's eye and saw the hot disappointment reflected back at him, swirled through with cold fear.

Lady Forester nodded briskly. 'I thought it might be. I'm afraid we are rather remote here. We rely on fair weather for these modern accoutrements. I suppose you're not confident here on your own. You look very young – you must be newly promoted to sergeant, I suppose? I'm afraid I don't know too much about the workings of the police force.'

'Not at all,' he said, offering no further explanation. He walked over to the mantelpiece. A Christmas scene painted on folded cardboard was in pride of place. It depicted a grand house. Snow lay on the ground in front of it and the pine trees surrounding it were frost garlanded. An evergreen wreath hung on the front door. To the side of the house a steep hill led to a winding path and, in the distance, a warmly lit village, windows alive with candlelight. With a chill Frank realised he was looking at a picture of the very house he was standing in. The muted red-brick facade with a wing, behind, to either side. The clock tower to the rear at the back with its black numbers on and brass bell above.

The painted scene was folded in on itself to either side, the central opening aligning with the centre of the red-brick house. Curious, Frank opened the flaps and saw the interior of the house intricately painted inside, furniture and fittings faithfully replicated: even tiny people going about their business. Each of the room doors had a number painted carefully on it and could be folded open – the first twelve had been folded back to reveal a scene, the rest remained closed. Interested, he prised one open – a child bathing their doll. That picture looked a little less carefully drawn than the others he could see.

Something about the cardboard scene jarred. It wasn't just that it depicted the house he was standing in. No. It would come to him. Frank studied it carefully and filed the image away in his mind to come back to.

'An advent calendar. They're the latest thing,' Lady Forester said from just behind him. 'I don't suppose you'll have seen one before – they're rather fashionable this year with the young. My daughter loves them. They are rather sweet.'

Her stony poise struck Frank, once again, as out of kilter. There was something guarded about her eyes, studied about her behaviour. Frank would have liked to get beneath it, see a little more of what she was made of. 'Are you worried about your mother?' he said, watching her carefully.

'My mother is dead,' she said flatly. No emotions crossed her face. 'She died many years ago; my father too. I suppose you mean Lady Abbott – an easy mistake to make. The Dowager is an old family friend.' She moved to a games table and picked up a chess piece. 'Yes, I'm afraid both of my parents died before the Great War. They were in their eighties; no one could say it was untimely.'

'You must have been the baby of the family.' A fine smear of dust was on the tongue-like leaves of the plant next to him in a copper pot. A mother in law's tongue, he thought – he had his grandma to thank for such knowledge; she was vinegar-soaked, but she had a love for plants that she'd shared with him.

'Not at all. I was the only child. A last-chance baby, I think they call it.' Lady Forester sat down on a high-backed chair. She picked a leaf from an ornate flower display on the small round table next to her and began to tear it into tiny shreds, her eyes fixed at a point in the near distance.

Frank picked up a Christmas card from the mantelpiece. *Forester Raw Iron wish you a Merry Christmas.* He glanced back at the door. Nothing. His ears were pricked for any sound, but all was silent. The fire in the mantelpiece looked as though it had died out some hours ago. They hadn't expected the guests in here in the evening.

'The family business is iron?' he said, opening the card and inspecting the looped writing inside. He glanced up at Dottie, sensing her tension. Eyes wide, she gave a quick, shallow out-breath. Her eyes were pinned to the door.

'You'll know the ironworks, I'm sure. It's done no end of good for the local community since Lord Forester's grand-father set it up. Not just jobs, but education and health. There are even art groups run by the local ironworks and supported by our charitable foundation. Of course, my own family were never in industry. Indeed, we can trace our ancestry back to the eleventh century. But I am proud to now be part of the Foresters. Unfortunately, we didn't have a son to carry on the family business.' She spoke slowly and loudly, without expression. 'But business is booming, thanks to careful management and a pioneering spirit.'

Frank picked up another card. Generous, untidy, looped writing. *With love, John and Anna Gray.* Another. *Cecilia Fox.* He moved to the table where Lady Forester sat. He picked up a chess piece from the board and put it back again. The white queen had check-mated the black king. 'Keen on chess?' he said.

'It's more of a man's game.' She smiled thinly. 'My husband's a keen player.' She glanced, involuntarily it seemed, at the door, and at Dottie standing there, hands behind her back, a high colour in her cheeks. Lady Forester stood up, a grey statue against the deeply shadowed emerald-green curtains.

'Hasn't iron rather had its day?' he said.

She smiled. 'Not at all. We were an early adopter of the open hearth furnace. It's a lack of innovation that destroys our competition, not the industry itself. Our income . . . I won't bore—'

Then a shot sounded loudly. Dottie screamed and ducked. Frank reached instinctively for Lady Forester and then made for Dottie, looking all around him. His ears rang with the sound of it. But there was silence. Dottie rose shakily to her feet.

'Just the pipes backfiring,' she said, a tremor in her voice.

But Frank noticed one strange thing. Lady Forester didn't jump or move an inch. She stood, stock still, a slight, fixed smile on her face throughout.

# CHAPTER TWELVE

## THE PINEAPPLE ROOM

'Where to now, Sergeant?' said Lady Forester levelly. 'Jessop will take you back to the billiards room to wait with the others,' he said. It really was extraordinary how accurately the cardboard scene – what had Lady Forester called it, the advent calendar? – had depicted the interior of the house. He could recall the tiny brush strokes that made up the coils of dragons in these carved panels. Lady Forester merely shook her head. 'I must insist,' he said.

'On the contrary, Sergeant, *I* must insist. I'm not usually in the habit of expecting guests to wander around my house alone, without a host or hostess.'

'I'm not a guest.' Frank quickly looked down the corridor and then opened the door on his left. He looked around, hand on his breast pocket. The room was empty. 'In you come for now, though,' he said. Dottie held the door open for Lady Forester, then followed, looking over her shoulder. 'Everyone has been drinking tonight, I suppose,' he said, quickly looking around.

'No more than you'd expect at a party,' she said.

The walls were covered with a riot of spiked pineapples and curled leaves. The room was tidy and well furnished, with a wardrobe, a bed, a small table and chair, and a chaise longue. 'Whose room is this?'

'This is Mr Bell's room.'

'When did he arrive?'

Dottie was at his elbow now. 'The guests arrive by teatime on Friday,' she said. 'It's the same every year.'

Lady Forester tutted and bent down to straighten the bed cover. 'These single men,' she said. 'They need looking after.' Dottie moved to Frank's side. Frank and Dottie exchanged a quick look, Frank wrinkling his brow and tilting his head towards Lady Forester, Dottie shrugging. Lady Forester banged a cushion loudly.

Frank flipped open the leather-bound book on the small table. It looked as though Mr Bell had neat, large handwriting. Scribbled notes. Sums of money. A hurried budget, perhaps, though it didn't seem to balance. Dottie peered over his shoulder at the pages.

'These pillows,' muttered Lady Forester, her back still turned. She plumped them violently, smashing them against the side of the bed.

Frank turned to the back of the book. He tried to slip his hand between the inside and outside cover. He turned to the front of the book and did the same, but this time his hand slipped between the paper cover and leather front and his fingers found a piece of paper, folded in two. He pulled it out, glanced at Lady Forester busy at the bed, and opened it with one hand. The writing was small and neat. *I wouldn't have thought you would want anyone to find out about your indiscretions. A small payment to cover my inconvenience . . .* He and Dottie met each other's eyes. He quickly refolded the page with the same hand and slipped it inside his trouser pocket. 'Tell me about Mr Bell,' he said.

Lady Forester straightened up and turned to face them. She smiled tightly: carefully. 'A charming man,' she said. 'He lived a charmed life, you might say. The high life. Wealthy, single, something of a playboy. Always another girl on his arm. A master of his world. Everyone liked him, wouldn't you agree, Dottie?' Dottie nodded. 'As I say, new money – you might say he needed to be liked. He never settled down. I believe he thought *settling* for anything was not for him,' she said, eyebrows arched – whether in disapproval or complicity Frank could not say for sure.

He wondered if his own life seemed easy and trivial to others. To him, the decision not to marry or have children didn't feel like a light one, but one born out of a hard-won philosophy of life: a seriousness of approach. But, of course, some company was nice, and he had not been born without emotions.

'How did he get along with your other guests?' Frank glanced at Dottie to check whether her expression tallied with Lady Forester's words, but her hands were behind her back and she was giving nothing away. She tucked a strand of wavy blonde hair behind one ear and her nose twitched. A pipe creaked and she jumped and looked behind her back, bit her lip and glanced at Frank anxiously, as if to hurry him up. 'Did he get on with the Grays?' He looked from Lady Forester's face to Dottie's to the door and back again.

'Of course,' Lady Forester said. 'He knew Mrs Gray from New York. They escaped that horrible bomb.' She grimaced and twitched the corner of the coverlet into place.

He tried to imagine Mr Bell as a gadabout, cruising between New York and England, but all he could picture was a man frozen on his back with a clawed hand and blistered face. Death had diminished him to a plate of flesh, as it did everyone. Outside, the snow beat fists against the windows, but Frank would rather be out there with the desperate elements than in this quietly murderous place. He'd begun to feel that it was the house that was watching him to see what he'd do next, that it was waiting for an opportunity to trip a switch and fry or boil him, to slip a cable out of its hook to crush him. What had these people done to anger her? Where was she keeping her final captive, Professor Webber? Was she torturing him or had she long since killed him?

'And Prince Rudolph? What was he like?' He noticed that Dottie flinched, almost imperceptibly, before quickly correcting her expression and standing a little more upright.

'Oh, all charm, as you'd expect. He's European royalty, after all. But it wasn't all roses. He's had to make some difficult decisions at times. That brings with it a certain steeliness of temperament, you know.' She sighed. 'Poor man,' she said, and gave Frank a rueful smile.

'What's through this door?' He pointed at a door on the opposite side of the room. It perhaps led to a dressing room or a small washroom. His bearings were clear in his mind and he could see that they would now be in the left wing of the house – the one that contained, right at the rear, the Roman bath where Mrs Gray lay in her finery, like an abandoned doll in a toy bath.

'That's the master suite,' said Lady Forester. 'When Florence – Mrs Radcliffe – was young this was the nursery.'

'We keep it locked when we have guests,' said Dottie. She added, in a different voice, 'Where is Professor Webber? I keep thinking I hear footsteps, but I turn around and no one's there.'

'Quiet,' snapped Lady Forester. She took a small bunch of keys from a fold of her skirt and sorted through them. Frank noticed a small brass one, with a head like a dog's at its bow. 'Yes, it was Florence's nursery when she was small,' she continued, 'but is generally locked these days. You wouldn't want someone wandering in on you in the night with nefarious intent. It's a bit of a fossil from my great-grandmother's era, when most large houses had interconnecting suites. We prefer to keep rooms for our regular guests. This is a house of entertaining. Or, at least, it was.' She nodded at Frank, in characteristically flat recognition, he supposed, of the deaths that had occurred there that night. Where Dottie's poise had a professional veneer and was punctuated with fear or grief,

Lady Forester remained stony faced and unreactive, her face untouched by whatever emotion lay beneath the surface.

'I'm scared,' Dottie said to Frank under her breath. She was at his elbow now.

'Stay close,' he said. Then, lowering his voice a little, he said, 'Can I count on your help?' She glanced at Lady Forester, seemingly torn, then nodded.

She unlocked the door as the clock tower struck twelve times.

# CHAPTER THIRTEEN

## THE FORESTER SUITE

'Wait,' said Frank, stepping forward. He held a hand behind him to keep them there, and then opened the door, looking around swiftly. 'Come through,' he said. Dottie's arms were folded, but she quickly unfolded them and put them behind her back.

The walls of the sparsely decorated room were the colour of spoilt milk and the wooden floor was covered in a plain rug. Blue curtains hung at the windows, and the two wooden beds were covered simply. Frank thought of Lord Forester's dominant character and Lady Forester's glacial stillness that, he felt, covered vast, tectonic rumblings.

The fireplace had been made up for a fire but not lit. Frank glanced over to the small bureau by the window on the other side of the room – an ink blotter, a newspaper, a sheaf of papers. Lady Forester plucked a displaced coverlet into place slowly. He gave her a long look.

There was a wastepaper basket next to the desk, with a single crumpled-up scrap of paper in – Frank glanced at Lady Forester, whose back was still turned, and then raised an eyebrow at Dottie. She flicked her eyes at the bin and quickly moved a couple of steps towards it. She eased the piece of paper out, looking over her shoulder at Lady Forester, and slipped it into her apron pocket, barely bending to do so; she looked like a silver birch arching in a strong wind. Frank nodded at her, approving of her instincts.

Still looking at Lady Forester, Frank nodded at the desk drawer. Dottie pulled at it, looking nervously at Lady Forester's turned back, but it was locked. The keyhole was small and gold-coloured, shaped like an animal's head. Dottie, hands behind her back again, moved efficiently to stand next to Frank. All of this time, Lady Forester had been fussing at the cover. He coughed and she looked up.

'I'd like to get you back to the others,' he said, 'I can tell you're a brave woman,' – she nodded in agreement – 'but I must put your safety first. You were in here dressing for dinner, I assume. And since then? When are the rooms made up?'

'After breakfast. And usually straightened again after dinner, before the day staff leave on a club night. They did it a little earlier today – after afternoon tea.'

A strange music drifted into the room like smoke, so quiet that Frank couldn't be sure whether it was real or a long-forgotten song in his head. It rose and fell, dropping in and out of tune like fairground music. The harder he strained to hear it, the more it eluded him. Lady Forester appeared not to notice anything. He shook his head quickly.

'Lord Forester does some of his business in here?' he asked, nodding at the desk.

'When we have guests it's easier to be tucked out of sight if it's just a matter of a little paperwork. Business is a round-the-clock concern, Sergeant, as I'm sure policing is.' She picked up a pencil from the bedside table and sat down on the bed, pressing the pencil into the table until the lead crumbled and, finally, the wood split. She put it down and glanced up.

'Of course. I'm sure you don't mind me glancing at these papers.'

'Certainly.' She sat there, grey and solid, watching him implacably.

He picked up the papers, which seemed to be a log from a cash book, or the workings behind one. Large payments in, he noted. 'Forester Raw Iron,' he said, 'that's the family iron firm.'

'Yes,' she said. 'Of course.'

He gave her a sharp look. 'I realise these are Lord Forester's business interests not yours,' he said. She nodded curtly. 'What does Lord Forester export to Ireland?'

'You'll have to ask Lord Forester that. There's nothing wrong with patriotism, though, Sergeant Glover.' She straightened a sapphire-studded bracelet on her sturdy wrist. 'Or, indeed, with business acumen.'

'Is this the door to the baths?' he said.

'That's to our bathroom. You're welcome to have a look. This door,' she pointed at an arched doorway on the far wall, 'is to the Roman bath.'

Frank took the few steps to the door and tried it, knowing it would be locked from this side, as it had been locked from the other side just an hour earlier, and that he'd have to wait for Lady Forester to follow and unlock it. But it opened. His heart jangling, he pushed. Someone had been this way – someone with a key.

The brass door handle was warm to the touch and fitted snugly in the palm of Frank's hand. He opened the door an inch, two inches. There was a sweet, chemical scent in the room that he hadn't noticed when it was filled with hot steam. He could just see the tiled room, the corner of the sunken bath, a hand. Like a doll in a bath.

A doll in a bath.

His heart quickened. He closed the door again.

Lady Forester was still standing exactly where she had been, at the foot of one of the two beds, her head tilted a little to one side.

Dottie stood next to her with a soldierly air, hands folded neatly in front of her.

'I'll come with you,' Dottie said hastily, though he hadn't spoken of moving.

'I think we'll return Lady Forester to the billiards room,' he said. 'We've been away long enough. But one second. Wait here.'

He strode quickly through Mr Bell's room to the morning room and took the advent calendar from the mantelpiece. The pictures behind some of the closed doors – a bell, a wreath, an angel – were painted in the same delicate watercolour as the house. Others didn't quite match as closely. He pushed at one with his thumb nail – it had been pasted on. A broken train. A sword in the library. A bolt of lightning in the electrics room. A clothed doll in the bath. These were all pasted-on pictures – just like the pasted-on words in the letter. He pulled open the other doors quickly, but how was he to decipher this? A ship, a toy soldier, a bell. He hurriedly pushed a fingernail beneath the other doors. This one – door twelve, in a corridor near the drawing room – hid what looked like a glued-on picture of a crumpled up body packed into a tiny space. He slipped the calendar inside his jacket.

He dashed back to Mr Bell's room. Lady Forester and Dottie were waiting at the door to the master suite.

'Quickly. Let's get you back to the others,' he said. 'What the hell is that music?'

Lady Forester snorted. 'That will be our musicians,' she said, almost gaily. Frank was startled by her tone. Face still set in a tight smile, she walked briskly to the door.

Dottie said to him quietly, 'They're not real, they're automated.'

'I'll go first,' he said quickly, and followed Lady Forester to the bedroom door. 'Right,' he said, opening it and looking around. He nodded at Lady Forester to walk on.

Dottie put her hand in her apron pocket and quietly handed him the scrap of paper that she'd pulled out of the wastepaper bin not five minutes ago. It read, in familiar, spiky capital letters, *12 November 1924. B.S. – It has been done. You can count on my discretion.* He put it in his pocket.

Jessop was standing at the head of the stairs. They moved quickly down the wood-panelled corridor towards him, lights flickering in their sconces as they passed. He seemed to be swaying slightly in an invisible breeze. One hand kept returning to his forehead, senselessly and rhythmically.

'Anything to report?' Frank said.

'No, Sergeant Glover. My Lady.' Jessop nodded at Lady Forester.

'If you wouldn't mind heading directly to the butler's room, Jessop,' said Lady Forester. 'That way, we can put calls between different rooms if we need to.'

'Very good.' He lifted a trembling hand to his forehead again.

'Where are these bloody musicians?' said Frank. He could sense Dottie's gaze on Jessop.

'In the drawing room,' said Lady Forester smoothly. 'We'll see them as we pass. They're one of the house's hidden surprises. Call for us if you need us, Jessop,' said Lady Forester, striding on.

'Yes, my Lady.'

Frank stole a look at Jessop. There was an almost imperceptible wobble to his face, like a blancmange that had been shaken. The hallway below them was swathed in shadows. He heard a creaking floorboard: perhaps a pipe. 'No,' Frank said. 'Come with us, Jessop. We don't know who's down there.'

'I am more than happy to do whatever her Ladyship wishes,' Jessop said, but his red hands were trembling and his eyes darted about the hallway like a cornered animal's.

'No,' he said. 'Come with us now. There may be safety in numbers.'

'There wasn't before,' said Dottie. 'Things happened quickly, unseen.' She looked at him reproachfully. 'Why not now?' The colour rose in her cheeks. 'You shouldn't have put Jessop here alone. I should have said so.'

'Don't worry about me, Dottie,' said Jessop.

'Oh, but I do!' Jessop put a gentle hand on her elbow quickly, as if to reassure her – or keep her silent – it wasn't clear. 'Jessop's nerves,' she said. 'How could you be so unkind?'

There was, it was true, a ripple of something unsteady creeping through Jessop's stubborn manner. 'Everyone stick together from now on,' said Frank, and he put a hand flat on Jessop's back by way of an unspoken apology.

They walked quickly through the picture gallery, glared at by stately portraits and more casual figures in modern paintings. The wind shook the windows, thin sheets between them and a world almost completely erased. The sense of the wind circling and the snow smothering was insistent and grim. The music got louder, dropping in and out of tune and time. Frank pictured a merry-go-round, his mother smiling and disappearing as he cantered out of sight, reappearing just round the next turn, still smiling. He pushed the thought away. 'We must hurry,' he said.

He pushed the door to the drawing room. Standing by the piano were three mechanical figures playing instruments – an accordion, a pair of cymbals, a triangle. Their faces were frozen into grins and their arms moved stiffly, juddering every now and then. They had white faces, red cheeks and fixed smiles. They stared straight ahead as they rattled out their cheap wails. They were fixed on some sort of rail that led back to an open cupboard door.

'Charming, aren't they? They were a gift from Professor Webber to mark the completion of the work to the house. He has a knack of finding the most unusual things. He set up a system for us where they roll into place and start to play automatically at the end of the night.'

'How do you turn them off?'

'They only play for an hour or so. You can't turn them off once they have started. As with all of our little modern conveniences.' She tilted her head at him, almost as if she were inviting argument. He had never found anyone so hard to read. 'Once they begin, they must play out to the end.'

They walked quickly across the room. Halfway across, he instinctively turned and he could have sworn he saw the shadow of a figure pass the door, but it was gone before he could fix his eyes on it. He rubbed his eyes and walked on.

He stood, alone, in the anteroom. He could hear angry, anxious, frightened, relieved voices greeting Lady Forester and Dottie on the other side of the door. He heard *stupid woman* and *need to stick together*. He could also hear crying. He couldn't hear Lady Forester's voice at all.

There were three doors from the anteroom – the door to the billiards room, the door to the electrics room and the door back to the drawing room. This was exactly where the sinister drawing of the small body crunched up in a cupboard had been pasted on the advent calendar. He stood there in the dim quiet, looking around him carefully. A slanting rectangle of light from the drawing room doorway spilled onto the tiled floor and gave him a vast shadow. He could hear his breath – in, out, in, out. He looked carefully at every doorway, every wall.

Then he saw it. There was a small hatch in the wall, next to the drawing room door, painted the same colour as the wall around it. It was almost impossible to see in the low light. Quickly, Frank lifted the hatch up and peered inside. A hole dropped down into the darkness, two ropes on either side. He reached out to touch the rope and it burned his fingers. It was moving.

He stood there for a second or two, thinking about what he'd seen. He glanced back at the billiards room door, then he quickly made for the stairs. He ran down them two at a time, following the corridor to the butler's pantry. There. Yes. His bearings were correct. His mind darted to Mary inside, but he had no time to stop. To reassure himself, he tried the handle of the pantry – it was still safely locked. Another small door in the wall, exactly like the one above. Breath fast in his chest, he threw it open. There was a small cupboard in there with two shelves, swaying just slightly. But it was empty.

He went swiftly back to the corridor. He felt watched. But the tall, shadowed room was empty and the only watching eyes were the portraits on the wall.

# CHAPTER FOURTEEN

## THE EBONY ROOM

F rank walked through the drawing room, the musicians grinning sightlessly at him. There, just outside the billiards room door, was Dottie.

'Dottie,' he said. 'Why are you out here?'

'Waiting for you,' she said resolutely.

'Are they all in there?' he said. 'You get back in there where it's safe.'

'Yes, they're all in there. I'll come with you,' she said. 'I can explain the house to you. The strange systems we have here. All of the automated devices. It can be a confusing place for newcomers. And if I can fetch some warmer things for the ladies upstairs while I'm at it, even better.'

He shook his head. 'You're safer here,' he said. He thought for a second that she was going to come with him regardless, but she just nodded. He took three steps across the room, hesitated for a breath, then he turned around.

'You can come,' he said, 'if you're sure.' How was he to know which was safer, and at least he had his wits and a revolver.

She nodded, pleased.

'Well,' he said, 'if we're in this together then we need to check all of the rooms upstairs and down for Professor Webber, or an intruder, or for any evidence of what has gone on here and why. Stick close with me, stay alert. If we see anyone, be prepared to get out of the way quickly. If I indicate it,' he gave her the smallest move of the eyes, '*like so*, get out of the way – behind a door, behind a table, wherever's to hand.'

She followed him. He took his hand from his pocket and brandished Lady Forester's set of keys. There were some advantages to having had an unruly youth.

The electrics room was dark and still. The figure lay as they'd left it, clawed hand clutching at nothing.

Frank observed everything quickly. He took a pen and paper out of his pocket and drew a quick sketch. 'Look,' he said, pointing at the controls. The lever that was marked 'funicular' was in the upright position.

Then he looked more closely at the body. The expensive suit was pristine. The nails were clean and neat. The bloodied right hand in the air was clutching at nothing. The left hand was at his side.

Dottie said, 'His hand.' A tiny scrap of what looked like blue paper showed through the flesh of his fingers.

'Yes,' he said.

He sat on his heels and with his pocketknife he gently eased the edge of paper out of the stiff hand. He kept an ear out for anyone leaving the billiards room, but heard no footsteps, just voices rising and falling. A tiny bit here, a tiny bit there. He adjusted his position and kept trying. Finally, there was a quarter inch of paper protruding from the hand.

Carefully, Frank pulled the edge and teased it out. It was a small scrap of blue paper, torn along two edges. Frank could see white lines and numbers, a few letters and words in small, very neat capitals. In the bottom corner the letters LKW. It looked like a blueprint, though a very tiny part of one.

*IGNITION. TIMER.*

'That's the same writing.' Dottie said. He nodded. Then she added, 'And it wasn't there before, was it?' She sat down on her heels opposite him, back against the wall. 'This isn't quite right,' she said. 'I feel as though . . . it's a stage, a play – do you? It seems that this, and the other pieces of paper . . . they're props. That people are acting and trying to make us say certain lines, do certain things.' She gave him a steady look across the dark room. 'I think someone put this here for us to find. And the other pieces of paper, the one in the bin, in the back of the notebook. We were supposed to find them.'

He nodded slowly. 'Yes, I agree.' He stood up. 'Let's keep going.'

'Where shall we go?' said Dottie. The billiards room was to their left, the drawing room to the right. They could hear raised voices, footsteps of someone pacing behind the billiards room door, a tense laugh. Mercifully, the strange mechanical music had stopped.

Frank took the advent calendar from his pocket and one by one prised the doors open with his fingernail. 'We need a proper look at this,' he said. 'Let's sit down a second.'

'Mrs Radcliffe's advent calendar,' she said. 'Why do we—' She followed him into the drawing room.

'Look,' he said, glancing carefully to all corners of the room before sitting down at a small table. He made sure she was sitting with her back to the near wall. He could see both doors. 'Some of the pictures aren't the right ones – they've had images pasted over the top; like the note they found. Look, here there's a toy train. Prince Rudolph died on the funicular.'

'Oh!' she gasped.

'Here, the doll and the bath. Behind the door to the Roman bath. Mrs Gray. Here, a sword behind the door to the library.' He looked up. 'Who gave this to Mrs Radcliffe?'

She shook her head. 'I'm not certain.'

He turned it over. 'There's no maker's name. Who had the opportunity to add to it?'

She shrugged, her brow furrowed. 'Just about anyone.'

He nodded. 'Now look, I can't make much of all of these yet – can you? But this one. This one bothers me. We need to go here next.' He glanced up at her. 'If you're willing, that is.'

'I'm willing.'

He closed the small door on the picture – a puppet lying prone on the floor – and folded the calendar in two.

'The ebony room. That's Miss Fox's.' She stole a worried look at the door back to the billiards room. 'She's unharmed, isn't she? Can you hear her voice?'

He nodded. 'Let's find out what's there.'


They walked quickly across the drawing room, keeping easy pace with one another. She was tall, her shoulders almost level with his.

'It's funny,' she said, 'how you almost get accustomed to danger.'

'Yes,' he agreed. 'But you'll find it hard to get out of that state of mind later when it's all over. When we're out of here.'

'If we get out of here,' she said lightly.

'We will.'

He turned back and glimpsed, at the drawing room door, the shadow of a man in a top hat again. 'Wait,' he said, and ran back. His heart caught in his throat. Professor Webber. He was there in seconds.

But the room was empty. Nothing. Just an odd stuttering sound next to the door that was, in a moment, gone. He breathed in, out, in, out. Nothing. Heart pounding, he walked back to Dottie, looking over his shoulders every few steps.

'I saw it, too,' she said. 'Professor Webber.' Her face was white. 'Where did he go?'

'There was no one there. It must have been a trick of the light.'

She shook her head quickly as if shaking off the untruth, but she didn't say anything.

He pushed open the door to the picture gallery and carefully scanned the room before holding it open for Dottie. The vaulted ceiling stretched above them. The large windows looked out over the snowy courtyard where he'd walked with Dottie – it felt like a lifetime ago, but it had been just an hour or two. Outside, the snowstorm was becoming a blizzard – tendrils of icy snow whipped around in the dark air, strangling the trees and covering the mouths and eyes of the house.

She cleared her throat. 'Isn't it an amazing house?' she said.

He recognised the urge to normalise and said, truthfully, 'I don't much like it.'

'It has everything. Steam heating, telephones, electricity . . .'

Frank cleared his throat. 'It has electricity, I'll grant you that. But is that a good thing? A house just outside Manchester burned down the first week it had electricity installed. The family were out at the theatre, showing off about their electricity to all and sundry. They got back and it had burned the house down.' He spoke slowly, soothingly.

'Now, now Frank. Don't be a luddite. Electricity is the future. Of course, there will always be teething problems, but engineering is where all our future is. It's . . . well, it's pure optimism!' Her voice shook a little still and her eyes were a little too bright.

They passed through the picture gallery, gazed at by dozens of mute, oil-stiffened faces. Frank listened by the door for a second and then opened it quickly, scanning the corridor before letting

Dottie through. The corridor was shadow muffled. The balcony dropped behind them into the dark below like a cliff edge.

'All quiet,' she observed.

The wind bayed mournfully at the windows. 'I shouldn't have left Jessop alone here,' he said. 'It was too much.'

'He's not had an easy life. First his parents died, then his sister – who was more like a daughter to him really – was drowned. He's all alone in life.' She gave him a clear-eyed look. 'He's not as strong as he could be.'

He nodded, accepting the implied criticism as a just one.

They quickly took the last few steps to the door to the ebony room, both wondering what they would find inside. Dottie took a deep breath. 'Shall we go in?' she said quietly. He listened intently and held out one hand as he turned the handle. The room was empty.

'She always has this room when she stays?' he said, eyes darting around every corner. He looked behind him and held the door for Dottie.

'Oh yes, all the guests have the same room each time they stay. Lady Forester wants it to feel like a home from home.'

'Except for the dead bodies,' he said, then regretted it. This wasn't a Marsh or Riley, with the dark sense of humour life in the force gave you, it was a country Lady's Maid.

'Depends what they get up to at home, I suppose,' said Dottie dryly. Frank gave her a quick glance. Perhaps he'd underestimated her.

The walls were a pale moss green, the furniture dark and brooding. The room had an intense gloom about it. A dark dressing table with a white bamboo-leaf pattern held a tall black vase and a large mirror.

Suddenly Dottie shrieked, hand to her mouth. He looked at her quickly and then followed her gaze.

In a dark alcove in the far corner of the room, a long, salmon-pink lace dress hung from the picture rail, a fur stole wrapped tightly about its neck. The arms hung loose and lifeless.

Dottie breathed out slowly. 'Just a dress,' she said. 'Sorry. It's just a dress.' He could see a tear forming in her eyes. Her lips were tightly pressed together. She wouldn't look at him.

'Now,' he said gently, 'don't take on. Don't take on now. It's just a dress, like you say. Tell me more about this house. There are great water wheels on the stream down to the river, aren't there? I saw them as I climbed. And the tin musicians, they are set by some kind of automated timed mechanism. And steam heating you say?' He spoke softly and slowly, keeping his tone level. All the while he scanned the room, looking for trouble – trouble that was already passed or trouble that might be coming.

Dottie nodded. 'The musicians are automated, yes. And we have hydro-powered electricity,' she said.

'Oh yes? What's that then?' He moved to the wardrobe and pulled open the door. There was an idea forming in his head, but he couldn't see the outline of it clearly yet.

'Powered by water. The lakes and streams on the estate power a turbine which generates the house's electricity. You might have seen the powerhouse – on the cliff? That's where it all happens. We've had electricity here for twenty years.'

'More like two or three, surely?' He moved towards the elegant, black bed. Dottie followed. It was made neatly.

'It is twenty years. The estate generates its own electricity thanks to Professor Webber's inventions. It uses a dynamo. We've got hydraulic engines too. Here,' she said, walking to the wall where the dressing table stood. 'Here's the vent for the steam heating. It's clever, though it's not an especially new technology. The Romans used it, you know.' Her eyes were brighter and she quickly wiped her cheek with the back of her hand.

'There are pipes throughout the house?' His mind was darting off with that, taking it in all kinds of directions.

'Except the servants' quarters, of course. We have the stove in the kitchen and fireplaces in our rooms. The ladies say the steam is good for their complexions.'

Frank pulled open the top drawer of the ebony chest. 'I'm not sure this is so good for their complexions,' said Frank, picking up a small, white porcelain jar, with a thin pipe protruding from its top. 'Mrs Gray and Miss Fox were close, I believe. You might expect Miss Fox to be more upset by her death. Perhaps she wasn't surprised?'

'She's always like that. She never shows her feelings. She has them, though, of course she does. She's just learned to keep herself to herself, her real self, I mean. It's locked away inside her. You get glimpses of it here and there, but I think that what is inside and what is outside are very different for her.' She sat down. 'You see a lot as a maid,' she said. 'If you're curious about people there's a lot to catch your interest.'

'What was Mrs Gray like? Did she sometimes seem drowsy or confused?' He opened the jar and looked inside, sniffed it.

'She was a beautiful, vibrant lady. And now she's dead. You shouldn't—'

'That she is. I'm trying to get a full picture. She wouldn't want it otherwise.' He examined the jar and pipe closely.

Dottie picked up a pillow, put it back down again. 'She might, you know. She had enough of people prying in her life without suffering it in her death.' She held the pillow in her lap and gave him a steady look. 'She was famous,' she said, as if he'd asked the question. 'Of course she did. Gossip, people wanting things from her, people talking about her.'

'Did she find it hard to manage, being well-known I mean?'

'She managed admirably,' she said, plumping the pillow up again and setting it into place. She picked up the next.

He put the jar back down and looked in the drawer again. 'You admired her?'

'She was beautiful,' she said, as if that settled the matter.

'You're more than that, though,' he said, quickly searching through drawer after drawer. They caught each other's eyes. 'Your interest in the house's engineering and all that, I mean.'

She nodded. 'My father taught me about engineering. We'd sit by the fire in the evenings and he'd tell me all he knew.' Her eyes glowed. She placed the second pillow down into place and stood up, automatically smoothing the slight indent in the covers she'd left behind. 'He said that to a father knowledge is a gift,' she said. 'You give all that you have of it to your children, just like mothers give love.'

There it was again. Pressed like an insect into the road. Frank's mind flared in horror and immediately froze. 'He's an engineer?' he said quickly, batting the thought away with habitual efficiency.

'No, he was a miner. He loved books. He taught himself.' The softness in her face spoke of sadness, grief. Love.

He noted the past tense. 'And taught you,' he said gently.

'He taught me to teach myself.'

Despite himself, he smiled.

Then he froze. Light footsteps, but footsteps nonetheless. They approached and then receded into silence. Almost immediately, another set followed in silence. Dottie and Frank stared at each other. He dashed to the door and pulled it open. The hallway was as they left it – empty, dark. The staircase was deserted. There was no one.

'We must have imagined it,' said Dottie, uncertainty rippling through her voice. They looked at each other, both knowing that they hadn't imagined it. Frank moved back to the chest of drawers. 'Look through the wardrobe, would you?' he said, as he opened drawers and quickly scanned the contents. 'There's no one out there,' he added.

'I don't like to,' she said, but she moved quickly to the wardrobe with the quick and efficient responsiveness of an excellent servant. 'What am I looking for?'

'Anything that seems unusual,' he said. 'You won't know what's unusual and important and what's just unusual at first. Nor will I, necessarily. The piecing together comes. For now, you are just looking for pieces of the puzzle.' He stopped, hands paused, then continued. 'And think on whether it's found or placed, as we were talking about earlier. Whether it may have been deliberately placed.' He heard the stiff ebony door creak and then the swishing of fabrics. 'You know her well,' he said. 'And Mrs Gray too. They come here often, to see Lord and Lady Forester? Not just for this annual party – they're regular visitors, or you wouldn't be so close to them, so distraught; so knowledgeable about their inner worlds.'

'Yes, that's right. They come often. All of them, more or less, but particularly the Grays and Miss Fox. Miss Fox's real friend is Mrs Radcliffe. They're alike, those two. They seem less similar than they are. They put on a careful show of being insubstantial, particularly Mrs Radcliffe. With Miss Fox the disguise is maybe a little different. But disguise it is all the same. Mrs Radcliffe is spoilt, yes, but she's sensitive, shy and full of desperate sadness. She did love Peter so.'

Frank could see nothing further of interest – just the sort of thing you'd expect to find in a society girl's bedroom. Maybe, he thought grimly, you might even expect to find opium paraphernalia among a worldly girl's belongings. Perhaps Mrs Gray was weaker than Miss Fox, had more to run from, more reason to do a little more than dabble. There aren't many situations that could make you unaware that you were being boiled alive like a lobster, but perhaps this was one.

'Just frocks,' said Dottie. 'And lovely coats.'

Then the footsteps again. This time they were even lighter and less solid. They moved quickly, getting closer and closer to the door, then they paused. Dottie and Frank stared at each other. The steps started again, moving quietly away from the door and down the dark, empty corridor.

# CHAPTER FIFTEEN

# THE READING ROOM

**F**rank was not normally one to prefer the station to the scene of the crime, but this was proving to be the exception to the rule. He thought of a busy room, many minds at work, the smart – and sometimes not so smart – jokes flowing. But here, the shadows, whispers, secrets of this place – its creaking walls, muted anger, its stubborn silences – they got into your blood.

The corridor was empty, as he knew it would be. He took his revolver out of his pocket again and held it lightly in his hand.

'Let's try to make sense of it,' he said. 'Most people here are guests. Most of the guests don't have a close family connection to the host and hostess. The connections are tenuous, you might say. Circumstantial, almost.'

'They're all members of the club,' she said. 'The Penny Club.' Her eyes brightened at his tone – he could tell she relished a puzzle.

'Right, and some introduced each other to the club and so on, so there are some closer connections there, but it's not comparable to, say, a family dinner or a party of close friends or business associates. And the club is a survivors' club, that's correct isn't it?' He looked over her shoulder as he spoke, listening keenly.

'Yes, I think so. Find a penny, pick it up, all the day you'll have good luck. That's the reason for the name. They all survived something important – they say it makes you into a different kind of person, being a survivor. That it's the making of you. I'm not sure that I agree. I think the mettle of you is something deeper than that. It could be that surviving something horrible may just reveal something about your character that was already there – that you'll stop at nothing, perhaps – rather than forging some kind of strength.' She hesitated, straightening her apron. 'Maybe what happened here tonight is just accidents, bad luck? Maybe their luck ran out. Maybe Mrs Gray fainted in the bath . . . and maybe Mr Bell just, I don't know . . . Like that story you told me earlier about the mansion house in Manchester that burned down because the electrics weren't safe. Maybe the electrics here weren't put in safely enough. Perhaps we're all hiding for nothing. The train crashed in the ice. And we've seen Professor Webber,' she said, though she spoke with less certainty now.

They both looked down the stairs towards the large entrance hall. The shadows of the bannister created bars on the stone floor. The driving snow battered at the tall window; the trees cowered under it. Frank had a sense of being trapped in a snow globe. 'Not a very easy-to-reach house, is it?' he said. 'Not exactly practical.'

She thought for a second. 'Maybe that's why they like it. Privacy. They can never be interrupted without knowing about it in good time.'

Once again Frank had the disconcerting sense that someone different to the person he thought he was talking to was looking out from behind her eyes. 'Where's tucked away that we might not have seen?' he said. 'Are there any smaller rooms, out of the way? I'm thinking where someone who was afraid might choose to hide out.' Or someone who was killing people. 'Where would you go, if Lady Forester hadn't led you to the billiards room?'

She tilted her head, thoughtfully. 'To the reading room,' she said. 'It's a small room, no one goes there much. It's out of the way. I'd have gone there, I think, and locked the door and waited for help.' She glanced at him. 'Not that I would have had any option but to do what Lady Forester wished.'

'Let's look there, then.'

Dottie led him away from the tall shadows of the empty hallway and back towards the west wing of the house, towards the picture gallery and the drawing room. All was quiet. If the small group in the billiards room were getting rowdy or angry or scared, then they couldn't hear it.

Back in the small anteroom that led back to the picture gallery she stepped neatly to the side and put the flat of her hand on a door that Frank hadn't noticed – like the door to the dumb waiter, it was panelled to match the walls and was easy to miss in the low light. A small, tarnished brass handle, almost the same colour as the wood, and the slender shadow of its outline were the only indications it was there.

He listened at the door. Nothing. Was the final missing person, Professor Webber, cowering in there in fear? Was he waiting behind the door with a weapon, ready to clobber him or stab him? Was he victim or perpetrator, on the attack or on the defence? He put his ear a little closer to the smooth wood. Nothing but muffled, inhuman silence. Could he hear the almost imperceptible creak of shifting weight on an old floorboard, the sigh of tension held too long and slowly leaking out? Then, very faintly, he heard something – was it a very quiet, low cough? Nodding to Dottie to keep back, he slowly turned the cold handle. Breath tight in his chest, one hand indicating for Dottie to wait, one hand on his revolver, he opened the door.

It was an empty, wood-panelled room. A desk was by the many-paned bay windows which, curtains open, looked out onto the snowy night and from there down across the gravel to the trees, barely visible now – just black shapes against the blacker sky, their outlines interrupted by snow. The floor was covered with a thick Persian rug, and pictures were hung on every wall – not the grand art of the picture gallery, but small portraits and photographs. More were on the mantelpiece. An easy chair sat on the other wall, looking out of the window.

Indicating for Dottie to stay where she was, he stepped into the silent room, gun in hand. But there was nowhere to hide in here – no cupboards, no hidden corners, no large pieces of furniture behind which someone could lurk. There was no one there. He beckoned Dottie in and shut the door behind her, putting the revolver back in his pocket.

'Let's have a look around while we're here,' he said. He made for the desk and started to open drawers. The first drawer had messily stacked writing paper and a series of pens, some missing their lids. The second contained a thick wad of letter-headed paper for Forester Raw Iron. The third contained a series of brown Manilla files, piled on top of one another. He pulled them out and sat at the desk.

'What are you looking for?' She was behind him, half peering over his shoulder.

'I won't know till I find it. Maybe even after that. You can look through some of these.' He threw a handful of files over to the other side of the desk.

She pulled up the easy chair and sat next to him. The file on top of his pile looked like a set of financial accounts. It was signed in each corner with a confident hand in thick, blue ink. The company was doing well from what he could gather. He glanced through it and opened the next.

'These are letters about raw iron,' said Dottie. 'Raw tool flow, it says at the top. I suppose that's what they call what they sell, which are tools, I suppose. So why raw? That's a strange term for a tool. Iron can be raw, but not when it's been processed and made into something.'

He looked up. 'True,' he said. He continued flicking through the files until he came across one with *Penny Club inaugural meeting* scrawled on the front in pencil.

'Ah,' he said. 'This could be useful.' Dottie looked over his shoulder, interested.

In the cardboard file was a sheet of paper with a date and a list of names, very like the one that was folded up in his pocket. He took that out, unfolded it and compared the two. The same notepaper, the same confident handwriting – slightly untidier in the older note – and the same, blue-inked names. The date at the top of the earlier piece of paper read *10 December 1921*. 'They always meet in December?' he said.

'Yes,' she said. 'It's their tradition. Lady Forester says it's good to remember the year that's gone with gratitude that you have survived it. And Mrs Radcliffe says it starts her Christmas season nicely.'

'I would have thought it's a bit of a boring mix of people for a young girl like her.'

'Oh, she's not so young. She's nearly thirty. She's already been married, you know. She seems younger than she is.'

He picked the piece of paper up and turned it over, leafing quickly through the rest and then going back to read them properly. 'Potted histories,' he said. He read for a couple of seconds then snorted under his breath. 'So, Mr Gray didn't have such an admirable war record as all that, then.'

'I don't know anything about that,' she said stiffly.

'Let's just say he didn't see much action. A month in the trenches before he was redeployed because of his nerves. That wouldn't go down well with the voters, would it? Resolute courage in making difficult decisions,' he read. 'For that read utter b . . .' he glanced at her. 'Anyway, who's up next?'

'Here,' said Dottie. 'What's this?' She handed him a handwritten note.

'Where was this?' he said quickly.

'Just here.' She pointed at the cubby holes at the back of the desk. Frank looked at them sharply, but they all looked empty. 'It was at the side, caught in the joint.'

He took it out of her hand.

*24 July 1924. B.S. – I will see you there at 6 tomorrow. It can easily be arranged. Would I ever say no to you? Particularly on such a project as this. It will take an hour or two, no time at all. If you are sure? I won't ask again. You know my thoughts on the matter. Yours ever.*

'B.S. again,' she said. 'Like the other note. That must be Baron Scarpside. And the same writing.' She put it down on the table between them. 'But it was quite easy to find.'

It was a small hand, letters very neatly formed, written in capitals. 'Professor Webber and Lord Forester – or Baron Scarpside, as he's also known – are loyal friends?' he said.

'Of course,' she said. 'But—'

'But?' he said quickly.

'Never mind. Nothing.'

He gave her a keen look but didn't press her.

'He's perhaps more loyal to Lady Forester,' she said after a while. 'There's a story he wanted to marry her, but she chose Lord Forester instead.'

He pocketed the note and carried on looking. The rest of the biographies told him, more or less, what he expected to know. Miss Fox, Mr Bell and Mrs Gray had survived the Wall Street bombing in New York, a bomb that had killed Mr Bell's younger brother. Mrs Radcliffe had survived the *Titanic* disaster. Prince Rudolph had escaped his homeland while it was under occupation. Lady Forester and Lord Forester had escaped the Irish War, as had Professor Webber.

'What did Lady Abbott escape?' he said. 'Why is she a lucky survivor?'

'Oh, I know something about her,' Dottie said, just as Frank picked up a newspaper clipping.

'*Mystery of lost crew of the Mary Celeste,*' he read. '*Found abandoned at sea intact, but all hands gone forever. No trace.*'

'Yes,' said Dottie. 'She escaped it against all odds.'

'It says all hands gone forever.'

'She doesn't talk about it very much,' said Dottie. 'She escaped in the dark in a rowing boat, she had to row for miles and miles alone. She must've thought she'd die out there. The rest of the crew, her husband too, they were lost without a trace; she was married to the captain, you know. It's a terrible tragedy in her life, took her years to recover. But she did recover, and she married again and she had a good life – a whole new life, a second chance. Lord Abbott died just ten years ago, after a long and happy marriage. Mrs Radcliffe will marry again too,' she added, almost defiantly. 'She'll recover too.'

He pulled open the next drawer – some pencils, a sharpener, a magazine. He flicked through it quickly and found a page with the corner turned down; though it had been folded back up again, the faint line in the paper was clear to see. It was an opinion piece about the conversion of factories to munitions during the War. The reverse of it was an advertisement. *Shorthand didn't give him time to think*, he read. *How much more work can a man turn out with The Dictaphone than with old-fashioned, round-about shorthand?* The next page was a witty comment piece about etiquette at the opera, the following page an advertisement for slacks. He closed the drawer and went to pull open the bottom one, but it didn't shift. It was the only one with a lock – a strange little keyhole in the shape of a dog's or fox's head.

'Anything else?' he said to Dottie.

'This last file is a memoranda of meetings,' she said. 'What do the initials WLW stand for?'

He glanced over her shoulder. *Scarpside requested sub-committee WLW be convened.* He looked at the date at the top – July 1920. He took it to read it more closely as the clock tower struck once for the hour. Paused at his work, he looked out of the window. It was hard not to be mesmerised by the snow outside the window. It fell in such soothing swirls, like the start of sleep. The shifting shadows out there could almost be someone struggling through the heavy snow. The dark shapes gathered into a person, out there alone in the dark. He blinked, looked back and they were gone. He rubbed his eyes. It was going to be a long night and it had barely begun.

'We'd better keep moving,' he said. Dottie nodded.

As they reached the door, he heard it – a stuttering, buzzing noise, almost as though the walls themselves were whispering. He bent closer to the wall to listen, but it was already gone.

# CHAPTER SIXTEEN

## THE GALLERY

As Frank and Dottie closed the reading room door behind them, Frank was overcome with a sense of how small his current landscape was. The whole world was outside these doors, but he could get to none of it. In some countries it would be morning now, in others lunchtime or the cocktail hour. People were going about their business, working, polishing their shoes, eating eggs, flirting, dancing, listening to jazz.

He was tugged back to another time, a short but precious few weeks, just a few months ago. She'd lost everyone as a child – first her parents and then her brother. Loss was a thread that linked him to Mary, though they never spoke of it. He reached his mind to the safely locked pantry door and then quickly back to the work at hand.

'There's something here with the trappings of the house,' he said. 'Don't you think, Dottie? Work has clearly been done by Professor Webber recently and it seems to have been done quickly, secretively even. And there is something to do with . . . never mind. It's not clear in my head yet. I wonder, has Professor Webber cooked this whole thing up? This strange theatre?' He was pacing up and down like he was in the station, working long hours to get to the bottom of a case. 'As revenge for Lady Forester choosing the wrong man?'

She threw a quick glance at the door. 'Professor Webber is more than an engineer, he's an inventor. Engineers find ways to make existing systems work, but inventors dream up whole new ways to do things or make use of what you have. Once you have the network,' Dottie was saying, 'anything can flow through it.'

He looked at her sharply. 'You're right,' he said. 'You're spot on. We need to know more about that.'

'They say it was a labour of love, this house, for him. That he lost money hand over fist doing it all hours at the expense of other paid work, so the other servants say. I even heard one of the maids tell that Mr Gray that Professor Webber had been desperate for money for many years, that he had turned to – what did she say – nefarious uses of his skills. But servants can gossip,' she said. 'That doesn't make it true.' She paused and then she added, 'He would do anything for Lady Forester, I would say that. And he did say to me last night that he'd have more money coming his way soon, so perhaps he was over the worst of it.'

'Anything?' he said, thoughtfully. 'Interesting. Now, our missing man isn't in any of the living quarters, it seems. Let's check the bedrooms now. We can ruminate on what you've said as we go. There's just one thing that's been playing on my mind. We passed it in the picture gallery. We'll take a really quick look while we're here.'

Frank was sure they'd left the picture gallery door closed. He made a point of closing every door he opened – he was always meticulous about that sort of thing. But the door to the gallery was open, swinging to and fro in one of the house's many drafts.

He found the painting he was looking for; he was certain he recognised the thing. It had been in the papers recently; what was the story? 'Horrible painting,' he said, conversationally.

'You don't have a good eye; that's the best of the bunch supposedly. Lady Forester is very particular about it not being touched
or moved. It arrived here in the dead of night in the summer. The
men that lifted it in looked more like gangsters than art handlers,
to be honest with you.'

'Did they now?' he said thoughtfully. 'I've seen what I need
to see here. Tell me more about Professor Webber,' he added.
'What's he like as a person?'

'I don't like him. He's not a very nice person. He's quite angry.
You never know if he'll shout at you or tell you off or just ignore
you. He told me off once for mentioning God. He's an atheist. He
says the concept of God is illogical.'

'So it is,' said Frank. 'So it is.' From where they stood in the
vaulted picture gallery, they could see through the door into the
drawing room, which was now opened by a good few inches.
'People are moving around. I want to know if it's them or our
missing man, or, indeed, someone else. We'll not stop long.'

She followed him through the drawing room, her feet tapping
in time with his on the soft rugs. The automaton musicians had
stopped playing, frozen, it seemed, mid-beat – one had its cymbals
raised, another had its mouth open in a horrifying rictus grin. The
lamps on the small bureau flickered, sending long shadows that
looked almost like human figures onto the pea green walls. The
curtain billowed out and sunk back to the window, revealing the
relentless snow and black sky.

He quietly opened the door an inch or two before it hit the
heavy bureau they had wedged there. Jessop stood by the door,
eyes bloodshot and strained, and moved to shift the barricade
out of his way. They were all in there – Mr Gray was sitting by
the window, staring at the snow, his arms wrapped around his
body. Mrs Radcliffe, Lady Abbott and Lady Forester were huddled in a corner, Mrs Radcliffe rocking backwards and forwards.

Lord Forester was pacing around the room. Miss Fox was potting balls at the table, one after another. None were speaking.

Frank closed the door behind Dottie and they all turned as one to look at him, dead-eyed. Then Mrs Radcliffe stood up, silently, and started to walk slowly towards him. Lady Abbott followed, and then Lady Forester. Lord Forester stood where he was, then slowly turned and began to move.

'Are they here yet?' said Mrs Radcliffe. 'Have they come to save us?'

'Where is Webber?' said Lord Forester. 'He's behind this. I respect the man, but think about it. He's disappeared. All the accidents involve his inventions. I've never entirely trusted him. He's our killer, no doubt about it. Driven insane by his own genius.'

'Or by his . . .' Lady Abbott lowered her voice, '*godlessness*.'

'Tempted by the Devil,' said Jessop.

'Lord Forester, may I have a quiet word?' said Frank. 'Just step into the drawing room, if you don't mind.'

Frank could feel Dottie's eyes on him, her desire to join them, be a part of the conversation and add her mind to the investigation. He didn't meet her gaze. He let Lord Forester go ahead of him and open the door to the anteroom. After he left, he closed the door behind them.

It was quiet and still. The snow lashed at the window. The light was low. Frank watched Lord Forester's back as he turned the handle of the door to the drawing room – a broad, heavy man, dark hair just curling over his neck. He remembered what Lady Forester had said about him needing to be looked after, but couldn't make sense of it – this brutish, bearlike man seemed anything but soft.

'The best room in the house,' Lord Forester was saying. 'Very important Regency architecture, you know. Can you see the detailing on the architrave? Small things like that, someone in the know would pick up on them straight away. Signals, if you like, to people of a certain class. We remodelled extensively. But we kept all those vital features that show how important the place is. There's still a little work to do – the new clock tower is not quite finished, though the clock is functioning. The stones need . . . oh, I forget. Lady Forester will know. Mortaring perhaps.'

Lord Forester sat down on one of the high-backed, pea-green chairs, upholstered to match the green walls. The back of the chair was intricately carved with foliage and animal heads, with a leering, hairless human head at the top.

'How is everyone?' said Frank. 'How are they bearing up under the strain?'

'Lady Abbott is blotto. Lady Forester is useless. And Miss Fox? Well, she's rather bloke-ish, so I imagine she's dandy.' He cocked an eyebrow and leaned back in his chair, glancing involuntarily behind him as he did so.

The sky outside was black. Frank would be feeling weary in normal circumstances, but the adrenaline was coursing through him. 'The family business is in raw iron, is that right?' He tapped out a scale on the table.

Lord Forester smiled coldly. 'Not quite right, no. We own an ironworks where we produce pig iron and now, of course, steel. But we also produce various iron and steel machinery parts and so on. We diverted to arms during the War of course, requested to do so by Parliament. We're now back to our core industry. Why the interest in our business, young man?' His arms were folded across his chest, his chin was lifted high. There was a dangerous glint in his eye. It read like anger, but Frank knew enough to be aware that it might also be fear.

'All information is important. And you run the business? It's doing well?' His eyes were on Lord Forester, but his peripheral vision took in the rest of the room and he listened for any slight sound.

'Of course. Can't trust anyone else to do it for you. Does it look like we're doing badly? We have not one but two beautiful houses, as a matter of fact. One back in Drogheda. Should be able to get back there soon, only my daughter and wife have got rather attached to this place. You know how women are. Sentimental. I expect they're hoping to get Florence married off to an English-man.' He smirked.

'Anyone got a reason to be angry with the family? Anyone might feel slighted, resentful?' He gave Lord Forester a level look. 'You know how people get.'

'Is there a man alive that someone doesn't have a reason to be angry with, Sergeant?'

'Perhaps not. Shall we go back in?'

'Glad to. Let's hope we all get out of here alive.' Lord Forester hoisted himself out of the chair. 'Stupid things,' he said and walked to the mute musicians and punched each one till it lay flat on the ground. 'Idiotic present for an idiotic woman,' he added. And he walked back into the billiards room as Frank watched.

A minute later, he and Dottie closed the billiards room door behind them, and stood, for a second, in something like peace; the peace of a battlefield in the seconds after guns are fired. They stepped quietly through the silent drawing room and on to the shadow-forested hallway.

# CHAPTER SEVENTEEN

## THE CHINOISERIE ROOM

The wood-panelled walls and narrow ceiling of the long upper hallway enclosed them. Lamps splattered thick, yellow pools onto the walls and floor. Wild animal faces peered out of the ornate wooden foliage. Bears, wild dogs, wild boars. Eyes everywhere, staring at them.

'Where do you want to go?' said Dottie.

Frank turned the stone over in his pocket. Once. Twice. 'We'll go downstairs,' he said.

'Do you feel like someone's watching us?'

'All big, old houses have that effect,' he said, but he looked around him all the same.

'Maybe it's because there are so many doors in them, and so many windows. They're what make a house look like a person. The eyes and mouth. I mean to our minds. I can't explain it clearly. Jessop would say we feel like we're being watched because we are being watched. He thinks the spirits live on. But then everyone he cares about is a spirit now, so maybe that's a comforting thought to him.' They walked, in silence, down the grand, empty stairs to the deserted entrance hall. 'Or we *are* being watched, somehow,' she added.

He thought of the amphitheatre-like balconied hallway. 'Yes,' he said. 'Now, let's work our way down there.' He pointed towards the empty dining room at the end of the long corridor; a busy dinner party wiped clean of people. Both of their minds moved to the pool of blood lying inexplicably and impossibly on the library floor, just out of sight, without any body or any sign of a body having moved or been moved. And on to Professor Webber, still roaming free, half-glimpsed at a distance. And on to the footsteps they'd heard. They made their way to the furthest closed door on their left, the Grays' room. 'Do you like working here?' he said, curious about her inner world.

She nodded. 'I like the ways of the house.'

'Its traditions?'

'No, the way it works. Here.' She reached across him.

'I'll do it,' he said quickly. He listened, heard nothing, and opened the door. The feathered fuss and sweet smell.

'My pa always said a room should be plain. He said it's not our place to mimic nature's beauty,' Dottie commented.

'I'm inclined to agree with him.'

'Oh, but it's so perfect for her. If you're in here it somehow feels like being with her. And Mr Gray, of course. He married a famous singer, after all. He'll have got used to the high life. He travels to all kinds of places, lives the life of Riley.'

'Did they have a happy marriage?' Someone had sat on the bed since it was straightened – earlier than usual today, after tea not after dinner. There was a streak of red on the floor, another on the mirror. There was a sweet, slightly chemical smell in the air – a familiar one.

'Some say it had run cold. They say he'd turned from her because her looks were fading and her blood was showing through.' Dottie's disapproval was in every line of her face.

'Her blood,' he said slowly. He bent down to examine the mark on the floor – it was a bright, waxy crimson.

'Her upbringing. It wasn't as high as his. He had his head turned, they say, when he married her.'

He moved to the mirror. The same substance.

'They say she was too concerned with her career to settle down and give him a family,' Dottie continued.

'Do they? And what do you think?' The red marks explained the how, at least, if not the who. He scratched his cheek with a thumbnail. Logic would dictate that it was Professor Webber; he'd written or received the notes, he'd altered the house and its strange gadgets only recently, he was the only missing person. And yet it was too staged, too deliberate, too one-dimensional.

'I think it's a good thing. She had a gilded life. She saw something she wanted and chose it. How many of us can say that? Most of us just find ourselves somewhere in life. She chose somewhere and made her way there.' Though she was animated, her skin was pale. He dropped his pencil as he tried to get his notebook out of his pocket and she jumped.

'How do you know she didn't just find herself there?' He picked up his pencil and made a couple of notes in thick graphite on the rough paper.

'Because I talked to her. She loved the limelight, loved being on stage. Said that's when she felt alive. She said that without it she felt empty, like a balloon that was let down. She had to get back on stage to fill up again.' She moved to sit on the bed, noticed that it had been disturbed and checked herself.

'Sounds like a curse more than anything, to me.' He looked around the room. What else? The sense of Professor Webber wandering around the house unseen made him glance over his shoulder at the door. Was that movement? Just the rattle of the window again.

Dottie had moved to the bedside and was looking at something nestled on the floor between the bed and the small table next to it. 'What sort of medicine is this? Is it for pain? Oh, poor Mrs Gray — she did get dreadful headaches.'

Frank crouched down on the floor. A brown bottle with a narrow neck. He knew the kind. He picked up the bottle. Rather a lot in there.

'You could say that.' He opened the lid and smelled it quickly. Yes. 'She was close to Miss Fox, you say? Had they been friends long?'

'Oh, years. They knew each other in America, you know. Miss Fox designs her costumes. Like this one.'

He followed her eyes and saw a figure, stock still in the shadows of the corner, watching them with sightless, blank eyes. He flinched. 'A clothes mannequin,' he said after a second.

'Yes, she likes to have one in her room so she can see her clothes properly. Look at this outfit, it's a stage one.'

A deep purple dress with gold feathers down its skirt hung on the cloth woman. Behind it a vast, ostrich feather fan was propped on a high, round table. 'Why does she need stage costumes for a dinner party?'

'She likes to travel with beauty, she says. She's a great inspiration to me. I may not need feathers and silk in my life, but sometimes I think I'd like them.' She stroked the skirt of the dress. 'She lived such an incredible life. Like a songbird – hunted down. If she came here to fix her lipstick, why didn't she go straight back? She must have stood in here just before she died.' She looked at the floor and then the mirror. 'It seems that she fell, just here, holding a lipstick.'

'Yes. Did she get on with Professor Webber? And how did Professor Webber get on with Prince Rudolph? And Mr Bell?'

'Professor Webber and Mrs Gray were very different people. You wouldn't often see them talking. He'd talk to the men more. He and Prince Rudolph were like-minded, though they'd argue about religion. Mr Bell got on famously with everyone. He was a charming man. I know what you'll say, you know the type, but he had genuine charm, I mean. He liked people. You can tell.' She rubbed the corner of one eye with a knuckle then straightened her back. She looked back at the lipstick mark on the mirror and rug, seemingly judging the distance.

'Unlike Professor Webber?'

'I don't want to speak ill of him. He doesn't have charm in the same way, but he is honest and clever.' She looked back at the mirror. 'That's not a natural angle to fall at,' she said. 'Your arm would be much more flung to the back or the side. She was placed down.'

Pleased, he said, 'You're right, you know. Dottie, you know the house and its workings well. Would it be possible to . . .'

'To what?' Her eyes flitted to the door and then to the window.

'Not to worry. I need to get my thoughts straight.' She nodded and smiled politely, looking like a dutiful soldier.

He turned the pebble over in his pocket, thoughts of intricately sprung mouse traps in his mind. He looked at Dottie more closely, biting the inside of his lip. *So, if* . . . 'Tell me more about how you got on with Professor Webber,' he said. He started to walk around the room slowly, looking at the walls carefully. He was counting under his breath.

'How do I get on with him, don't you mean?' she said. 'Not how did I.'

'Of course.' He paced from the door to the far wall. Bent down and peered at the corner of the room – the walls, the deep skirting boards. What if the whole place was a stage set?

'I don't like his need to argue all the time. To put people right and debate. I like a conversation, but I don't like anger.' Her fists were clenched and the set of her shoulders was high and tense.

'I like a heated debate, myself.' The work had been done a month ago. But it had been done in league with the owners of the house – how else could it have been, of course? They *could count on his discretion.*

'You'd get on with him then, unless you're very godly. What are you doing?' She was staring at him.

He ignored the question. He was running a finger over the corner of the room. 'Oh, I'm a heathen. We all are, my lot. You have to go back a long way to find a God-fearing man.' Despite himself, he half-smiled to himself, thinking of his old dad and his sister Beatrice, and evenings spent in fierce discussion until the fire sank into the hearth. As his thoughts drifted to his ma, he batted them neatly away.

'He'd like you, then. I was interested in what he knew about engineering, but he never wanted to talk to me about it. Have you found any clues about what's happening here?' Again, almost involuntarily she glanced at the door. There was a thick tension in the air, as if they were both waiting for someone to burst through the door and attack them; to enter, stage left, right on cue.

Frank paced back from the door to the next wall, counting steps under his breath. 'I suppose he doesn't talk to women about that kind of thing.' He looked at her. 'I'm not saying I agree with him,' he added. 'I'm sure your questions would be very intelligent. If he listened, maybe he'd learn something.'

She nodded, accepting the compliment quietly. 'I suppose the question I'd have is, is the whole thing accident or design?' she said. 'If it's design, then you'll find a more obvious pattern to it.'

'That doesn't sound like a question that would get you *out* of a heated debate with him, if that's what you don't like. That's a godly question.' While he was talking, he was calculating the distance between the two of them and the door, and the distance between his hand and his pocket. Every creak sounded like a step, every sigh like the intake of breath of a man who was standing silently behind you ready to strike.

'I don't mean that. I'm talking about . . .'

Frank would be glad to be out of this room, dark and full of hidden nooks and crannies as it was. The painted scene on the wall to the side of the bed kept dragging his eyes towards it, but it struck the kind of false note that he hated. A clouded sky over what he guessed was supposed to be an oriental landscape – ornamental trees and strange, multi-tiered buildings. It didn't look, to his eye at least, well painted – the trees didn't look real at all, and the animals in the landscape looked flat and lifeless, except the lone dog that strolled towards the tall house on the mountain – that looked real enough.

His eye was drawn to the painted house again and again and he couldn't work out why. Something about it made him feel peculiar.

Then he saw it. In one of its ground-floor windows – the fourth along, just like this room – a man stood at the window looking out. Behind his painted figure you could just make out a woman's pale face and dark dress, watching his back as he stared out of the window, oblivious to her presence. He jumped, but calmed himself quickly enough. It was just a strange painting. Or were they pasted on too?

Perhaps to reassure himself, he moved to the window and opened the curtains to look out into the grounds. The skin between his shoulder blades prickled. The first few rooms of this main corridor were set back a little from the dining room, which, with the library, formed the grand corner of the east wing of the house. Those last rooms stood proud of the rest of the facade, their large bay windows protruding deep into the gravel path outside. From this window you could see the dining room's bay window splashing yellow light onto the snow-smothered gravel.

No.

He stared, heart pounding, fear shrieking through his brain.

The glass of the bedroom window reflected a woman in black standing right behind him.

He let out an *oh* and turned around. Just a reflection of Dottie. But she was standing in the corner of the room, looking at her fingernails and glancing nervously at the door.

Heart in his mouth, he turned back again. And then he realised. It wasn't a reflection at all. There was a woman standing at the dining room window staring right at him. But before he could focus on her, she was gone.

# CHAPTER EIGHTEEN

## THE GARDEN ROOM

Frank's father was not an unkind man. He did his best. He knew that Frank and Beatrice were being brought up without the benefit of a woman's touch, and he tried to be gentler and more loving than his nature allowed to make up for it.

Frank hated it. He couldn't stand the touch of his father's hand on his hair, the way his voice dropped when he talked to him about the softer things in life. He wanted none of it – wanted the real thing or nothing at all, certainly not some sort of make-do. He'd bristle, move away from his father's hand with the anger rising in his chest. He couldn't help himself.

His father accepted this anger passively in a way that infuriated Frank. If his father had shouted, he could have shouted back, thrown a punch even, but he just stood there waiting for the blow.

Once, early on, he'd had such a vivid dream about his mother that he could smell her – the warmth of her skin, the scent of apples on her fingers, the soap powder on her dress. The disappointment on waking was too much to bear. He'd cried into his pillow. He'd felt his dad standing in the doorway watching but he couldn't stop.

'I know, lad, I know,' his father had said quietly, and he'd walked away.

Frank just wanted him to be a father. He preferred it when his father talked about the nobility of hard work or took him bird watching on the marshes or showed him how to knock a nail in straight. Those times he felt a kinship, so long as his father didn't mention his mother and reveal just how alone Frank was with a grief no one but he could understand. The only person who would have understood was gone.

'Who the hell was that?' He turned to Dottie. 'Who was it, I said?' he repeated, because she was just standing there behind him, not moving quickly to the window in the way that he wanted her to; she was just standing there and looking at him.

'What?' she said eventually. 'What do you mean?' He saw that fear was gumming her up rather than rousing her.

'There was someone there, watching us,' he said. Then he added, because he didn't want to frighten her any more than she already was, 'that or I imagined it, or saw your reflection in the glass here,' he said. He could see her chest rising and falling quickly and he could sense her trying to contain it, to check and calm herself.

'Yes,' she said, a slight tremor in her voice.

'Now then. I'd like to keep looking for Professor Webber,' he said, 'and get a few things straight in my mind.' She didn't answer, her mind still slowed with fear. 'I can escort you back to the billiards room,' he said. 'You'll be with the others there. Tucked away at the back of the house, safely inside. You can wait there for help to arrive.'

'There is no help coming,' she said quietly. 'You couldn't get them on the telephone, remember? There's no help coming. I'll stay with you, if you don't mind. I'd rather that. You normally work with your colleagues, I suppose,' she added, an attempt at lightness, he could see. 'I'm a poor substitute.'

'I don't mind working alone,' said Frank. 'Never have.' He glanced at her. 'Though you don't make a bad colleague at all. Calm, astute.' He considered it. 'Brave,' he added.

'I'd make a good lady detective, I think, like in the novels.' She smiled her watery smile again.

'You're a reader, then? My father would approve.' He was trying to keep her eyes on him and buoy her up. Hours together in this godawful place and he was starting to feel like they were in a bad dream together.

She blushed. 'Yes, I read whenever I can. I don't understand people who don't. You can try out all kinds of different worlds. Be someone else. Do something different.'

'Maybe not murder,' he said, forgetting again that he wasn't talking to Riley or Marsh, who welcomed a bit of dark humour. She didn't seem to mind though.

'Except that,' she said, 'though it would be interesting to hear the reasons and ways.'

'You'd have made a good copper, then,' he said, both of them knowing there was no way in their world that this was possible. Maid was her only option, or perhaps seamstress. 'Now,' he said. He was trying to get the vision of the white-faced woman out of his mind – he wasn't able to make out her features with two panes of glass and the driving, slicing snow between them; but the way she'd just stood and stared . . . 'I want to pace something out in the corridor.'

She watched as he listened at the door, turned the handle carefully, looked all around him and then nodded at her. Quickly she followed and shut the door behind her. She, too, looked up the corridor and down it. He paced from where the room started to where it finished.

'I thought as much,' he said.

'What?'

'It's not real.'

'I see,' Dottie said, and followed him as he walked a little further towards the dining room. 'I'd like to look in here now,' he said at the next door. 'I haven't been in here yet. Keep your eye out for anything strange.'

'Tonight, everything is strange,' she said, and she followed him in.

The room was a mess of yellow and green wallpaper, acid-bright glass forming a half circle of sunbeams over the double doors. Stiff white chairs with carved arms and legs looked like seated, headless skeletons. Just one wall sconce was lit, throwing peculiar shadows across the room. White marble heads, blood-less and blind, stood on column tables by the garden doors. The heads all looked in the same direction – towards the door Frank and Dottie had entered by – towards them.

He realised he had been in here before, of course, when he'd first arrived – this was the room that the crows had flown out of, though that seemed weeks ago now. 'So, someone left through this door earlier,' he said, 'but perhaps didn't return through it.'

One of the garden doors was open just a touch, enough to let the snow in, though he had shut it firmly earlier when he'd startled the crows. Frank pushed at it with his foot and looked out at the raging storm. He shivered. 'Ah,' he said.

Dottie came and stood at his shoulder. 'Footprints.'

'Yes.' The prints were frozen over, engraved in the snow, lead-ing neatly towards the pine trees in the distance from the garden door.

'A man's prints,' she said. 'Look, they're men's shoes, aren't they?'

'Yes,' he said.

'There's none coming back, though,' she said. She was quiet for a second, two seconds. 'We maybe saw those earlier,' she said, 'at the back of the house, remember? Coming towards the butler's room.'

Though his blood was still running high, he was beginning to piece it together. His emotion always led him in feet first, but his logic helped him find his way around once he was in there. He pushed the door a little further ajar with his foot, pulled his coat more tightly around him and took a step into the blizzard.

'I suppose everyone turns their hand to what's needed in a war situation,' he said. The snow was thick and crisp, frozen solid beneath with snow still falling on top. He pushed his scarf under his coat. Dottie hurried next to him, her coat a burgundy splash against the white.

'I suppose so,' she said. 'My sister worked on a farm.'

'Did you know Lord and Lady Forester during the War?' he said. 'I forget the dates of your employment. Did they turn their hand to war supplies?' He bent down to inspect the footprint. It was a deep imprint with clear markings from the sole.

'I did, yes, by the end of it anyway. I expect they did something like that.' She bent down with him. The footprints weren't evenly spaced – two prints close together would be followed by a bigger gap and then two next to each other, like the person who had made them stumbled and stopped occasionally. 'Someone heavy,' she said.

He nodded. 'Yes, exactly. And Professor Webber – does he work for their company too? The ironworks, I mean.'

'I wouldn't have thought so. He's an inventor, not a business-man. I think he calls himself an engineer.' She was still looking at the footprints. 'He's not a particularly heavy man, I wouldn't have thought.' She thought for a second. You could see the thoughts flitting across her face. 'Unless he was carrying something heavy,' she added.

'Something heavy – or someone.'

She met his gaze and held it a second, two seconds. Neither of them said anything.

'How long has he known Lord and Lady Forester? I'm sure you've already told me, my apologies.'

'I think they're old friends.' Her hands were shoved deep in her pockets. The snow swirled around her bare head. 'Not since childhood, but since early adulthood, perhaps.'

'That must have been a difficult time for all of them, the war in Ireland. The bad feeling against the English was high, I'd imagine. In war we all do patriotic things, that I suppose the other side would think of as troubling.'

'I don't think anyone has anything against a farm worker,' said Dottie.

'Ah, yes. Your sister. And what did you do during the War?'

'I worked in a munitions factory,' she said. 'I loved it. I've never felt so ... well, so alive. That probably sounds stupid to you.' She shook the snow off her hair and plunged her hands deeper into her pocket. 'What's this?' She brought her hand out. 'Oh, just a hanky. Hold on.' She unfolded it and a familiar sweet, chemical smell drifted towards Frank.

He looked at the hanky quickly. 'Whose coat is this? Is it yours? Jessop's?'

She shook her head. 'No.' She lifted the hem and showed, at the bottom of the coat, a jagged rip in pale pink silk, the deep red of the wool showing through. She hesitated. 'It's Professor Webber's. He brought it to Jessop tonight and asked for it to be mended. Jessop hung it up in the boot cupboard and I was to mend it after the main course was served.'

He nodded slowly. 'Let's get in from the snow.' He looked uneasily towards the dining room window, but there was no one there. 'We need to look in Professor Webber's room.'

They walked through the snow-stacked courtyard. 'Why would he do this?' she said quietly. 'Why would he kill these people, his friends?'

'I don't know. Yet.'

Dottie nodded. They walked on.

Back inside, he closed the door behind them. The garden room felt still and silent and incredibly warm. His ears rang with snow and his skin prickled with the sudden heat. 'Tell me some more about Mrs Gray. I know you liked her. What did other people think of her? The other servants, say. I'm sure you all talk.' The alabaster heads all stared at them, a dispassionate, audience.

She nodded. 'She was well liked, mostly. More than Mr Gray, perhaps.' She folded her arms over her chest and looked towards the door to the corridor. 'One of the maids did say it was unfair that . . .' She looked up. 'Was that someone?'

'No. Just the pipes creaking.' He opened the door to the hallway, looked both ways carefully then stepped out, beckoning her to follow. He waited there a second, two seconds, and then nodded. They started to move along the densely patterned rug towards the dining room, walking under an arch and passing a gilt mirror, its surface clouded by age. They reached the oil painting of the old-fashioned couple.

'Hold on. Did you hear something?'

They both stopped, halfway up the dark hall towards the entrance. The flickering light from those damned wall lights fluttering over the oil painting made it look like the eyes were following you.

'What?'

'Maybe it was the snow falling. Or the pipes again.'

They both stood, shoulder to shoulder, in the low light. He could feel the warmth of her arm.

'Voices,' she said, her eyes wide. 'Voices,' she said again, less softly this time. Not ghostly, whispering ones but loud, well-spoken, angry ones. 'It sounds like Mrs Radcliffe.'

They both walked quickly. He almost started to run but stopped himself. Nearly breathless, they arrived at the entrance hall. At the top of the stairs two figures were arguing loudly. They were outlined by the light at the top of the stairs, looking like shadow puppets against the gothic wood of the elaborate carved banisters and railing. The two stags' heads, mounted high up on the wall, seemed as though they were about to charge. Mr Gray was pointing at Mrs Radcliffe's chest. She was pulling back angrily.

'. . . you take me for?' Mr Gray was saying.

'You're not what you pretend to be,' Mrs Radcliffe retorted. 'We all know that! I've heard the rumours, we all have. Do you think we don't know? Even the servants know!' Her face was folded up in fury. 'You're a liar.' A tear streaked her cheek.

'What's going on here?' said Frank, loudly. 'What are you doing? It's not safe.'

'Just a moment,' said Mr Gray, not looking at him. 'Mrs Radcliffe, I—'

'Do I need to arrest you? Get back to the billiards room.'

'No, you don't,' said Mrs Radcliffe. 'Though you might want to arrest *him*.'

'The hypocrisy is astounding,' said Mr Gray. 'If it wasn't for your friend, you'd have sunk to all kinds of depths years ago. Don't you think we all know she's your conscience, scurrying around after you, tidying up your messes, hiding your temptations from you. Really, you—'

'Both of you, back to the billiards room now. I don't want to arrest you, but I will if I have to.'

'Very forceful, Constable,' said Mrs Radcliffe. Her face was lit from within by anger.

'He's a sergeant, ma'am,' said Dottie with a slight flush. 'And I think you should do as he asks. Normal rules don't apply. People have died.'

Mrs Radcliffe shrugged, expressionless. She looked, suddenly, like Lady Forester. 'It's just the way this house is. Things crash, things explode, things break. We don't need a policeman; we need someone to take the bodies away so we don't have to sit around with a lot of corpses.'

'Young lady,' said Mr Gray. 'You have a lot to learn about sensitivity.'

'You've got a lot to learn about a lot of things.'

Frank took the stairs two at a time. Dottie followed.

'Right,' he said. 'Off we go.' He took Mrs Radcliffe by the elbow. She shrugged him off.

'We're not children,' she said. Mr Gray folded his arms and leaned against the wall.

'Come on,' said Dottie. 'Take some blankets back with you. Get everyone comfortable.' Mrs Radcliffe's face thawed a little. Dottie continued, 'It's been a long night and it's not over yet. Let's make ourselves useful.'

Frank waited while Dottie knelt down on the landing and pushed at the wooden wall. A section of the panelling sprung open, and Dottie pulled out a pile of yellow blankets with foliage and animal heads embroidered on the corners. She handed an armful to Mrs Radcliffe, one to Mr Gray, to his apparent surprise, and then took out another pile for herself. What looked like a wire was looped across the side of the cupboard, a space that was about a foot and a half deep. Frank bent down to take a closer look. Dottie stood up and closed the low door with her foot.

They walked in silent procession through the picture gallery and drawing room. Frank had such a strong sense that they were not alone that he took his revolver from his pocket. His eyes darted around the dark rooms. But he saw nothing. By the time they had reached the far end of the drawing room, he could hear voices.

'. . . off gallivanting with that wet young politician, probably bedding him . . .' It was Lord Forester's voice. Lady Forester replied, 'Charles, for . . .'

The billiards room smelled of whisky. Cushions were scattered about and Jessop was crouched in the corner over what looked like a spillage of wine. Billiard balls were rolling on the floor and a cue was slung across the rug.

'Florence,' cried Lady Forester. 'Where have you been? Don't go anywhere. Why is John with you?' She strode to Mrs Radcliffe and gathered her into her arms.

Mrs Radcliffe stood there stiffly. 'I was just showing him something.'

'The last thing the man needs is another wife,' said Lord Forester. 'Particularly not one like Florence. Peter was a very indulgent man, but not all men will be. Stop babying her, Sophia. It drives me mad.'

'What do you mean by that? I was the perfect wife to a perfect husband. I don't want another man, I want him.' Mrs Radcliffe started to cry. She stayed poker stiff, with her hands over her face.

'Well, you can't have him; he's dead.' Lord Forester's face was pink with fury. 'The sooner you get over it, my girl, the sooner you'll move on. Forget about whatever morbid thing it is you keep blathering on about. His lungs, his—'

She moved her hands from her wet face. 'I loved his lungs. I loved all of him.' She glared at him, then she rested her head on Lady Forester's shoulder and cried.

'He wouldn't have known anything,' said Lady Forester.

'He was in hell. He knew everything. Every last thing, believe me. He suffocated on his own dissolving lungs – do you not think you'd know about that?' She lifted her head up and stared at Lord Forester. 'I'd rather be dead too. I wish everyone was dead.'

She stared at them all and then walked over to Jessop, picked up the whisky from the table next to him and took it to the chair at the end of the room, tipping some into her mouth on the way. Her red dress trailed behind her like a seeping wound.

'That's it, my girl,' said Lady Abbott. 'I'll join you. Forget your troubles.' She stood up a little shakily and walked unsteadily to Mrs Radcliffe.

'Come on,' said Frank quietly to Dottie. 'Are you coming with me? You can stay if you prefer.'

'Coming,' she said, and he was glad to hear it. As he closed the door, he could hear Mr Gray's voice, raised above the others. 'I think someone should keep watch,' he said. 'Jessop . . .'

He turned to Dottie, her sure, calm face suddenly feeling like a refuge. 'Can you take me to Professor Webber's room?'

'That's the ivory room,' she said. 'It's next to the ebony room.'

'Very apt. Named by someone musical, I suppose.'

'If you say so,' she said blandly, disappearing behind her mask again.

They walked in silence through the picture gallery and then the drawing room. Frank listened hard, but there were no sounds. It was just Dottie and him moving through the quiet, empty rooms. The rooms felt malevolently, claustrophobically quiet – there was an electric energy about them. For a second, he heard the low stuttering buzz again. He stopped and listened. Now nothing.

They passed two doors, the carved wooden heads next to them grimacing in the shadows. As they reached the third, Dottie nodded. Frank put his ear close to the door. Behind the wood all he could hear was that stretched out silence that lay paper-thin above the house's creakings and shiftings – the soft grumbles as she adjusted her position. He turned the handle slowly and motioned for Dottie to stay where she was, checking behind her towards the cavernous entrance hall and the other way, towards the morning room. All was quiet. Frank noticed that it was an unusual handle – he'd thought the door handles were all a sort of hammered brass, but now he could see that they were a curling snake or tail.

He turned the handle slowly and quietly, then quickly opened the door a crack and carefully looked in, hand by his revolver pocket, ready to meet a killer.

# CHAPTER NINETEEN

## THE IVORY ROOM

The room was dark, lit only by the moonlight reflected from the snow. The walls were bone coloured and no pictures hung on them. The carpet was pale and faded – muted flesh pinks, tooth-white, old bull's blood red. Twin beds with brass bedsteads were almost the only furnishings. At the window, a desk looked out over the side of the house – the watchful trees, the driving snow.

'Professor Webber must spend a lot of time here at the house.' He imagined looking out of the view through Professor Webber's eyes, seeing these skeletal branches with the soundtrack of someone else's thoughts and feelings.

'Yes,' she said. 'They're great friends and the house project has taken up a good deal of their time.'

'And he consults for the ironworks,' he said casually, looking at her face closely as he said it. 'He started doing so in the War, but why not continue?' The beds were both neatly made. There was no sign which of the two Professor Webber used. 'As you said earlier, once you have the network, you can move anything through it. He's a useful man to know if you want to change your business to something a little riskier.' He moved to the desk. 'I'm wondering if perhaps he got a little too confident, though, and started striking his own deals without them.'

'What do you mean?'

There was a small, printed piece of paper placed neatly on top of the desk. – *Please take notice that your pledge – unless you redeem your pledge* . . . He couldn't read the scrappy handwriting. Dottie moved to stand at his side. 'If that's his chitty,' she said, 'maybe the rumours are true. I always thought he was a well-off man. The last person who'd need to use a pawn shop.' She looked down at the piece of paper. 'It's rather easy to find, though,' she added, 'for something so private.'

'So, we're meant to find this,' Frank nodded. 'But why the bread-crumb trail?' He opened a drawer and took out a leather-bound diary. He flicked through the pages, but the entries were sparse – an appointment here, a reminder there. He seemed to have a meeting with Lord Forester and Lady Forester, annotated *C&S*, every week or two, going back right through the year. An entry for 25 July read *Bss. 6pm*. The writing was precise, and very small.

He flicked to the back and there he found a faded photograph, taken perhaps thirty years ago, but he quickly recognised the straight set of the mouth, the steady eyes, the implacable expression. In this photo Lady Forester looked more joyful than he could now imagine her looking. There was something about the face that softened it – was it hope? Or belief in something or other, something vitally human like fairness, or love?

He showed it to Dottie. 'Do you think Lord Forester would be surprised that his great friend Professor Webber kept this photo of his wife?'

'Her Ladyship,' she said, taking it from him. 'She was so pretty back then.' She stared at it for a while. 'I don't know if he'd be surprised,' she said, looking up from the photo. 'But I'm not particularly. It's clear Professor Webber has very strong feelings for her Ladyship, always has. He'd do anything for her, says so by what he does, rather than words, if you understand me. And by how he looks at her.'

'And Lady Forester?' Strangely, she just shrugged, as if that was irrelevant.

'It was Professor Webber's writing,' she said. 'The notes we found earlier. Look – it's the same.' She got the scrap of paper she'd found in the wastepaper bin out of her apron pocket and laid it next to the diary on the desk. Frank took the blue fragment of paper that he'd eased out of Mr Bell's hand from his pocket, smoothed it out and compared the three.

'Yes,' he said. 'As we thought.' He looked at them. 'So, the breadcrumb trail is to lead to Professor Webber. But why?'

He flicked back through the diary, glancing instinctively over his shoulder as he did it. One entry gave him pause. It was on the 23rd of August of that year; just a few months ago. Dottie peered over his shoulder. '*Wolf*,' she said. 'What does that mean?'

'Does Professor Webber like games?' asked Frank. 'I mean, would you say he likes . . . I don't know . . . playing with – toying with – people?'

'I don't think so. He's the opposite of that. He's quite direct.'

'If he was worried about someone being a threat to him . . .' He closed the diary.

'He'd say so. I don't know him very well, but he is the sort to go in fists flying, as my pa would have said.' There were dark circles under Dottie's eyes.

'They're all of a type, the Penny Club, aren't they? Would you say they all have darker aspects?'

'Everyone has more than one aspect. That's what makes people interesting.' She gave him a serious look.

'Birds of a feather flock together.'

'You sound like Jessop now. Him and his spirits.' She folded her arms across her chest. 'I feel like Professor Webber is watching us. Can we get out of this room?' Her eyes darted about the dark corners of the empty room.

'Yes. Let's move on in a second. I'm interested in the steam heating you were talking about,' he said. 'How is it distributed through the house?'

Her face brightened. 'There's a duct system. It's actually a very old technology, but it was forgotten for centuries. Professor Webber put the ducts in. It was a big job, as you can imagine. The water is heated and then the steam moves around the house and comes out through these grills.' She pointed at a small section, low down on the wall.

'How can you do that to an old house? How does it travel?' He gathered up the papers and the diary, tapped them on the smooth wood of the desk to tidy them and put them in his pocket. He could feel the stiff shape of the advent calendar in there. He flicked through all the calendar's pasted-on images in his head, the newspaper, the letter, the bell, the toy boats, the toy soldier, the toy car. It didn't make enough sense yet. He pulled it out and flicked open the door to the ivory room with his thumbnail. What looked like a toy rocket – or a firework.

'That's the clever thing!' she said. Zeal shone from her eyes. 'That's the brilliance of it. You see a problem that's impossible, so would most people. Professor Webber just worked out a solution. The walls you see around you? Almost all of them are false. He built them in every room. Ceilings and floors too.' She glanced at the calendar. 'A bomb?' she said.

He looked back at the calendar. A bomb. 'You're right. The blueprint in Mr Bell's hand was the design for a bomb – Professor Webber's design. The trail of breadcrumbs was to show that.'

'Professor Webber killed Mr Bell for knowing?'

He shook his head. 'No, I don't believe so.' He thought for a second. 'How big are they, the passageways for the steam? Around a foot and a half?'

She held her hands out. 'Just this big. But everything can fit in there – the steam pipes, the electricity cables, the phone cables, everything.'

'People?'

'Oh no,' she said. 'It's too small for that. I wouldn't fit in there, you certainly couldn't.' She gave him a steady look – she'd picked up on his thinking. 'Nor Professor Webber.'

He folded the calendar back in half and stowed it in his inside pocket. The room had a musty smell old places had, beeswax furniture polish, smoke from fires that had been lit earlier in the evening and on top of those comfortable, everyday smells a familiar, sweet, chemical scent. 'Are there any plans for the house? Blueprints, that sort of thing?'

'Of course,' she said. 'There's a plan chest downstairs in Professor Webber's working room. They call it the inventor's room. I'll take you there,' she said, rubbing her hands together in something that looked almost like glee – a bright curiosity that was papering over her fear. He thought of her, an engineer trapped in a maid's life, and he felt a sharp pang of empathy for her.

# CHAPTER TWENTY

## THE INVENTOR'S ROOM

They hurried down the grand, upper corridor towards the stairs. Frank walked quickly, his mind turning over the problem again. If the killer was Professor Webber, he had to be located fast. But with growing certainty he felt that it wasn't as simple as that.

'Tell me about Lady Abbott,' he said. 'How do you think she survived the disaster at sea?'

'Everyone likes her,' she said. 'She brightens up a room. She's more practical than you'd think, she's had to be. She isn't high-born – she didn't have money till later in her life, you know, through a second marriage – she lived a very simple existence till then. She's a survivor – they all are, I suppose they'd say, but perhaps her more than most. It's said that pirates attacked the ship and she escaped on a boat, just the two of them—'

'Two of them?' he said quickly.

'Her and her baby. I heard it was taken on by another family because she was a young, penniless widow. Anyway, Lady Abbott said that she didn't believe it was pirates. She recognised one of them and it was another captain, a rival of her husband's. She thinks they were all murdered. She seems happy, as a person, but she's carried that around with her all her life. You can claim the cargo if you rescue the ship. It's said the captain went on to be

175

a captain of industry in New York, you know. She told me his son—'

'But if the other captain hauled the ship in and claimed its cargo, they would know he'd got rid of the crew somehow. Unless—' He turned the stone in his pocket again and again. The lines of this case went a long way back and crossed in all kinds of ways.

'Unless he waited a while and said he found it deserted.'

'Yes.' The broad stairs were quiet, with no signs of life other than the delirious wind screeching and harrying at the tall window-panes. Dottie led them down the wide staircase and into the hall, but this time she took them out of the main hallway and down a short corridor to a door at the end. The handle – the same as all the others – was a tail, not a snake, he realised. He checked the room quickly – it was silver-lit by the frosted snow and it was empty. He beckoned her in, closing the door promptly behind them.

'Right,' he said. 'We need to work quickly, if my thinking is right.'

The snow was piling thickly onto the domed glass ceiling, creeping up the sides to choke them entirely. Frank could just see the sulphur moon through the blizzard. The vivid mustard of the walls was sickly, like the moon, but brighter, hung with framed elevations of the house. A table with a reading light was positioned precisely under the centre of the domed ceiling, with three straight-backed chairs pulled up around it. To their left was a plan chest.

'Shall we start here?' said Frank. A neatly stacked pile of drawings and architectural blueprints was inside the first drawer. He carried them to the table, Dottie close behind. 'All's not as it seems,' he said. 'Professor Webber is still in the house. The house has secrets.'

'Looking for us, to kill us?' she said.

'No,' he said. 'I suspect he's dead. Which means someone else is committing the crimes.'

'Dead?' she said, stopping in her tracks. 'Why do you say that? But didn't we see him earlier – we saw the shadow of him passing just an hour or so ago.' She passed a single forefinger across her furrowed brow. 'I can't begin to . . . how can . . .' She looked down at her hands.

She moved some hair out of her eye, throwing her arm to the side as she did so, half yawning, half stretching. Her arm passed in front of the lamp light and made a monster on the wall.

'Yes!' he said. 'That's how.'

'What's how?'

'I'll show you later,' he said. 'A trick of the light. Automated, perhaps.'

She joined him at the table. 'Here,' she said, leaning over him, her hand trembling just slightly. 'This is the original plan, long before Professor Webber's work. He redrew them. You'd think, if you didn't know, that it was the plan now, unchanged – that's how clever the work is. If you looked around you, you wouldn't know you weren't seeing the original house.'

His heart started to beat more quickly. A theatre set within a house, effectively. 'And this one?' he said.

'That's the same set of plans,' she said. 'There are around ten of them. Look, there's the date in the corner.'

*1712 redrafted 1914*

'Right.' He lifted them all quickly up until he got to one with a more recent date. 'These are the more recent ones?' he said. 'So, it should be dated this year.'

'It takes years to do this sort of thing. The work started seven years ago, before they escaped from Ireland. It was finished five years ago.'

She straightened up and stood with her hands behind her back. It reminded him of himself, that trick of retreating behind a mask, finding a private place where you couldn't be hurt. He looked up. 'Maybe you could explain them to me,' he said. 'I'm not very good at this sort of thing.'

'Of course,' she said. 'I'd be glad to. Do you see the double lines,' she said, 'here and here and here? Everywhere. One in thicker ink. That's the false wall I was telling you about. This line represents electricity, see, and this one a steam duct, see. These lines are telephone lines. And this, here, is the maintenance access point . . . Here, see, in the Italianate room. On the first floor. Lady Abbott stays there when she's with us. It's one of the best rooms.'

He nodded. 'We'll go there next. You'll need to be careful. Be even more watchful and stay close to me. Alert me straight away at sight or sound of anything peculiar. We're getting closer. Think of a cornered animal.' He marched towards the door then doubled back on himself. He'd seen a second drawer, this one with a dog's head on the keyhole. Or perhaps a wolf's, looking more closely. He pulled Lady Forester's keys out of his pocket, looked for a small brass one with an animal head on it. He found it and put it in the lock.

It turned.

Frank pulled the drawer open and discovered a third set of plans. 'Good,' he said. 'These are the ones.'

'These must be earlier,' Dottie said. 'They're different. Look. They must be ones they didn't use. See, here, there's a staircase marked on; and here, there's a whole passage we don't have.' Frank recognised Professor Webber's hand in the small pencil writing. But the date was 1924. 'That's strange,' she said, her gaze following his, 'that's long after all the work was done. Just this year.'

'Where is this?' He was so near he could taste it.

'That's the dining room, here, and the library, here. The passage seems to link the butler's room to the library. And the staircase starts in the library and leads to . . .' She lifted the plan up and revealed the one underneath. 'Yes, here, to the pineapple room. That's very interesting. I wonder why they didn't do it.' She looked at him, plan still in hand. 'Or perhaps they did.'

'Let's go to the Italianate room,' he said. He was getting hungry for an answer now. 'Quick,' he called over his shoulder. 'And stay very close.'

It was moments like this that got his heart pumping, his mouth salivating. His prey was in sight. He was almost running, taking the stairs two at a time.

'Wait for me,' gasped Dottie. The landing on the first floor was long.

'Sorry.' He slowed down.

They walked down the empty corridor, sometimes jogging a step or two. His breath was coming quickly.

They reached a closed door and Dottie said, 'Here.'

He pushed the door open and stepped inside, his hand ready for his revolver. He assessed it quickly and nodded her in. 'Where's the maintenance door?' he said. 'The one on the plan?' The room was dark and messy, shadowed with secrets. A green cape with a fur collar was thrown over a dressing-table stool and pieces of glittering jewellery of all colours were scattered over the powder-dusted surface of the dressing table. Three pairs of very small shoes were tossed in the corner. A narrow evening dress was laid out on the bed, almost little enough for a child. He looked around the room.

'Quickly!'

'Here,' she said. 'It will be here, behind this bureau.'

'Help me,' he said. With him, she pulled it forward until it was clear of the wall.

'It doesn't look . . .' he said, looking at the smooth, deep yellow wall.

But Dottie was already busy tracing the smooth wall with her capable fingers. 'Let me see,' she was saying under her breath. 'Yes. That's it. Here.' She traced her fingers down and gave a little push and a door opened out from the wall.

Frank stepped closer. 'Almost invisible,' he said. 'Very clever work. Right. We've no time to spare.'

Behind the door was what looked like a dusty cupboard. In the low light Frank could just make out the original walls – the older, larger ghost of the room. They were around, as Dottie had said, a foot or so back from the new walls, plainer, with a simple picture rail and high skirting board. Wallpaper was peeling off in places.

'See, here is the heating pipe – you can see it diverts towards that grid. That, up there, is an electricity cable. Below it, the black one that's hanging a bit looser, that's the telephone wire.'

'That voices and electricity can pass through cables . . .' said Frank, forgetting himself.

'It be a wonder,' said Dottie, 'to us simple folk.'

'You're teasing me. What's this then?'

Dottie bent a little closer to look. She straightened up. 'It looks like a voice pipe,' she said. 'This house had a voice pipe system once. But it would be on the other side of the original walls, you would think, if it was the original system. It wouldn't have been visible. It would have been tucked behind the plaster and wallpaper.'

'Where does it go?'

'Hard to say. Towards the pineapple room or the master suite, or perhaps nowhere at all. It could be a relic. We never use it.'

The whispering sound was back, a little louder now, just to his right. And then it stopped.

'I wonder . . .' he said.

She raised an eyebrow.

'That whispering sound we hear now and then, does it remind you of anything?'

She thought. 'It's a little like the crackle of a gramophone record. But not quite.'

'Yes, my thoughts exactly.' He chewed his lip. 'It will come to me.'

'I've been thinking,' she said. 'Won't the motivation match the means? Don't people do things in ways that reflect how they feel about them? Maybe a killer who felt a close, personal emotion would kill someone up close, with a knife, say. Maybe if you felt someone had pushed you over the edge—'

'You might push them off a cliff?'

'You make it sound silly.'

'Not at all. You might have something there.'

Frank was gauging the gap. As Dottie had said, it wouldn't fit an adult. Perhaps a child. But there were no children here. 'Would you fit down there?' he said.

'Not if I wanted to come back out again.'

'No.' He was thinking hard.

He glanced back at the closed door and worked quickly through the room, opening drawers, pulling out papers. In the drawer of her bedside table he found a gold pendant, cheaper looking than the rest of the jewellery. He turned it over in his hands.

'It's a locket,' said Dottie, next to him. 'It opens here, see.' With a capable fingernail, she prised open the necklace and revealed two pictures inside. An old-fashioned portrait of a young man with a stiff collar and a small, chubby-cheeked child in a lacy white gown.

'Poor woman,' said Dottie. 'Imagine losing your husband and then not being able to keep your own child.'

'She married again.'

'Doesn't mean she didn't love him.'

'She gave the child away.'

'Maybe because she loved it not because she didn't. She never had another.' Dottie had a forensic eye for the emotional truth of a situation, for its heart, and he liked her for it. But he didn't like dwelling on such things as parents without children or children without parents. He walked around to the other side of the bed and pulled open the drawer. A Bible. A book of poetry. He flicked open the book and something dropped out and fell to the floor – a photograph. The same photo that he'd seen in Professor Webber's papers – the portrait of Lady Forester as a young woman, her smoothly curving limestone cheeks, her hope-lit eyes.

'Like family,' Dottie said slowly. 'Almost like a mother to her, she always says. She is her mother. She is Lady Forester's mother. Lady Forester is the baby she gave away.'

He pictured a maze of interconnected lines, relationships, resentments, acts of revenge. A trail of breadcrumbs led through it, but at every turn there were thorned branches to snag your way on, false turns, hidden ways through.

'There will be more entrances and exits,' he said. 'Let's go back to the dining room.' They were close. So close. The blood rushed to his skin and his thoughts moved faster than words. So close he could smell it.

# CHAPTER TWENTY-ONE

## THE CONCEALED PASSAGE

F rank and Dottie stood in the corridor looking down towards the balcony. The silence was strained, like a bomb waiting to go off. His racing thoughts filled his head.

'Something's different,' he said. 'What is it?'

She stood, nose in the air like a gun dog, looking, listening, sniffing out information. 'The wind,' she said finally. 'It's calmed. The storm must be slowing.'

She was right. Where the screeching wind had been smacking sheets of snow against the walls, now there was a muffled silence. It was as though a wild dog had been tossing them around for hours but had now swallowed them whole.

'Help should come soon,' he said. 'At the station, they'll know I've not returned. There's a system to say you've got home safe. I brought it with me from Manchester. They had nothing here before.' He made his way quickly down the corridor to the balcony – where on the strange advent calendar the picture had revealed theatre box seats – trying to ignore the feeling of malevolent suffocation. 'Perhaps they didn't need it,' he added.

'Don't be too hopeful. The pass will be totally inaccessible in this weather. That's why all the staff went home. You'd need a sturdy pair of skis to get down.'

'Went home?' he said quickly. 'Or were sent home?'

'Sent home, of course' she said. 'Lady Forester told them to leave.'

'After the snow had started?'

'No, this morning. Yesterday morning now, I suppose.'

He was flipping through this quickly in his mind. 'Before the food was prepared?' They had made it to the wide staircase, the banister smooth and warm beneath their fingers. His heart was thumping. They were at the top of the stairs, looking down into the entrance hall below, white snow pressing hard against the windowpanes.

'They prepared it early, on her request. The evening before and then in the early morning. There was just heating up to do last night.'

'When the weather was known to be bad,' he said. He walked quickly down the wide, shallow stairs. He felt all of the house's close, malevolent attention focused on him.

'No,' she said slowly. 'We didn't know about the storm until the morning papers arrived.' She stole an anxious glance back up from the balcony to the door to the picture gallery and, beyond, to the billiards room. 'What if they're unsafe?'

'They're locked in. How could someone kill them all silently without anyone raising an alarm?' There were ways, of course, but he was fizzing with the desire to beat the puzzle while it was fresh in his head. 'Come along,' he said. 'Or are you flagging?'

'Certainly not!'

He could see it was a matter of pride with her, staying courageous. He liked her for it. He took the rest of the stairs quickly and she kept up.

The dining room looked lost and forlorn, abandoned plates pushed away next to glasses, empty chairs pushed out of place – none with even a jacket or a shawl thrown over it in haste, though there had been a shawl here last time Frank was in the room.

Frank noted the place setting with the glass with the red lipstick mark on, its chair pushed back towards the far wall, its napkin thrown down to the right. The chair next to the head of the table was pushed straight back towards the end of the room. The napkin had been folded in on itself into a very small square. He moved to the seat next to the head of the table and crouched at the table, as if he were sitting.

'Whatever are you doing?' said Dottie.

'Sightlines. This was Mr Gray's seat, next to Lady Forester?'

'Yes. She asked Mr Gray to take the seat tonight, said it was in celebration of his recent election victory.'

He nodded and moved his quick gaze to the blood spots, the blood splatter, the pool of thickening burgundy on the library floor.

'Mr Gray killed Professor Webber here,' he said. 'On impulse, more or less. If you look at the sightlines from the table, the only person who could possibly have seen Professor Webber at the site of the blood fall was Mr Gray – and, interestingly, Mr Gray claimed no one could see the library from the table. The lie always leads to the perpetrator. The fall of the blood suggests he was attacked from behind. Two wounds, I'd say – perhaps an initial strike and then the throat slit – the pool being the second wound. There are no significant signs of blood between the desk and the dining room, other than a couple of small dots, perhaps from Mr Gray's hands, by the door. I'd say he put his gloves back on around there. You'll notice, he's not taken his gloves off all night, though he's certainly wanted to. He's a nail-biter. He'll not want the evidence so on display. He's avoided pulling his handkerchief from his pocket too – I'll warrant there's blood on that. The body will still be in the library somewhere. I expect we'll find it shortly.'

'What? It doesn't make any sense. Why would Mr Gray kill Professor Webber?' There were dark thumbprints under her eyes and a tiny tremble, a sub-surface shudder, to her hand. 'And we've seen Professor Webber moving around since then.'

'He was a threat,' he said. 'To his career, and possibly to something else . . . It will become clear soon.' He walked back towards the bookcase, stopping next to it to think. He stepped to the side. 'As for the sightings of him – so much here isn't true, isn't real. We'll need to get a better look at the drawing room doorway. I think there'll be a small cut-out figure, a lamp light that's perhaps automated. We didn't see Professor Webber at all – there will have been a deliberate trick of the light. A shadow puppet, if you like. The light was perhaps automated to come on, just as the musicians were. Someone wants us to think Professor Webber is behind this, still around and dangerous.'

She took a deep breath in and let it out. 'Or,' she said, 'they wanted us to keep thinking it for a little while. Just long enough.'

'Just long enough for what?'

'That I don't know.'

'Dottie,' he continued. 'You're good at reading plans and so on. The extra passage that was marked on the plan. Where would it be, if it existed?' The walls curved around her, stacked floor to ceiling with books. It looked exactly like a shelf of books – could there really be a door in there? His heart was beating quickly – if he found Professor Webber in there, then perhaps all of his thinking was correct. The whole thing could start to fall into place. He looked up to see her looking at him as if he'd not responded to something she'd said. 'Sorry. Miles away. Careful there.'

She stepped neatly around the blood without looking at it, but the trembling in her hand increased. She stood next to him and looked at the wall of books, scanning it with her eyes. 'Here,

I'd say.' She took a step forward and one to the left. 'Yes. Here, more or less. Yes, that would be it.'

'If it was a door, how would you open it?'

'It's a push,' she said. 'Just so.' And she pressed firmly at waist height on the polished wood of the bookcase.

The bookcase opened towards her. She stepped back.

There was a second's silence. And then she screamed.


He took Dottie by the elbow and gently guided her to the easy chair at the other end of the room. Her hands were over her mouth and she was shaking. He knelt next to her and put an arm around her.

'Calm yourself,' he said. 'Calm yourself.' She put her head on his shoulder and he could feel the wet of her tears. Her shoulders were shaking. 'Come on, now. I've got you. Be calm.' Then they heard footsteps thundering and voices calling. The footsteps stopped at the top of the stairs.

'Where did it come from?' Lady Forester's voice.

'From the dining room,' said Mr Gray.

'Oh, surely not Dottie, dear Dottie,' said Lady Abbott.

'Where's my Flo?' said Lady Forester. 'She's disappeared again. Was it her?'

'Come on, this way.' That was Lord Forester. And the footsteps crashed down the stairs towards them.

Dottie lifted her head up and wiped her eyes. Frank gave her an enquiring look and she nodded. He went to meet them at the dining room door. Lord Forester was leading the way. Behind him followed Lady Abbott with Lady Forester, and then a pale-faced Mr Gray, and after them all was Miss Fox, her black cape floating behind her as she strode down the hallway. As they got to the bottom of the stairs and entered the hall, Lady Abbott reached to the side and instinctively flicked off the entrance hall lights. Frank looked at her sharply, in swift recognition.

'Nothing to worry about,' Frank said. 'Dottie's fine. She's had a shock. Come and sit yourselves down.'

'Where is she?' Lady Abbott demanded, walking into the muddled dining room. 'Where *is* she, please?'

'Please sit down, your Ladyship. The library's—'

'Certainly not!' Lady Abbott's precise features were drawn fiercely together.

Dottie appeared at the library door, looking poised. Frank could see she was still shaken. 'I'm fine,' she said. 'Like the sergeant says, it was just a shock.'

'Oh, my dear,' said Lady Abbott, rushing forward. 'You had us worried. Such a blood-curdling scream.' She put her hand lightly on Dottie's arm. Her eyes crinkled in concern.

'It certainly was,' said Mr Gray flatly. His arms were folded, his mouth set in a disapproving frown, but his eyes flicked around nervously.

'I'm glad you are well,' said Lady Forester. 'We were concerned.' She stayed where she was at the dining room door, still as a figurehead on a sinking ship.

'Why on earth is the girl screaming?' said Lord Forester. 'She's making everyone even more on edge than we already were.'

'Was, Charles,' said Lady Forester. 'She's not screaming anymore.' She looked up at him with hard eyes.

'Oh, do shut up,' he said. His fist was clenched at his side. 'Do bloody shut up or I'll silence you myself.'

'Certainly,' she said, and she smiled coldly.

'I'm fine,' said Dottie. 'Sergeant Glover will explain.' And she looked at him and nodded.

'*Sergeant Glover will explain*,' jeered Mr Gray. There was a tiny froth of spit on the corner of his mouth and his eyes were bloodshot. He'd run his hands through his hair and it stuck up over his head in thin, pale brown tufts.

'Could everyone please sit down.' Frank waited. 'I'm afraid that we have discovered Professor Webber's body.'

'Oh God,' said Miss Fox. 'Poor Leon. This is just awful.' She sat down at the dining table, in Mr Gray's seat, and picked up his place card, folding it in half and half again. 'Everyone is dying. Who next?'

'When?' said Lord Forester. 'Good God, man, is the killer still about? Are you sure he's dead? When did this happen? It must be that damned blue-blood murderer. So, Leon was innocent.'

'Early yesterday evening,' said Frank. 'Before I arrived.'

'How do you know?' said Mr Gray. 'Where's the evidence?'

'He's definitely dead,' said Dottie. 'We found him.'

'How do you know when?' said Mr Gray to Frank, ignoring Dottie.

'Where was he?' said Lady Abbott. 'Where was he all this time?' She stepped across the dining room to peer around the door. Frank blocked her way.

'He was hidden out of sight,' Frank said. 'I'll have to ask you to stay where you are, I'm afraid. The room must not be disturbed.' He folded his arms and stepped across the doorway to the library.

'But any old servant girl can poke around, eh?' sneered Mr Gray. 'Be careful she's left no fingerprints. Could be incriminating.' He cocked an eyebrow. 'Or perhaps she did it? Who is more perfectly placed to slip around doing foul deeds to get her own back on us all than a bitter, envy-drenched maid? Keys to every room, slipping around like a rat all the time, practically invisible. The perfect criminal.' He laughed. 'I've done your job for you, Sergeant. You can go home now. The maid did it.'

'Where are Jessop and Mrs Radcliffe?' Frank, with half an eye on the room, stepped towards the door to the hallway where Lord Forester and Lady Forester stood and saw Jessop, pale and drawn, eyes like black coals, waiting silently to the side of the door.

Just then, Mrs Radcliffe appeared at the top of the stairs, cheeks pink, red dress seeming to glow in the half light.

Dottie had moved to stand next to Frank. 'Professor Webber has a smear of red on his lips,' she said quietly. 'Did you see?'

'Yes.' He took a step or two away from Lord Forester and Lady Forester and glanced back towards the dining room to check that no one had moved.

'And Mrs Gray's lipstick was smudged. Professor Webber killed Mrs Gray, didn't he?' Her hands were behind her back and she was looking ahead at Mrs Radcliffe on the stairs, an anxious look on her face. 'Mrs Radcliffe doesn't seem—'

'Yes,' he said. 'That's right. Because she knew about his secret dealings, I'd guess – his rather more scurrilous inventions, you might say. Making bombs for a decent pay packet. She could have got him in hot water, so he put her in hot water. But why would he kiss her?'

'Because he could,' she said flatly. 'But who killed Mr Bell and Prince Rudolph? Was it Mr Gray or Professor Webber?' Mrs Radcliffe was standing with a hand on the newel post, like an actor on stage about to deliver a speech. Her face was flushed and her eyes looked too bright. 'Mr Bell knew he made bombs. Maybe he killed Mr Bell.'

'No. That scrap of paper was placed there for us to find – the blood on the hands. It was put there after he died. You said it yourself earlier. Your words stuck with me. Match the ends to the means. Professor Webber killed Mrs Gray with hot water because she could have got him in hot water. And Mr Gray stabbed Professor Webber in the back because Professor Webber planned to stab Mr Gray in the back. So maybe – just maybe – someone who'd had a terrible shock killed Mr Bell,' he said. 'But it was decades ago, the shock. It's been reverberating for years.'

Dottie wrinkled her brow.

'Everyone!' called Mrs Radcliffe from the top of the stairs. 'Everyone! Gather round.'

Frank heard footsteps behind him and chairs being pushed back. 'Out of interest,' he said, 'who's the servant in charge of running the electrics room? That may help us piece that one together.'

Dottie smiled. 'That's me, of course. Who else?' And, soldierly as ever, she put her hands behind her back and faced Mrs Radcliffe as if waiting for her orders.

# CHAPTER TWENTY-TWO

## THE STAIRCASE

'Gather round,' Mrs Radcliffe called from the top of the stairs. 'Gather round.' Her skirts swirled around her ankles and her voice echoed around the large hallway.

'What on earth does she want?' said Lord Forester, his voice flashing with impatience.

'I have no idea,' said Lady Forester. 'Why don't you listen to her, and you might find out?' She stood motionless in the doorway, facing the stairs. Lady Abbott was the last to leave the dining room, reaching behind her to flick a light off as she left. Everyone began to move slowly down the dark corridor towards Mrs Radcliffe, a rowdy, overdressed funeral procession.

'What rubbish has she got in her head?' Mr Gray said loudly, walking just behind Frank and Dottie. 'The girl's brainless, between you and me. Not her fault of course, she's been spoilt all her life. She's never had to confront reality.' His voice was a flat drawl, self-consciously firm, but there was an edge to it.

Mrs Radcliffe stood there at the top of the stairs in her column of red silk, dark lips half-smiling, cheeks fuchsia now. Her eyes sparkled unnaturally. 'Gather round, gather round,' she said loudly. 'I have an announcement.'

'Don't listen to her,' said Mr Gray. 'Don't give her the satisfaction. It's a desperate plea for attention.'

Mrs Radcliffe laughed. 'Get all your objections out of the way, John, while people are still prepared to listen to you. That will all change soon, won't it?' She thrust her chin into the air.

'No one will believe a word you've got to say. You're drunk – if not worse.' Mr Gray stepped forward, pushing past Lady and Lord Forester, and made his way to the stairs.

'Everyone's drunk!' said Mrs Radcliffe. 'Everyone's always drunk. None of us can stand the sound of our own thoughts, isn't that right? All of us get away from them whenever we can, don't we? Lucky survivors? Hardly. None of us has survived. We're all flotsam and jetsam. We'll all be washed out to sea sooner or later. Ladies and gentleman,' said Mrs Radcliffe, 'I'd like you to meet John Gray: politician and criminal.' Mr Gray was now at the bottom of the stairs. Frank quickly followed.

'What crime?' said Lord Forester from behind them.

'No crime!' spat out Mr Gray. Frank took him by the arm. Mr Gray tried to shake him off.

'Obscenity,' said Mrs Radcliffe shrilly. 'Hardly fitting for a politician, is it?'

'What on earth do you mean?' said Lord Forester. 'He's an upstanding—'

'For God's sake, Charles,' said Lady Forester. 'How stupid are you?' The yellow moonlight through the tall-paned hall windows gave her skin a reptilian gleam.

'Gross indecency,' said Mrs Radcliffe, 'is a criminal act. Am I correct, John?'

'What utter . . .' He pulled his arm, trying to free it from Frank's grip. Frank held on grimly. He looked quickly down the corridor. Just Jessop walking slowly towards them, a strange look on his face, as flat and beaten as a glove puppet without the hand.

'His marriage was a sham,' said Mrs Radcliffe from above, giddy on triumph.

'Well, that's no crime,' said Miss Fox, 'or half of England would be in prison.'

'But where did his true passion lie? With men!' she spat out. 'With men. With Cleveland Bell!' She folded her arms and stood there, speech delivered, eyes bright.

'Rubbish!' said Mr Gray. 'I . . .' He relaxed his arms. 'You can free me, Sergeant. I'm not going to waste my ti—'

'My dear, what nonsense,' said Lord Forester. He gave a hollow cough of a laugh.

Miss Fox leaned back against the corridor wall, directly beneath the Elizabethan portrait of a severe man in a black doublet and white collar. 'Of course it's true,' she said. 'Not that it matters a jot. Don't any of you have eyes in your head?' She smiled in Mr Gray's direction – a genuine smile, though a brief, sad one.

'Unfortunately, it does matter,' said Lady Forester. 'I'm sad to say it, but the law is the law.' She gave an almost imperceptible shrug and sat down on the hall chair.

'How does prison sound, John?' said Mrs Radcliffe shrilly. 'Prison for buggery!' Her eyes were wild now and there were two tiny red dots on her cheeks.

'I'm afraid it's all made up by a little girl who didn't get her own way,' said Mr Gray. 'As you all witnessed, she tried to seduce me. Of course, I said no. And this is a petty revenge.'

'Ha!' said Mrs Radcliffe, pulling a pile of envelopes out from behind her back. 'I suppose I faked these love letters too?' Mr Gray made a sudden move for the stairs again. Frank tightened his grip on his arms. He could smell Mr Gray's anger and fear. 'They're rather saucy, in fact,' said Mrs Radcliffe. 'I learned a thing or two.'

'You foul girl,' said Mr Gray, trying to pull away from Frank.

'Don't make things worse for yourself,' said Frank. He added, under his breath, more to himself than anyone else, 'Revenge, I suppose.'

'Yes,' said Lady Abbott, at his elbow, 'an eye for an eye, eh, John? Happy to send her husband to his death, weren't you?'

'He didn't die in the trenches!' Mr Gray's eyes were bright with indignation again.

'No, but he caught Spanish flu in France, didn't he?' said Mrs Radcliffe. 'And you knew very well what you were sending him into.'

'It's war,' said Mr Gray. 'You're very naïve if you think there was a genuine choice.'

'He drowned in his own lungs!' cried Mrs Radcliffe, her voice high. 'He was only twenty-two. We had our whole lives ahead of us. Meanwhile, you huddled in an office somewhere, too scared to face the music.'

'I faced the music.' His mouth was set in a line.

'A month of it! Then you cried off and got a cosy job.'

'Peter was a brave man,' said Lord Forester. 'No doubt about it.'

'He was a boy,' said Mrs Radcliffe. 'A boy, not a man.'

'A lot of brave men were lost,' said Mr Gray. 'The war was a terrible thing.' His expression was pleading.

'Unfortunately, you weren't one of those brave men,' said Mrs Radcliffe. 'You were a cowardly one who sent people to their certain death, either by enemy fire or by some disgusting disease – you didn't care which so long as it wasn't you.'

'Not anywhere near true.'

'Well let's see how you enjoy the firing line of the press! And how you enjoy the disgusting conditions in prison.' Her voice rang out into sudden silence. Everyone stood in the hallway watching her as she waited on the balcony, flooded in red silk, staring down at her audience. Then they looked away, looked at their feet or their own hands, shuffled uncomfortably. Outside the four walls there was muffled silence. The house was folded deep inside itself, deep inside snow, deep inside night, deep inside an empty land- scape, and under a vast black sky.

Then Miss Fox spoke. 'Who cares who he loves?' she said. 'Why do any of you care?' A thin smile played around her lips as she leaned back on the wall, an elegant, monochrome shape against the dull wood.

'Love!' said Lord Forester. 'Hardly. I suppose you killed Cleveland,' he said to Mr Gray. 'Because he knew your foul secret.' His close-set eyes were full of hatred. 'Arrest him, Sergeant,' he spat at Frank.

'I certainly will not,' said Frank. 'I'm not here to police people's private lives.' He released Mr Gray's arms, which were now soft in his grip. Mr Gray fell forward slightly but didn't right himself.

'Of course not!' said Mr Gray. 'Why would anyone . . . He's a wonderful man. A good man.' He passed a shaky hand over his forehead.

'He can hardly be good, my dear man, can he?' said Lord Forester, not meeting his eyes. 'I suppose if you'd kept it under wraps, been more discrete. But love letters! What are you, a pair of girls? It's against Christianity, for God's sake.' His face was red and he spoke in clipped tones.

'Heaven forbid he would actually love and cherish him,' said Miss Fox. 'Leave the man be. He's lost someone dear to him.' She stepped towards Mr Gray. 'I understand,' she said. 'I saw it. I saw your grief when he died, your relief when you could openly grieve when we found out about poor Anna. It's a dreadful strain keep- ing these things pushed down.' Mr Gray just shook his head.

'Exactly. You weren't upset about Anna at all,' said Mrs Radcliffe. 'It was your lover boy you were crying over.' She smirked. 'It was all faked.'

'It's not fake. I loved Anna.' His voice was broken now, the bluster gone from it. 'It's not a matter of loving one person or loving the other, you know. You can care about more than one person, in more than one way.' His breath left his body in a long, low shudder. 'And now they're both gone.' Frank could sense some of the moral certainty leaving the room, or at least being laced with something less sure.

'Don't worry,' said Mrs Radcliffe, but her high voice was now threaded with doubt. 'I telegrammed the papers yesterday. It will be everywhere by the morning. I've sent them some of the letters too.' She stood at the top of the stairs, as if she was trying to keep hold of her righteousness, despite it seeping out of her. Her thin sneer faded, her eyes got softer, her shoulders sank. She looked at Mr Gray nervously and then at the rest of the small crowd, scanning their faces, it seemed, for approval.

Frank stole a glance at Dottie. She was looking sober, her mouth a straight line, but he couldn't read her thoughts.

Mr Gray straightened his shoulder, sensing the shift in mood with a politician's opportunism. 'You're a silly little girl,' he said. 'Jealous. And what's more, you're peddling narcotics!'

'Don't be ridiculous,' said Lady Forester, standing up.

'Whatever do you mean?' said Lord Forester, turning to face Mr Gray. Miss Fox threw Mrs Radcliffe a sharp look.

'She's a witch,' said Mr Gray. 'You should know this about your precious daughter. She dragged me off to my bedroom. Tried it on with me and then tried to get me to take some opium. A very large dose, by the looks of it. Could have killed me if I was stupid enough to take it.'

'About time you knew what real pain is. It's a shame I couldn't show you how Peter felt when his lungs dissolved, but this is the next best thing to watching you froth at the mouth as you died from opium poisoning. It's a shame you didn't take it. You'd be better off dead. You'll be wishing you were soon enough. Just wait till morning. I've hidden it now so don't go changing your mind! It's too late. The hounds will come for you.' And she walked off. 'Show over!' she called. But her shoulders as she walked away were bent as if by a terrible burden and she looked uncertainly over them, uncomfortable in her shoes and with the part she had chosen to play.

For once, there was a hushed silence and then the clock tower chimed three times.

# CHAPTER TWENTY-THREE

## THE PRIVATE STAIRCASE

The entrance hall and corridor were silent.

'Back to the dining room, please,' said Frank. 'Jessop, can I count on you to stand at the door and watch them?'

'Where will you be?' said Jessop, looking frightened. Frank's mind was galloping on.

'For God's sake, stop treating us as criminals or small children,' said Lord Forester, his face erupting into anger again. 'We should all have got out while we could. Why did we let my wife talk us into hiding out in a billiards room? I could be asleep in a comfortable bed now in the nice little inn in the village.' He looked around, as if searching for someone to punch. 'Instead, I'm stuck here, a sitting duck, waiting to be murdered.'

'Someone's a criminal,' said Dottie. 'Maybe more than one person. Sergeant Glover is trying to keep everyone safe and do his job.'

'Lock us in with the murderer, then!' said Mr Gray. 'Look, this is madness. There's someone working their way through us, killing us all. It's been hours and what has happened? No answers and more of us are dying. We'll all die if we don't do something. I for one am not going to be locked in a small room with someone murderous. I'm leaving.'

'There's no way out,' said Lady Forester. 'You'll have to stay.'

'I'd rather keep everyone where I can see them, I don't know about you,' said Miss Fox. She patted Mr Gray on the arm then gave his elbow a quick rub. She murmured, 'Don't worry, old friend,' under her breath.

'Come along,' said Frank. 'In you go.'

'Aren't you worried that Mr Gray's right?' Dottie said quietly at his elbow. 'That we're trapping innocent people with a killer?'

'There's no alternative,' he said, moving back towards the dining room. The group all shuffled in front of him, their bombastic spirit departed. 'They'd be more vulnerable separated. We're looking at a series of carefully concealed, carefully planned revenge killings. That's not the sort of thing that's done in full view.'

'Jessop,' said Lord Forester from the rear of the slow caravan, 'get the whisky, there's a good man.'

'Certainly not,' said Frank. 'You can manage without alcohol for an hour or two.'

'We've all had a shock,' said Lady Abbott. 'A series of shocks, in fact.'

'Best keep your wits about you, then,' said Frank. 'What you have left of them, anyway,' he added, more to himself.

'The cheek,' said Lady Abbott unsteadily and winked at him. She swayed a little as she walked down the hallway. Frank noticed she had a small, silver hip flask in her right hand.

Frank and Dottie stood at the rear, watching them all make their way into the dining room. 'Go ahead,' said Frank. 'And keep them out of the library, if you can. I'll stay here and usher them all in.'

'How about the other way around?' said Dottie. Frank remembered the sight in the library, the awful gaping throat like a second grin, and agreed. He looked up the stairs, but Mrs Radcliffe was nowhere to be seen. He followed the ragged crowd.

'Keep them in here,' he said to Jessop. And he made his way to the library and half closed the door, so he could see them and hear them but gather his thoughts at the same time.

Frank stepped carefully over Professor Webber's prone form and peered into the dark corridor. Wider than the false wall cavity for air ducts he and Dottie had looked into earlier, it would easily fit a man or a woman. He walked in the dark, a hand on each wall, the bright doorway to the library behind him.

The air was stale in here and the walls were rough to his touch. He walked a dozen or so steps but then the corridor came to an abrupt end. He felt the wall in front of him for a door – nothing. Professor Webber would have had a reason to be in this corridor – he had fallen, not been dragged. He felt the wall to his left, the wall which would be on the courtyard side, and found just bricks. To his right, the wall with the main corridor, there was no obvious door, but he remembered how Dottie had opened the hidden doors. He searched blindly, feeling his way with his hands and pushing at waist height every now and then. Suddenly a wide crack appeared in the wall.

He shoved at the opening and saw the dim light of the main corridor beyond, the door to the empty garden room in front of him. From here Frank would be able to enter and leave the garden room, and return to the library, without anyone seeing.

He sat back at the library table with his hands flat on the top. He took a deep breath in and out, leaned his elbows on the table and his fingertips against each other. He leaned his forehead into his forefingers, and he thought, hard. Then he took an envelope and a pencil out of his pocket. He wrote down three names and drew a circle around them. Then he drew a second circle around all of them. Three different killers, but ultimately . . .

He took the advent calendar out of his pocket and smoothed it out. The firework – or bomb – in Professor Webber's bedroom, the bell in Lady Abbott's, and the boat in Mrs Radcliffe's. The toy car in Mr Bell's room. He ran his finger over the small, cardboard doors. In the Roman baths, a dressed doll in a tin bath. In the library a sword. In the electrics room a bolt of lightning. And in the master suite a gun. He looked at it for one second, two, and then stood up, pocketing the pencil and envelope. He shut the library door behind him and walked to Jessop at the dining room door.

'I'll be a short while,' he said. 'Go in there and try to keep them calm. Can you keep them in there?'

'I can try, Sergeant Glover.'

'Ring the exchange if you need help. I'll be sure to hear it.'

Jessop stepped inside the room.

'Where's he going now?' It was Lord Forester's voice, crackling with irritation.

'Ask the constable to bring the wine back with him,' slurred Lady Abbott.

'He'll have better things to do,' said Dottie.

Indeed he did. He strode down the corridor to the main staircase. The world outside the house had the deadly muffle of deep snow. He took the stairs two at a time, and sprinted down the corridor towards the morning room, turning towards the master suite. But outside Mr Bell's room he heard what sounded like a sharp cough.

He stopped. And he turned on his heel. He listened carefully. Again. But it was not a cough, so much as a . . . He pushed the door open quickly.

He wasn't alone. Perhaps he shouldn't have been surprised by who it was, at any rate.

'How on earth did you get here?' he said. Then, 'Of course. The concealed stairs from the library. You knew about those too.'

Mr Gray was white with grief. He was sitting on the bed, head in his hands. 'What did he look like?' he whispered. 'Did he seem at peace?'

Frank hesitated. 'Yes,' he lied.

'Was his face ruined? He'd have hated to be on show like that, seen at his worst.'

'Not at all,' he lied again. 'It was clearly instantaneous.'

'That someone can just be gone in the time it takes to switch on a light!'

Frank shared that horror. He nodded grimly.

'Do you believe in an afterlife, Mr . . . Sergeant?'

'No. I'm afraid not.'

Mr Gray sank further down. 'How will I bear it?' he whispered.

'Because it must be borne,' said Frank. 'That's all. That's all there is.'

The two men occupied the room in silence for a few heartbeats, both weighed down by a burden that they knew would never release them. Outside was dead silence. Frank would have given his career and his freedom, his mind and his eyes, to know that the dead carried on in another room, however unreachably. But he knew with a grim certainty that it was not the case, that nothing remained, that there was nothing to hold on to – nothing at all.

Then Mr Gray sat up a little straighter and looked Frank straight in the eyes. 'Professor Webber must have killed Cleveland and Anna,' he said. 'Perhaps even, somehow, Prince Rudolph. I'm glad he's dead. It was less than he deserved. He must have been drunk on power.' His pleading eyes met Frank's, begging, it seemed, for an answer. 'Or mad, perhaps. You know, he was far from a saint. He wasn't above using any means possible to push through legislation that would suit him, for instance. He wasn't a discrete man. He wanted to get into politics. I was being pressured to pass certain bills for him, cover certain costs, pay him a little to not talk about his, shall we say *encouragements* to me. I'm sure you know what I mean. He's hardly a great loss to mankind. Even one of the maids said so to me, just last night. Even she could see that he was a man full of vice shouting about his virtue. She'd asked him for a loan of money, would you believe, and he'd brushed her off. Mind you, she'd asked Mr Bell for a shop girl job too, I believe. He said no; she's a little too common for an upmarket store.

'And Professor Webber was blackmailing Mr Bell,' he went on. 'Did you know that? Perhaps that's an even better reason to be far from sorry he's gone. You know about his connections with the Foresters, I assume?' Mr Gray had the air of a drowning man who planned to drag everyone down with him. Frank thought he'd do well to keep him talking.

'I know some of it. I'm sure you know more.' He sat down at the chair by the desk; his ears, his eyes, on high alert. The house was silent.

'You're aware Professor Webber wasn't just an inventor of, I don't know, heating systems and the like? He put his talents to more practical uses. Consider the two wars – the Irish War, the Great War. How might an industrialist and an inventor make themselves handy?' Mr Gray's face was crumpled with sadness, but his eyes began to look clearer as he talked. 'You know, Professor Webber took it upon himself to take what he knew and apply it to other weapons and pass them into extremely unworthy hands. All for the rush of power! God forbid this man be lauded as a genius after his death. Think transatlantic acts of terror.'

'The Wall Street Bomb killed Mr Bell's brother, did it not?' As Frank spoke, his ears were pricked, listening for any small noise that might betray a commotion in the rooms below them. He could hear nothing. Did he have time to get down there if he heard something?

'Yes. The code name was Stacy.' He shrugged. 'You may as well know.'

'Professor Webber's code name?'

'No, no,' he was irritated now, 'not Professor Webber's code name, the bomber's code name. State secrets are less secret than you'd think, once you get into the right room. Once you get a seat at the table. His brother's death crushed Cleveland, but he didn't stay down for long. But Professor Webber got more and more confident, less and less discrete. He had the power to end my career and he'd have done it sooner or later. Ironic, isn't it, that Mrs Radcliffe has done it anyway? That bitter little girl.'

Mr Gray's eyes were wild now. Frank recognised the look and he wanted to clear the room of Mr Gray's grief. His own grief was too heavy for him to take on someone else's. It was always there, always waiting for a moment to come back – he was constantly on the lookout for it, trying to kill it before it could kill him.

'I think . . .' he said, meaning to move Mr Gray onto a different topic, a different room.

But Mr Gray stood up, looking dazed, and walked a couple of steps, only to stand in the middle of the room, looking helpless. He picked up a jacket that hung on the back of the dressing table chair. 'Oh God,' he said. He took his black jacket off and put the other jacket on, tears running down his cheeks now. He stood stock still, staring straight ahead of him, as though there were an executioner with a raised gun behind him.

Frank opened his mouth to say something impatient, then he saw something in the cast of Mr Gray's face, in the crumpling of his forehead as if everything inside had been smashed to pieces, and he closed his mouth again. He sighed. They stood there for a second, two seconds. And then he removed his hand from Mr Gray's shoulder and said, very quietly, 'It's time to go back.'

Mr Gray nodded and he walked to the corner, pushed at a wall-papered panel and disappeared, seemingly, into a deep, black hole. Frank followed.

A wise man had once said to Frank that it was a mistake to assume everything in a complex situation was connected. Having a head-ache at the same time as a stomach pain does not necessarily mean you are suffering from an illness that carries both symptoms. It was advice that had stayed with him throughout his fledgling polic-ing career, when the networks of motivations were often complex and subtle webs, with many broken connections and surprising threads. He had learned to look for both.

The staircase was narrow and dark. The treads were steep and travelled down in a narrow spiral. He felt as though he were in the belly of the monster. He'd never suffered from claus-trophobia, but he was glad when the winding stairs came to an end and he heard a familiar, dull clicking sound. Suddenly light flooded into the tight space and they were in the far corner of the library, concealed, it seemed, from all of the dining room. Mr Gray stepped out first and stood in the low lamp light. Frank followed.

'Wait here,' he said to Mr Gray, who looked relieved.

He stepped quietly across the dining room. The guests were slumped in chairs, heads on their hands, or sitting against the wall. Dottie sat, back straight, hands folded in her lap, in a corner. The rest of them seemed dazed, their anger and terror spent into a dull, grit-eyed torpor. He opened the door to the hall, slipping out into the shadow-thronged corridor.

'Jessop,' he said quietly. 'Here a second. Can you try the telephone line for me? The snow has stopped, I believe. Perhaps the line is open again.'

'Certainly, Sergeant.'

Frank watched Jessop walk slowly down the corridor, as if he was carrying a heavy sack of potatoes over his shoulders. He looked back at Lady Forester through the half-open door. Was she concealing a grief? Had she just found out her lover had been killed? It wasn't clear from her face, if so. She was implacable as a polished spoon.

'Any luck?' he said to a returning Jessop.

'Afraid not. Not likely to be fixed until the morning, or beyond.'

'Not to worry. I can make use of the time.'

'Right you are, Sergeant.' His knees looked like they were ready to buckle under him.


Mr Gray was sitting down with his back against the book-lined wall. His legs were straight out in front of him on the wooden, rug-strewn floor and his head was thrown back against the dark spines of the books.

Frank took his notebook out of his stuffed pocket. 'It's time for the conversation that I'm sure you knew was coming,' he said. 'Can I ask you a few questions?'

Mr Gray shrugged. 'I'd happily be hanged,' he said. 'It's better than living with this pain.' He looked up at Frank. 'It will never go away, you know.'

Frank pulled up a chair next to the round table by the window. The rawness of Mr Gray's grief was like salt sprinkled on a wound. He flipped open his notebook. 'I will need to note down your exact words. You understand.' He looked back at Mr Gray who gave him a desperate, grief-drowned look. 'I know,' he said, more gently.

'Yes, yes.' Mr Gray bowed his head and looked at his shoes. His jacket, trousers and feet were black as deep shadows against the wooden floor, the shadow of a cut puppet.

'You didn't intend to kill him. It was an impulse. A horrible impulse. You hated him and were afraid he'd ruin you. And of course, he was blackmailing Mr Bell. You saw him in the library on his own. You had a knife in your pocket and you just went in there and stabbed him. Perhaps someone suggested you took the knife with you to dinner, or planted the idea at any rate. Suggested it and the idea took hold.'

Mr Gray just shook his head.

'You stabbed him first. After you stabbed him you panicked that he'd make a noise, so you slit his throat and pushed him backwards into the passage and shut the door and left him there. That's why the blood was pooled by the desk and splattered towards the shelves.'

Mr Gray was motionless.

'And then you went back into the dining room, of course. What else could you do? That accounts for the single drop of blood by the door to the library. You put your gloves on to hide the blood. You put them on afterwards, not before, and you haven't been able to take them off since, for fear of incriminating yourself.'

Mr Gray shook his bowed head. He released a deep, rattling sigh.

Frank put his pencil down. 'And who told you about the hidden butler's passage and staircase?'

Mr Gray looked up, face tear-stained. 'Maybe the lady of the house wasn't as shocked by her daughter's little theatrical reveal as she implied,' he said. 'Blind eye, and all that. That's what the perfect hostess does.' One foot tap, tap, tapped against the wooden floor. His gloved hand was on the floor next to his hip.

'Of course. And where was your wife while you were in the library?' He could hear the low murmur of voices in the dining room, now and then squalling up before settling back into silence. But he believed that the relative calm was deceptive; temporary. That the true puppet master had yet to be revealed. Mrs Radcliffe, Lady Abbott, Lady Forester or Lord Forester had altered that calendar, had pasted that note together. One of them wanted to set their actors on a stage and let them do their worst; give them their lines, even. Ensure they'd be heard and recorded.

'She went to freshen up between courses,' Mr Gray said.

'Perhaps she'd have gone out for some air? Maybe through the garden room?'

'I can't see why she'd do that. If she'd wanted air, why not go out through the front door?'

Frank agreed with this verdict. The sweet, familiar smell in their room, the heavy, footprints leading from the garden room, the handkerchief in Professor Webber's pocket – she'd been carried, unconscious, from there to the baths. Rather a long way with a heavy burden. Tired and concerned about how long he'd been absent, Professor Webber must have risked returning to the house through the butler's room, gambling on it being empty and Jessop being in the kitchen.

'So, everyone else was in the dining room.'

'Yes, except for the servants of course.'

'Where were they?'

'Jessop and Dottie would have been in the kitchen. They were serving us. The little maid was probably in the scullery. And then we saw that note from the blue-blood killer. And we all got extremely frightened and went for cover.'

'You surprised Professor Webber on his way back from killing your wife, you'll perhaps be interested to know.'

Mr Gray looked up, surprised. He stared at Frank, his face expressionless. 'Good,' he said eventually. 'Another excellent reason for him to die. But why would he want to kill her? He was a rational man, not particularly led by emotion, not particularly interested in Anna.' He flicked at his teeth with his gloved thumb.

'Ah, well you see it wasn't a murder led by emotion; interesting you should say that. It was a calculated killing. Mrs Gray knew his worst secrets, knew he sold bombs to terrorists, and she was an alcoholic who couldn't be trusted. Professor Webber needed to get rid of her before it all came out. He rendered her unconscious in your bedroom, surprising her from behind with a chloroform-soaked cloth. She dropped her lipstick, marking the mirror and floor. He carried her through the garden room to the baths in light snow, deposited her unconscious there, and then turned the heat up. He, of course, knew about the hidden passages too, having designed them.'

'She'd have known nothing.' Mr Gray didn't phrase it as a question because he needed it to be beyond doubt. 'She was a bright spirit, a candle in a dark night, but she wouldn't have coped with pain, or with fear.'

This time Frank could be truthful. 'No. She wouldn't have known a thing. And then Professor Webber made his way back. He kept out of sight of the kitchen by using the hidden passage for a second time, coming out of it again in the library. Unfortunately for him you met him there. Now, would anyone have been able to go and adjust the cable for the funicular at any point?'

'No, of course not. I don't know what you're talking about.' He sighed. 'Prince Rudolph,' he said, drawing the word out like a dying breath. 'The train must have slid on the ice. Always did seem a ridiculously rickety thing.'

'You were all together from that point on?'

'Well, except for my wife of course. And later Cleveland went to—' He bent over and sat there on the stone floor, shoulders shaking.

'We'll leave it there. Can you stand?'

Mr Gray stood up and waited to be told what to do.

'This way. Come on.' He put a firm hand on Mr Gray's back and gently led him towards the dining room, where he sat him down at the table. Frank nodded at Dottie, who sprang up immediately. He locked the dining room door behind them.

# CHAPTER TWENTY-FOUR

## THE EYRIE SUITE

Frank and Dottie walked quickly down the dark, wood-panelled corridor. The house was enclosed by a thick layer of snow. It was silent; waiting for the next act. The one thread to the outside world had been neatly snapped off.

Their steps were loud. It was the very dead of night – the witching hour, his ma had called it, when he woke up with a bad dream. As they passed the butler's pantry, Frank paused. He reached for the handle, but she'd be asleep now – there was plenty of time. He gently turned it to reassure himself; it was locked, as he'd left it.

His ma would be proud of him now, they all said, but the truth was she'd be heartbroken not to be there with him. She'd be glad he was using his brain, was working his way up through promotions, but he knew for a fact there were things he'd done that would have disappointed her. She was a woman of principle and she could be impatient with lesser souls who made mistakes. For the first time in years, he let his mind rest on her for a second or two. He'd have given the world for an opportunity to disappoint her in person and make up for it in person too.

'I haven't yet been to the suite at the top of the house,' Frank said now to Dottie as they approached the entrance hall. 'The one on the second floor. Now we have found all our missing parties and have some clear ideas on who did what. But there are some gaps to fill in.'

She nodded. 'The royal suite,' she said. 'That's what they call it, though we don't get a great deal of visiting royalty.' She hesitated. 'It's awful,' she said, 'that they would kill each other like savages. That they would—'

He agreed. 'People are pushed to things,' he said, 'by their anger, their fear. No one's a monster,' he said, 'or at least very few are. I believe what they're seeing is all part of the theatre they've created with themselves as players. All part of this Penny Club. This sense of them as lucky survivors. So, I think you are safe.' He glanced at her. 'But stick close to me, just in case.'

Dottie led him away from the entrance hall. 'I hope you don't mind a climb,' she said. 'It's right at the top of the house. It's called the eyrie suite. Like an eagle's nest.'

'I don't mind a climb. Miss Fox wasn't keen on Prince Rudolph, was she?'

'What makes you think that?'

'I believe he made a play for her? That she didn't appreciate him being on the make too much?'

'I'm sure she's used to that kind of thing.' She led him to the narrower staircase at the side of the house. 'Here. Two flights, but the second one's steep and long. She wouldn't have appreciated it, like you say, but she takes things like that in her stride. She's not one to hold on to a grudge.'

'It didn't sound like he was particularly chivalrous.' The stairs were dark, lit by moonlight that reflected off the quiet, unspoilt snow and bounced in through the tall windows. The newel posts at each turn threw long shadows onto the floor, shadows that looked like dark sentries if you caught them with an off glance.

'I don't expect he was.' Dottie's mouth was set in a firm line that Frank was starting to recognise.

Frank was tired. He knew it was important to stay alert when you were starting to flag; he knew it was vital to keep your thoughts organised and clear.

'Here we are.' Dottie opened a small door at the top of the stairs. A steep and winding staircase corkscrewed further upwards. From here Frank could hear the wind again. As they started to climb the stairs he glanced over his shoulder, suddenly feeling vulnerable. Anyone could grab him in the dark and pull him back down the stairs. He took his revolver from his pocket and kept it quietly by his side.

'Why make royalty climb the worst stairs in the house?' he said under his breath.

'It's the best room and the most private. And it has the best views. There are four rooms up here – two bedrooms and a sitting room. And a very grand bathroom. Prince Rudolph liked it. He said it reminded him of home. The mountains and trees, I think.'

'He escaped from occupation during the War, is that right?' These stairs were narrower, the dark treads smooth beneath his feet. The silence gathered thickly around them.

'Yes. Lucky for him. He bribed one or two of the locals, gave some sort of sleeping draught to a guard – so it's said – and escaped across the Baltic by boat in the dead of night. Maybe it was less lucky for the people left behind. I hear a few of the guards were blamed for his escape and hanged.'

They reached the top of the stairs and he was glad that the claustrophobic space had opened up again. They were in a small hallway leading off to a number of rooms. He opened the first door to reveal the first of the two bedrooms, a large space with a vast four-poster bed. The ceiling was swathed in swags of fabric in yellows and bright blues. He looked around carefully. 'It's empty,' he said. 'Have a careful look around here. I'll carry on.'

The second room was a smaller bedroom with two single beds in and a window overlooking the snow. The outer wall curved slightly – they were in a tower, of course. He had a good look around – the room hadn't been occupied. The third door led to a sitting room or study. The curved wall had window seats overlooking the view, not that there was much to see at present. A chair with fabric swags. A desk with round, sturdy legs, like the calves of someone who did a lot of walking. He took a closer look.

He didn't have to look far. On the top of the desk, centred on it, in fact, as if the writer wished it to be found, was an envelope.

*Mr. Bell*

*And anyone else it may concern*

He hadn't seen the handwriting before. The black letters were elaborate and looped, the writing of someone with careful education and time to spare. He turned the envelope over. It was unsealed.

He pulled the letter out and read it, whistling between his teeth. Well, no wonder. A sorry bunch they were, he thought. All vain, selfish and ruthless. Less lucky than prepared to push others aside in order to survive and thrive.

It was just a matter of connecting everything else now. Light at the end of the tunnel. His heart began to lighten.

Dottie was standing at the door, a hand over her mouth catching a yawn. 'Nothing interesting,' she said, 'as far as I can see.'

'Not to worry. I think I have what I need.' The letter was folded up in his pocket. He could feel it pushing against the breast pocket of his shirt. 'A connecting line.' Outside the window the trees threw out their white arms and looked to the sky. The heat of fatigue and tension and hours spent feeling like he was being watched sprung into his brain like a jazz tune. For a split second, a mad second, he imagined asking Dottie to dance. Then he shook his head and walked towards the door.

At the dining room door, Frank beckoned Miss Fox over. With her habitual wry look, she made her way across the room, rubbing her eyes as she walked.

'This is turning into a long night, isn't it, Sergeant?' she said.

'I've had longer.'

'Oh, so have I! But it was more fun than this.'

'Can I have a quiet word?' He nodded towards the hallway. Dottie stepped neatly around them without catching his eye.

'I'm being summoned for questioning.'

'Not at all. Just a private word, please.'

She smiled at him, though the smile didn't reach her eyes, and followed him out of the room and into the dark hall. She was slim, but not slight. He examined her cape while her back was turned. No snags that suggested she'd been trying to get through an impossibly narrow space – anyway, there was too much of her, she was sparely built but on a large, elegant frame.

'Here.' He handed her the letter and waited. She looked at the addressee but didn't open it.

'It's addressed to Mr Bell. Such a lovely man. He's my investor, you know. Or was. He's been so good to me.' She held the letter carefully, two fingers holding it on each edge.

'You, he and Mrs Gray escaped the Wall Street Bomb together?'

'Oh, yes. It was rather awful. We were in a meeting with his accountant, Mr Bell and I, right at the top of the building, when there was this dreadful explosion. It shook the building to its bones. We ran down like the wind, the three of us. Moments later, the building started to topple. We'd have been done for, for sure – a lot of people died that day, including Cleveland's brother, you know. We saw Anna, Mrs Gray now, of course, though she wasn't then, running towards us down the centre of the road like a horseman of the apocalypse. She was wild! Mr Bell got us all into his private car and away.' She hesitated. 'We had a little extra room. I suggested we stop and get a few more in. Anna wasn't keen, she was rather highly strung, but Mr Bell agreed eventually. We all had quite a hoot in the end, the three of us and these five strangers. After a minute or two I asked them to stop the car and I got out and went back into the thick of it to try and round up some ambulances. It was mayhem out there.' She opened the envelope, unfolded the pages and started to read. Frank looked away, giving her a moment of privacy to come to terms with the contents.

He heard a snort and looked at her quickly, expecting to see her crying, but she'd thrown her head back with laughter.

'Oh, Rudolph. It's hilarious! Thank you for this. What a gift.' She wiped her eyes and read on.

'It's not true, then?'

'Of course it's true. Every word. What a prim little madam he is, isn't he? You can practically hear his voice in this. It's priceless.' She turned the letter over. '*I regret to inform you.* Oh, he's too funny. I can't bear it.' She refolded the letter and put it back in its envelope. 'Thank you for this, Sergeant. Just what I needed.'

'It could have ended your career and a very important business relationship with Mr Bell.' He was thrown by her jollity; it was so out of place with the contents of the letter.

'Not at all. He would have found it hilarious too.'

'Not a secret worth someone dying for?' He thought of Rudolph's unrecognisable face.

'Very little is worth dying for. Do you mind?' She nodded towards the dining room door. 'May I?'

He held out his hand for the letter, but she kept hold of it and walked back into the dining room.

'Listen everyone,' she said, holding the letter out in front of her and unfolding it again. 'I have something rather amusing to share with you. Rudolph's last words, if you will. I'm sure he'd like you to hear them. In fact, I think that may have been his precise intention. Are you all listening carefully? Then I shall begin.' She cleared her throat.

Frank could see Lady Abbott dozing in the corner and Jessop looked dead eyed, but everyone else seemed reasonably alert.

'*Dear Mr Bell.* That's how it begins. I'll just read the rest out to you straight. I'm sure you'll find it extremely entertaining; I know I do.' She assumed a posture that Frank's mother would have described as theatrical and carried on reading. '*I'm afraid I write with some rather unfortunate word of your business associate, Miss Fox. I am sorry to be the bearer of bad news, but men must stick together,*' she snorted, '*and help each other out. You may instinctively have half guessed some of this but the full truth of it will appall and disgust you. Miss Fox, and I'm afraid I have this on sure confidence, indulges in many nefarious practices, not least . . .* Not least! . . . *not least dressing as a gentleman and frequenting what I can only describe as specialist establishments in London and New York and engaging in relationships with other morally bankrupt young women.* Shall I go on? The rest of it is mostly bluster about how sad he is for me, and so on.'

The room was silent.

'Oh, my dear,' said Lady Abbott, blinking. 'What did I miss? I must have dozed off.'

'Don't worry, I'm sure the others will fill you in.' Miss Fox's face softened into earnestness and her eyes filled. 'I have no secrets, you know. I don't care what anyone knows about me. My only private life is in my thoughts and my feelings, and those I trust to very few. I wasn't unique. Prince Rudolph was a horrid man and a pest, but I wasn't the only one to receive his attentions. He pestered Florence too, many a time, practically under her parents' noses.'

Lord Forester burst out. 'What a dreadful lie!'

'And he tried it on with Stacy.'

Frank swallowed. 'Stacy?' he said. His heart dropped towards his stomach and his mind was ice-cold. Stacy.

'Yes. Sorry, that's my pet name for her. I forgot myself. Mrs Gray. Anna.'

'That's a strange shortening. Anna to Stacy.' He deliberately said the words slowly to disguise his racing heart.

'Stasia,' she corrected him. 'Anastasia. I believe her parents were Russian. It's an old Russian name, anyway.'

Lady Forester was sitting up straight, very flushed now.

'Stacy,' said Frank slowly. So that was how she knew Professor Webber constructed bombs – because she set one off. That was the final piece of the Professor Webber puzzle.

'We've heard enough, Cecelia,' Lady Forester said. 'No one cares about your grubby little ways. I've been saying for hours now, no one is listening. We must go and find Florence. She disappeared and no one seems worried.'

'She can't come to any harm,' said Frank. 'The killer, or killers, are all in here. Those that are still alive, anyway.'

'What a damned cheek,' said Lord Forester. 'Sophia, ensure a complaint is made.'

'I will certainly be complaining, about the abandonment of Florence.'

Frank said, 'I understand your anxiety but I'm sure she's safe. I'll go and look for her, if you wish.'

'Florence will be taking opium like a street worker,' said Mr Gray. 'Like the grubby little wretch she is. Why none of you have worked that out about her . . . She'll be lying on her bed, dreaming foul narcotic dreams. She tried to drag me down to her level, but I had none of it.' He stood up and clenched his fist and then started to pace around the dining table.

'Maybe you shouldn't have killed her husband, then,' said Lady Forester. 'And with it all her chances of happiness. Don't wrong people if you don't expect revenge to be taken.'

'I confiscated her little kit,' said Miss Fox. 'Sometimes you have to patronise people a tiny bit with little deceits for their own good. As soon as she can take her mind off Peter and move on with her life, she'll be fine.'

'It's not just that,' Lady Abbott swayed, eyes slightly glazed. 'It's not just grief, my dear, it's shame. Boiling, rotten shame. Shame that Peter died in her arms and that she couldn't save him. She's wracked with it. It's a killer, shame.' She sat back down. 'It's eaten her up, poor girl. It's destroyed the sweet girl inside her. That bitter anger you saw from her. That's the shame talking. There was a sweet girl once in its place.'

'And so she shamed Mr Gray,' said Dottie quietly.

Frank gave her a steady look. 'Anger can be a killer too,' he said. 'Especially when it brews over decades, can't it, Lady Abbott?' He glanced quickly at Mr Gray's grief-streaked face. 'Mr Gray, would you be so good as to fetch a bottle of whisky from the butler's pantry? Everyone has had a terrible shock.' He waited a second or two for the footsteps to recede before continuing in a lower voice. 'Imagine being so angry about the shock of your husband's death that you felt justified in killing,' he said.

'Quite,' Lady Abbott said. 'Poor girl. Hold on a minute, who has Florence killed?'

'Not Mrs Radcliffe, Lady Abbott, but you. And not the *Titanic*, but the disaster at sea a generation earlier, when your husband and all the crew were killed by a Captain Bell, who then claimed the cargo of the ship as his own. His money . . .'

'. . . built a fortune and a vast sense of entitlement for all of his family!' she spat. 'All this talk of how charming, how lovely, how elegant Mr Bell was. That man was the spitting image of his father in every way. Just like his father, his charms were entirely superficial. Maybe he never murdered to get rich, but I'm sure, like his father, he would have if there was a profit to be made. My husband would have lived, my daughter could have stayed with us if that awful man had never lived. Who knows what lives are saved by Mr Bell being dead? Revolting man. He only got his due. Someone needs to pay their dues, even if it does come a generation too late.'

Frank nodded.

'Daughter?' said Lord Forester. 'What is this, Lady Abbott? What daughter?'

'Sophia, my dear,' said Lady Abbott. 'I hope you always knew.' There were tears on her cheeks. She walked to Lady Forester and took her hand in hers.

'Not always,' said Lady Forester. 'But for a while now.'

'Shame the old dear's off to the gallows,' said Miss Fox under her breath, 'just as the family reunion starts.'

Mr Gray walked through the door with a decanter of whisky in one hand. He thrust it onto the table and sat, mute, his back against the wall.

'Lock them in, Jessop,' said Frank.

'How did she do it?' said Dottie quietly. 'I can't quite believe she would.' They walked down the quiet corridor side by side.

'It was clear from the start that it wasn't an accident,' he said. 'The body wasn't in the right position to have fallen there – it was

224

too neat. The arm was up in the air, whereas if someone had a shock and fell, or a shock leading to a heart attack then fell, their arm would be thrown to the side. It was positioned carefully. That all showed it was a deliberate act. As for it being Lady Abbott, I suspect she changed the controls so they weren't earthed – she knows how to do that – and planned to fake a call for the funicular. She didn't need to in the end because I called it. She took her opportunity and told Mr Bell to go and pull the lever. You'll remember they all said that Lady Abbott sent him, when logically it should have been Lady Forester or Lord Forester.'

'She was missing, moving around the house alone when we went upstairs to find everyone.' Dottie frowned. 'For hours. It seemed a dangerous thing to do.'

'Yes, highly unlikely she'd do that without an extremely good reason. Remember, Mr Bell was not the only death at this point – they'd all fled in fear from a threatening note and a pool of blood in the dining room. Only someone wanting to cover their tracks would be that foolhardy. After Mr Bell had been gone a few minutes, she made her excuses and went out to check it had gone to plan – she slipped out early, you'll realise, before they barricaded the door; she wouldn't have been able to slip out unseen with the bureau in place. She prised his hands off the lever by turning the power off – that's what the blackout was when I arrived. She had to use a little brute force too – a knife that she went downstairs to find, though she claimed she'd only been upstairs, powdering her nose. Her shawl had been in the dining room, but she retrieved it at the same time – it was gone next time we were there. And she switched all the lights off – you'll have noticed that it's a habit with her, switching a light off when she leaves a room. And when we went back downstairs the lights were all switched off. Anyway, once up there, she managed to get him onto the floor – though not in a position that anyone would ever land in naturally.'

'She must have known he would be found—'

'She hoped it might pass as a heart attack. That's why she mentioned he had heart problems – his heart stopping probably did kill him, after all. She was in there when we first went to the billiards room – we heard a floorboard creak. And before she came back into the billiards room, we heard the sound of a light switch being flicked off – the drawing room light that time.'

Dottie sighed. 'How very sad,' was all she said.

He nodded. The house loomed, silent, around them.

'So, Professor Webber didn't do it all,' said Dottie. 'He killed Mrs Gray, but not the others.'

'Yes,' he said. 'She really did know Professor Webber's worst secrets. The last thing he could afford, given his finances were so bad he was turning to blackmail and pawn shops to stay afloat.'

'It doesn't quite add up, though,' Dottie said. 'Something else was going on. The note – who left that? You were telephoned, but none of us telephoned you. It wasn't me, I can't see that it was any of the guests. They would have been having champagne in the drawing room an hour before dinner.'

'Someone will have been getting about unseen using the space behind the false walls. That wasn't Professor Webber – we now know he was dead by then. So who? And, going back a bit further, I was telephoned at 7.15, before the lines went dead. In fact, before dinner was served – before any crime had even happened. When I arrived, the candles were only burned down half an inch, dinner hadn't been served more than thirty minutes before. Yet I was telephoned nearly an hour earlier. I'd guess the line was cut deliberately straight after that call.'

The house was silent. There was no sound from the dining room.

'There's someone behind the scenes,' said Dottie. 'Some of the clues seem like they've been left for us to find. I'm not a detective, but I've worked with people all my life and I know that they don't leave their darkest secrets out on desks to be easily seen.'

'Yes, someone else was behind all of the murders,' said Frank. 'I was supposed to find that they'd done each other in, but I'd say not that it had been staged – not that people had almost been given lines to say; that they'd been provoked into being their worst self.'

She gave him her clear-sighted gaze. 'Doing someone else's dirty work, you could say. Why would anyone want all of them gone?' she said. 'Who would hate so many people, so much? Had they all done something so awful to one person?'

They stood together on the balconied landing. Behind them the grand staircase dropped to the ground floor, with the entrance hall's two tall windows standing sentry. In front of them the claustrophobic, wood-panelled corridor that led to the morning room and East Wing.

'This way,' Dottie said, opening a door off the main landing. 'This is Mrs Radcliffe's suite.' Frank thought of his quiet house and his thick door and his bed – it wouldn't be too long now before this was all wrapped up.

The room was a vibrant green. Even the wood panels were painted with it. The windows were swathed with green curtains with a riot of foliage on them. There were mirrors on two walls, a sea-blue chaise longue by the window and a large vase of red silk poppies on an elegant wooden cabinet. A red dress was draped stiffly on the low sofa, the opium pipe from Miss Fox's room and the bottle of opium from Mr Gray's room at the sofa's feet.

Only it wasn't a dress.

Dottie gasped and ran to the sofa.

'No,' she was saying, 'no, no, no. Please. No. Florence. Mrs Radcliffe. Wake up. Wake up, Florence.'

Frank ran to Dottie's side, grabbed Mrs Radcliffe's wrist and tried to find a pulse, but he could tell by the set of her skin. There was a bloody froth on her lips and nose.

'Wake her up! Wake her up!' Dottie was screaming. She started to shake Mrs Radcliffe. 'Wake her up, Frank! Don't just stand there. Florence, please wake up. It's not time for bed. It's not time yet. Frank. Frank!'

He put his hand gently on her shoulder.

'No!' she screamed. 'Don't do that! Get her back, Frank, get her back. How do you do it? I'll do it!'

He put his arm on her shoulder. 'Dottie,' he said. 'Dottie. She's gone.'

'No. No, she hasn't! Why are you saying that?' She started shaking Mrs Radcliffe's shoulders. Mrs Radcliffe's head sagged on her neck. There was blood-mottled foam around her lips, down her neck, staining the bright dress. Her eyes were fixed. What had inhabited them was gone.

Dottie sank to the floor, face in Mrs Radcliffe's silk dress and sobbed. 'She was just a young girl,' she said. 'She had so much she hadn't done yet. Who did this to her?' She looked at him with pleading eyes. 'I've worked with her so long, since I was almost a child, since she was barely out of childhood. We grew up together.'

'I don't know that anyone's done it to her,' he said gently. 'Come on, Dottie. There's no sense—' Outside, the wind picked up into a squall for a second, blowing icy snow off the black tree branches, then settling again.

'It doesn't make sense.' She stared at him, damp eyed, sighed and wiped her nose with the heel of her hand. She looked around the room and almost immediately her gaze snagged on something.

She stared at the doorway through to the bathroom. Frank followed her eyes.

'Mary,' he said.

She was standing there, staring at them, pale-faced, leaning against the door frame, the floral drape falling against her tiny frame like a ball gown. She had a half smile on her face that flickered and fractured every few seconds, like a stuttering projected film. Frank stared at her, disbelieving.

'Mary,' said Dottie slowly. 'What are you doing there? Why did you just watch that happen and do nothing? How could you watch her die?'

'Hello, Frank.' Her eyes were wild.

'Mary. How did you get here?'

'Why did you not help Florence? Look at her! Mary!' Dottie was standing in front of Mary, blazing with anger.

'Mrs Radcliffe isn't the type to help others in need, so why should I help her?'

Frank's mind was racing. The blurred image in the window. The narrow, hidden corridors, cramped dumb waiters.

'Mary, what have you got to do with all this?' He took a step closer. 'Tell me what the hell is going on here.'

Her shaky half smile sank and she looked away. 'You underestimated me, Frank.'

And she turned on her heels and left. Frank stood in the middle of the room, staring at the draped doorway to the brightly lit bathroom where she'd been standing. Her image was burned onto his eyes even though she had gone – a shadow version of her shape.

'Frank,' said Dottie, a voice from another world. 'Frank. Frank! We can't just leave Florence here like this. We must tell Lord and Lady Forester. We should tidy her up, we have to make her nice.'

He brought his attention back to the room. To Dottie. To Mrs Radcliffe. 'We can't move her, I'm afraid. We'll have to wait for help to get here in the morning.'

'We can at least cover her.' Dottie went to the wooden chest by the bed and opened a drawer. She walked back to Frank with a silk scarf. There were tears on her face. 'She deserved better. We knew she'd disappeared. We could have caught her in time. She was so young. She had her whole life to live. She would have got married again, had her own house. I'd have stayed with her as she got older, had children, threw parties. I know people judged her for seeming silly and spoilt. Maybe you did too. But there was more to her than that. Inside she was hurt and lost. She wasn't always kind, but she was capable of being better and she would have been, given the chance to grow and learn, like we all have to – she would have been a better version of herself. But she won't have that chance now. She didn't deserve to die. You know that Mary saw it all,' she said, more slowly now. 'She killed her. She stood there and let it happen. She murdered her. She was there in the bathroom all along, wasn't she? Watching, not helping. She was there all the time we were there and for longer, otherwise we'd have seen her walk past us.'

'It was the opium, Dottie, nothing else.' But he knew she was right.

'If you watched me walk off a cliff edge and did nothing, would it be the cliff edge and nothing else?' Her eyes were bright with anger. He didn't say anything. 'She's a nasty piece of work, that girl. She was jealous of Mrs Radcliffe. Always saying things to other people about her, horrible rumours. It was jeal—'

'Rumours about Mrs Radcliffe? What sort of rumour?' he said quickly.

She pursed her lips in irritation at the interruption and passed a hand over her forehead. 'That she pushed people aside – children aside – to get on the lifeboat. You know, when she escaped the ship.' Her eyes filled. 'Mary does that a lot, you know,' said Dottie, her eyes flashing with anger still. 'Puts ideas in people's heads.'

'How exactly would Mary know that?'

'I don't know. You seem to know her better than I do.' She folded her arms.

He turned the stone over and over in his pocket. 'Who did Mrs Radcliffe push aside? Supposedly?'

'I don't know. A young Irish girl,' she said. 'I'm not saying it was right,' she added, her eyes a little more muted.

'An Irish girl who got separated from her family as a result? Never saw them again? Had to . . .' He sighed. '. . . Had to hold on to a boat in the middle of the night to survive.'

He strode out of the room.

# CHAPTER TWENTY-FIVE

## THE SERVANTS' QUARTERS

'Mary!' His voice echoed around the empty hallway. Mocking him, the wind whistled back. 'Mary!' His heart was shoving hot blood around his body, pumping into his chest and cheeks. He ran to the main corridor, his footsteps loud on the stone floor. She was standing at the top of the stairs, stock still.

'Yes?' she said. The smooth curve of her cheek; her shoulder, as delicate as a sparrow's wing.

'We need to talk. Now's your chance to set it all straight. You know you can trust me. What's going on?'

She frowned. 'Why would I want to set it all straight? You're so concerned with things being straight.'

'Thank God you're alive. Four people have died.' He stepped towards her, but she took a neat step backwards. 'The thought I could have saved you in Manchester only for you to—'

'Five,' she said.

'Why did you let Florence die? What have these good people done to you?' Helpless he let his arms fall to his side.

'They are not good people.' She threw her shoulders back, lifted her shaking chin up. 'These people, they think they're better than me; they think they're better than you – they do, you know. I've lived for years as someone invisible, worthless, walked all over by people who think they have some kind of . . . what would you say . . . *grace* . . . when all they have is position. That's it!

Luck of the draw, Frank, luck of the draw, nothing more. Deny me some money when I need it, deny me interesting work when I want it, deny me the same sort of respect you get as a singer when I get none as a poor nightclub waitress, deny me dignity, make me the toy of rich men. Rich men with bad breath.'

*Rich men with bad breath.*

'Who denied you money, denied you work . . .?' But already he was piecing it together. The little maid who'd asked for work, who'd asked for a loan.

'Professor Webber wouldn't give me just a few shillings that I needed to make a fresh start in life! It's nothing to him. Mr Bell wouldn't give me a little job as a shop girl in his store in London. Neither of them even remembered that they'd said no. I was nothing to them, a bit of dirt on their shoe. Off you go, forgotten. I tell you, I hate them all.' Her eyes were gleaming with a wild blaze, the sort that starts with a quiet crackle at the edge of a leaf and turns into a forest fire. 'I've known them all for a while now, Frank, longer than you have. They never did give me what I deserve.' Her shoulders fell.

Frank's breath was quick as he pieced it together. 'You work for . . . the wolf,' he said. 'The war loot wolf. Or raw tool flow, when it's above board.'

She placed a hand on the balcony, leaned towards it. He moved towards her again, but again she edged away. 'You've been working for the Foresters and their darker business interests for years, haven't you?' He took a shuddering breath, the realisation running icily through him. 'Not just here, in this house, for the last few months, but for years – and not just as a maid . . . The stolen Picasso, that . . .' That came to the Forester's house in the summer. He stopped and stared at her helplessly. 'In Manchester – you weren't the witness, were you? You were the . . . Oh, God. I helped you get away . . . I put someone in jail . . .'

'If you say so.' She was smiling shakily again, but her eyes flashed now and then with uncertainty, hollowness, a need for something – he just didn't know what. 'You are foolish Frank, despite your big job and everything. How do you think it works? They just hand guns out to war lords, do it themselves? To criminals? In a neat parcel tied with string? You need a network of hands holding hands. And then anything can go through it. Guns. Money.' She was rubbing her forehead again and again with a shaky hand.

'You've been listening, haven't you? Walking around the air duct passages, going up and down the dumb waiter. Eavesdropping. Doing the Foresters' bidding. Back in Manchester – it was *them . . .*'

She shrugged. 'Maybe.' The corner of her mouth tried to lift.

'But why are you involved here? You don't need to be a lackey. You're better than that.' He took a step closer to her, to where she was standing on the balcony like a promise to fly, but she stepped away again. 'They're just using you,' he said.

'Don't forget. Don't you forget – I hated them all. Every last one of them. The haves. The push-a-poor-Irish-girl-aside ones. I hated them all. Let's go somewhere private and talk.' She let a soft breath out and looked away. 'I thought they needed me,' she said. 'But perhaps they never did. Perhaps I was nothing to them.'

He didn't move, didn't go to her, though he wanted to. 'That's not all you've been doing,' he said. 'You wandered around making sure the clues were easy to find – the note in the paper basket, the scrap of paper in Mr Bell's hand that showed Professor Webber sold bombs, the evidence Professor Webber was running out of money, that he was blackmailing Mr Bell. You made sure it was clear that they all had motives to kill each other. Like Dottie said – it was too neat.' He was flitting through the pieces he'd added up already. He just hadn't joined them to her. 'You were ensuring that the threads all pointed to each other so no one else could be blamed. You put the note together, added the pictures to the calendar.'

'Did I?' she said. 'Come and talk to me. We have a lot in common. A lot more than you might think. Come and talk with me, like old times. Let's have a proper chat. You'll see it's not as bad as you think.' The house was dead quiet. Perhaps everyone was asleep now. Outside was silent too, the wind calm. 'This way,' she said, stepping back away from the balcony without taking her eyes off him. 'Come on Frank, you're all I have now.' The corner of her mouth twitched downwards.

He took a step forward as she moved back. It was as if an invisible cord bound them, her pulling the thread that moved his limbs.

'Good. We see things the same, you and me.' She opened the door behind her, the small, plain door that led to the back, servants' corridor. 'We both of us hate unfairness. We both of us think people shouldn't have power just because of what — because of what family they're born into. How's that fair? This way.'

Shaking his head, he followed her into the servants' quarters.

A plain oak door frame led to a hallway with two doors.

'This way,' she said. She gestured at the closed door to their right.

He didn't move. 'What are you doing? You could be so much more than this. It's not too late.' If he could just convince her, steer her back to the right path. 'Get a proper job in a good house. It's honest,' he said. 'It's steady. It's the road to self-respect.'

'Who needs honest? The world doesn't work like that.' She placed a hand on the curved wolf-tail handle.

'Some of it does.'

'What makes you think I want that bit of it?' She'd tilted her head as if the very idea was puzzling. Her hand was still on the brass wolf's tail. 'The world's dangerous, isn't it? Better to be on the right side of that, with the right people. I'm a good worker, a trusted one – they trusted me, didn't they?' She looked uncertain. 'I did my job well. Didn't I? I got them all nice and worked up. I got them all to do their bits. I got you here, didn't I, just like they asked me to? And now you've seen it all. I did it all perfectly, and it wasn't easy, getting away at the right time, getting it all set up, just so. Putting a fancy voice on and making a telephone call. Cutting through a telephone wire, oh Lord! I'll be given a good job for this, see that I'm not. I'll have enough money, I'll have respect, no one will treat me as a fool. I'll be seen, Frank.' She looked down, rubbing her pale forehead over and over again. 'They'll notice me. Won't they – won't they, Frank?'

He just shook his head and shrugged.

'You know,' she said, looking back up, 'We're the same, you and me. We don't play by the rules, we don't get all settled in a boring life, accept whatever life's dealt us. These aren't good people, Frank. Let 'em kill each other. It's a few less of the bad 'uns about. You're more like me than you know. I hope you don't know it too late.' Her feverish eyes were alight again, crackling with growing flames.

'I'm not like this.' He recoiled from the idea. She'd done her job – he was right. There were two circles here. Mary prompting and hiding and whispering and helping. And the person pulling her strings.

'Come and sit with me.'

She opened the door.

He saw all of it in a flash. A black lace shawl was thrown across the bottom of the unmade bed. A wooden trunk next to the bed was open, revealing a tangle of clothes. The walls were plain. A tin cup on the small table held some coins. A pair of stockings was flung onto the windowsill, next to a pot of powder and a little tub of rouge.

He shook his head and sighed.

# CHAPTER TWENTY-SIX

## THE KITCHEN MAID'S ROOM

Frank heard the clock tower strike. It would be light soon. Outside Mary's room the black sky was stretching out and fading to a deep charcoal. He could just see the top of the pine trees out of her small window – the snow sat inch thick on the branches.

'Come and sit down,' Mary said, patting the bed next to her. 'Make yourself comfy.'

'I'm fine standing, thank you.'

'Come on, Frank. Don't be so standoffish with me.' Suddenly he heard a man's voice. A crisp, well-spoken voice he recognised. *Testing, testing. Testing the new toy*. He stared at Mary, looked over his shoulder. Where was Lord Forester? Then a woman's voice he didn't recognise. *Come and sit down, Lord Forester. Next to me. That's it. Make yourself comfortable.* He looked around the small room, but they were alone.

*Take your jacket off. That's it.* The woman's voice again. She had a strong Manchester accent. You could hear a hint of theatrics in her voice – she sounded like a tired woman play-acting confidence and enthusiasm. There was a wheedling note too; a slight but sharp note of desperation. Now Lord Forester's voice again. *I'm tired, Daisy. Charlie's tired. It's been a long day.*

Frank walked away from Mary's room and into the hallway. It was empty. The voice was just as loud here. It was coming from the walls of the house. That was the noise he recognised – the stutter and crackle of a recording, like a gramophone record. They were listening to the ghost of a past encounter played out over the voice pipes. It all made sense.

The female voice again. *You relax, sir. I know how to help you relax.*

He made his way back to the servants' quarters. There was a crackle in the voices now and then.

Lord Forester spoke again. *You always know how to relax me, Daisy, even better than little Mary does. Let me see you. That's it. Show Charlie. That's right. But tell me what you're doing too. Say it out loud. Tell Charlie a naughty little story about what you're doing.* Frank wanted to run into the room and get her out of there, but this had happened already – she was already somewhere else, doing something else. *Like this, sir? You like this, don't you. You like me to put on a little show for you.*

He walked back into Mary's room. She was sitting on the bed, examining her nails. Her eyes had deep black wells underneath them. Her skin had always been pale but now it looked paper white. Another crackle and the voice changed, a man's voice that Frank didn't recognise. *Ah, Charles, come in. Good to see you. How's business?* And back to Lord Forester. *Rudolph. Good evening, old friend.* There was a shuffling sound, as if furniture, perhaps a heavy chair, was being moved. A cough. Then a long crackle. Then Lord Forester's voice continued . . . *girl is fine. But can you get me something a little more imaginative, a little . . . ah . . . inventive?* Rudolph spoke again. *There's a girl – you've dined with her after my introduction before, I think – one who doesn't mind her friends being a little rough with her. I could put you in touch with her. Mary. Ah, I see from your face that perhaps you're looking for the opposite?*

A last crackle and silence. So, Rudolph arranged girls. He'd known there was something rotten there, something to do with sex, but he'd not spotted this.

Mary nodded. 'Interesting, isn't it?' she said. 'People's private lives. Never what you think.'

'Who do you work for?' he said. 'Prince Rudolph? Prince Rudolph could be the wolf, the head of this little crime network. But no, I think it's Lord Forester, isn't it? He's got you here doing his dirty work, hasn't he? Clearing up his mess, getting rid of people who know too much about his part in the more criminal side of the business, people who know who he is and who can't be trusted. Much simpler to get them all to take care of each other. All you need is someone to encourage them all in the right direction – play to their weaknesses, their insecurities, their fears. Then plant a solution. And who better to do that than a maid? A clever way of keeping his hands clean and getting the story to make sense. While he was at it, why not get a policeman here to witness it and make sure that all the evidence is there for their motivations to kill each other. Someone to witness the theatrics and make it a matter of public record.'

Mary gave a thin smile, on firmer ground now. 'It's just a matter of putting the idea in the right head. Plant a seed and watch it grow. They sprout pretty good with this lot. Professor Webber didn't want anyone to know he wasn't a good 'un. Bombs for Russian terrorists! Mr Gray's so easy to talk smooth to. A little angry boy.' She leaned back against the wall, widened her eyes.

'Perhaps you killed Rudolph,' Frank says. 'Perhaps you unhooked the cable. You're good at making yourself unnoticeable. You slip away and get things done.'

'Oh no, that's not true at all. I was with your little friend Dottie the whole time. She can vouch, she can tell you.'

'And Mrs Radcliffe. You'd met her before, hadn't you? She pushed you aside to get a place on the lifeboat, didn't she? Stood by and watched while your chance slipped away. So you did the same to her. You let her die. May not have been your wisest move, since she's your boss's daughter, though.'

She shook her head, her trembling hand reaching for her forehead again. 'She did that herself. I didn't stop her. But why would I, anyway? She didn't look out for me, did she? She should have died on that ship, but she got a few extra years, didn't she? She still came out on top. She wouldn't have lived through what I did. Clinging on to that cold wood in the dark, waiting for the waves to take me, feeling my breath freezing in my lungs. I drifted away from the ship, sailed off into the dark on my own. All I could do was just hang on. And that's not all. I thought my dear old brother, my only brother, that he was dead because of it. He'd brought me up as my dad and I thought him dead for years – and he thought I was gone too, washed into the bottom of the ocean. We lost each other. Mrs Radcliffe would have given up and drowned but I gave her a few extra years. She got to court that boy she loved so, Peter, and marry him. If anything, she should have been grateful, should have been glad. She wanted to die now, anyhow. She saw nothing left to live for. So, as I see it, I did her a second favour letting her slip off instead of dragging her back to where she didn't want to be, didn't I?'

'Maybe. But maybe in a month or two she might not have wanted that.'

'It feels good, revenge does,' she said. 'You should try it. It makes you feel good. It makes you feel strong.' But she didn't look strong, her slight shoulders bent, her face pale, her hand trembling and her eyes begging for reassurance.

'And Lady Abbott and Mr Bell. You whispered in her ear too, I suppose, about how cruel it was that his father had killed her husband and that Mr Bell had lived an easy life off the money his father stole from her husband. I suppose that was everyone who knew that the Foresters were more than iron barons. Everyone taken care of. Everyone set on each other like dogs.'

He was revolted, despite himself. At the needless death, at the long, simmering anger in every direction. But perhaps most of all, at the ease with which they'd been manipulated into killing for revenge. It said something dark about the human race he was a part of; its single-note fury, its malleability, its senseless selfishness. He felt sickened by Mary's part in it – at her unshakeable certainty that she'd done no wrong.

'An eye for an eye,' said Mary. 'It's all so easy. Everyone's so angry and so vengeful. I even showed her where to change the electrics!' She frowned. 'So easy. *Here you go, my Lady, cut that and it's lethal! You don't want to do that!*' She laughed, catching his eye as if expecting him to join in, then looking away.

He left Mary on her bed, putting some lipstick on and checking her reflection in a small hand mirror.

'Dottie,' he called from the landing. 'You're coming with me. We need to go downstairs. Stay close.' He could hear shouting and banging from the dining room downstairs. 'It's not safe here.'

Dottie came out of Mrs Radcliffe's bedroom. Her eyes were red and her cheeks were wet. She was hugging the big, wine-red coat around herself. 'I always knew Prince Rudolph was a bad man, but Lord Forester—' she said. The banging was louder. They were rattling the door like caged animals. 'I know Prince Rudolph is not a good man,' she said. 'He wasn't respectful. It doesn't surprise me at all, what I heard.' She stopped at the top of the stairs. 'Sounds as though they're angry,' she said, nodding towards the staircase.

He dipped his head in agreement, but he didn't move. 'What else do you know? About his connections to the Foresters' iron-works, to their factories? What do you know? It's important, Dottie. I need to know.'

'I don't know anything. I didn't even know *that*, but it doesn't surprise me one bit.' The banging was a fearful racket now. He could hear Lord Forester shouting. 'It was the voice pipes, you know,' she said. She took a step towards the staircase.

'Think of the footprints in the snow. One set were Prince Rudolph's but the other were a different pair of shoes, with more worn soles. The footprints by the funicular cable were not the footprints of a wealthy man.' He started towards her, but something was holding him back. 'And they'll match Jessop's shoes.'

'No, Jessop wouldn't do anything bad!' Her eyes were fierce.

'I think Jessop's had a few surprises in the last day or so. Where did you say he was from?' There was a thread pulling him, stopping him going downstairs.

'I didn't. Ireland.'

'I thought so. Hold on. Stay here.'

He ran back to Mary's room, but it was too late. The room was empty. Her maid's dress was lying on the bed. She was gone.

# CHAPTER TWENTY-SEVEN

## THE TELEPHONE EXCHANGE

F rank stayed in the dark bedroom for a second, two seconds, three, staring at the empty bed, the empty chair, the black sky outside. Who was she? There was a part to her that was sweet, steady and smart, he was sure of it. Why did she run from it? They could have been happy together. But now it would be impossible to get back to that.

He stared at her bed, her clothes, her hairbrush, her sheets. Where was the person he'd loved in all of this? She'd always felt so beautifully strange, so out of reach. He'd longed to pin her down. Just to have her sit in a room with him for more than half an hour without talking to anyone else. To listen to her private thoughts. He knew he could have made her into the person she always could have been, if only she'd trusted him.

He pictured Mary . . . Mary. Mary with a knife in Dottie's shoulder blades, a silk scarf twisted around Dottie's throat, placing a glass of arsenic-laced milk in Dottie's hands.

He rushed back out. But there Dottie was, just where he'd left her. At the top of the stairs, straight back, clear eyes, serious mouth.

'Let's go,' he said. He glanced at her. 'I need your help. I couldn't have done all this without you.'

She nodded and frowned and yawned, covering her mouth with her pinprick-marked hand.

'It'll be light soon,' he said. 'It won't be long till help comes.' And they could see through the grand entrance hall window that the slate air was fading to pearl. The shouting and door rattling had stopped and everywhere was deadly, deathly silent. All they could hear were their own footsteps, in sync with each other, patting softly on the stone floor. She habitually walked quickly, as did he, but now they were half marching, half running, down the stairs and into the hallway. There they paused, listened, and marched on.

Jessop wasn't in his place at the dining room door. They walked quickly to the butler's room. Jessop sat at his desk, head in hands. The square wooden box with thirty-one numbered doors was on the wall above him. As they watched, the light above door thirty-one went red and there was a single, short ring. Then the light went out and the bell stopped.

Dottie stepped forward. 'Je—'

Frank held her arm and put his finger over his lips.

They watched as Jessop opened his desk and pulled out a telegram machine. He typed four short words, sent the message and put the machine back in his desk. Then, without looking back, he stood up, walked to the back door, opened it and walked out, shutting the door behind him.

'What was he doing?' said Dottie quietly.

'I'd say it's an instruction,' he said. 'Door thirty-one will be the standard code, I'd have thought: the signal to send a certain message. Which room is that?'

'The library.'

'We'd better go there.'

They turned to go and saw Jessop standing behind them, shadowed in the doorway with the wood-panelled hallway stretching behind him. He smiled thinly. 'I thought I'd see what you were up to,' he said. 'I heard voices. Dottie seems to have abandoned me for you tonight.'

'Your accent. I've been trying to place it. It's Irish, isn't it? Dottie was telling me some of your family history. I suppose you were pleased to be reacquainted with your sister after all this time of thinking she'd drowned. You practically brought her up as your daughter, didn't you? You must have been devastated when you heard the work Rudolph had her doing.'

'We were brought up good Catholics.' His eyes were wide, haunted looking. 'We were brought up to be aware of sin,' he said. 'Aware of the consequences of it.' His hands shook badly. 'Some sins aren't forgivable,' he said. 'Some sins can't be washed off.'

'You would have been furious with Prince Rudolph, I'd have thought. Murderous, even. I'm sure it was easy to convince you that the man who'd been peddling her out like a freshly baked loaf should perhaps be finished off. I'm sure Mary had a hand in suggesting it to you, as well – that was her job, after all, to persuade and convince and plant ideas. She'll have given you the why and perhaps even the how.' Dottie stood next to him, her sharp eyes watching both of them keenly.

Jessop snorted. 'How could you possibly know that? It's a guess. A bad one at that.' The yellow lamp light from the hallway made a halo around his dark outline. He swallowed, licked his lips.

'Hours ago you knew that the train had crashed, though I'd never mentioned that. You just walked down and unhooked the cable. Easy. There were your footprints on the hillside, there was fresh mud on your shoes.'

Jessop just shook his head, blankly. Dottie threw him an intense, pitying look.

'Your sister might have some answering to do when her boss catches up with her,' Frank said grimly. 'I don't think Lady Forester will be too pleased that she watched her darling daughter die. That won't have been on Mary's jobs list. Sit down. We'll have to lock you in, I'm afraid.'

Jessop didn't reply, but he moved heavily to the small, stiff chair and sat down in it. His eyes were hollow and glassy, as if his soul had been eaten out of his body. He looked at Frank blankly. Frank gave him a small nod and shut the door. He was relieved to be away from Jessop's haunted, hollow stare.

'What has Lady Forester got to do with it?' said Dottie. 'Did she turn a blind eye to Lord Forester's criminal activities?'

'She has everything to do with it,' said Frank. 'For a while I thought it was Lord Forester, but of course it was Lady Forester. She was the one who had Professor Webber's blind loyalty, not him. She was the one who planned all the renovations to the house. She was the one who ran the business – the cheques were signed in her hand and pen, the same as we saw on the calling cards. She knew the details of the business in a way that he didn't. She was the one with the ambition, with the drive, with the cool head. Unfortunately, those who knew she was the wolf were a problem. She used this party as a way of getting rid of them and, cleverly, she was careful to keep her own hands clean. Careful to make sure the evidence was all there to be found – evidence of who had killed who and how and why. Mary was a useful go-between to ensure all that evidence was there and that everyone stayed to the bitter end, creating even more distance between Lady Forester and the murders.'

'But now *we* know,' said Dottie, looking worried. 'And what about Lord Forester's secrets coming out? And Mr Gray's secret? She can't have been behind those things.'

'I think perhaps she was. A good way of ruining them and making their word worth nothing without having to get blood on her hands.' He thought of Mr Gray's deep grief and his pity flew to him.

'She wouldn't do that to her own husband,' said Dottie.

'She might,' said Frank. 'She just might, at that, if you think of years of mute fury at his ways. It was relatively easy to do, once Professor Webber had set the voice pipes up for her. Another reason to get Professor Webber killed off, of course. He didn't realise he was digging his own grave. Loved her too much to see it, perhaps.'

'She'll want to kill me now then,' said Dottie. 'And you.' Her eyes were wide. She swallowed hard and looked back towards the dining room door and then to Frank again.

'Stay with me,' said Frank. And he threw open the dining room door.

'Lady Forester,' he said. 'A word please?'

'What is it now?' said Lord Forester. His face was red and his eyes were wild. 'It's the middle of the night. We've dealt with more than enough for one evening. Just as we thought we might find some peace and quiet, some awful piece of make-believe theatre starts playing out, blasted every which way. Utter lies, of course.' His fist was clenched by his side and his chest was puffed out.

Lady Forester's expression was volcanic. 'How devastating to hear such things,' she said. 'Charles, you must be so ashamed that you want to die. And to think of it hitting the papers in the morning. Your reputation, my dear, is as intact as a burnt-out car.'

'Do shut up, Sophia.' He walked towards her then stopped, as if he wasn't sure what to do next.

'Oh, I won't shut up. I won't shut up. I've had enough of being silenced, ignored, made to feel small, treated as some sort of worthless idiot. Enough, do you hear me, Charles? Enough. At some point or other everyone gets to a point where they won't take any more. But I think *you* will be shut up now. I don't think anyone will listen to you anymore. Will they, Charles? See how that feels. See how you like being treated as worthless.' She was stock still, fists closed at her sides as if she was trying to hold them there.

'Not in front of our guests, Sophia. You must calm down. You're getting hysterical. Practically foaming at the mouth – not attractive. Someone had an axe to grind. That's the sum of it. It will all be water under the bridge in no time. I think, my dear, you've overestimated the interest anyone has in an important man's peccadillos. No one cares but you. And you've made a fool of yourself, yet again.'

'Lady Forester?' said Frank. 'Please? A word?'

She was standing by the dining table, a slow look of dawning realisation on her face. 'You're finished,' she said, less confidently.

'I do hope,' said Lord Forester, 'you'll look to make an arrest for libel or whatever it's called. Someone has been broadcasting lies about me.' He shot Lady Forester a look. She didn't meet his eyes, standing rock-still. Her body looked as though lava was coursing through it.

'Lady Forester?'

'One second,' she said. 'One second.' She walked quickly to the library. They heard the sound of a telephone receiver being picked up and then, almost immediately, it being replaced. 'I do apologise,' she said, wiping her hands on the front of her skirt as though there was something sticky on them. 'Do lead the way, Sergeant.'

'Dottie, stay in the dining room with us,' said Lord Forester. 'You're our servant. Your place is with us.'

Dottie hesitated.

'She's staying with me,' said Frank. He shut the dining room door behind them. The grey dawn light was creeping through the double-height window in the entrance hall, giving the hall a pearl-ised half-light. 'I'm afraid, Lady Forester, that I'll need to place you alone in a room.'

'Whatever can you mean?' She peered down her nose at him.

'For your own safety,' he said. 'A lot of people have died here tonight and I'm afraid you could be a target. There's a crime ring involved, I'm afraid to say. And unfortunately, it involves your husband.' He started to walk down the grey half-lit hall. Lady Forester followed, Dottie close behind.

Lady Forester laughed joylessly. 'Well, you make him sound awfully clever, I'm sure. You say he deliberately killed our guests, that he's, what, a criminal?' She gave another short, clipped laugh. 'Well, perhaps you're right, Sergeant, perhaps you're right.' She shook her head. 'I suppose it will be prison . . . or worse . . . for him.'

Their feet tapped on the cool, stone floor. Outside, the trees were dropping steady pats of snow and ice onto the cold ground. 'And you gathered everyone here for him, like sitting ducks – without realising it, of course,' said Frank. 'It was so easy for him to line them all up and shoot them down. Or perhaps should I say to line them all up and get them to shoot each other down. He could rely on the perfect hostess to get them here and give them the most wonderful party until they were ready to be slaughtered.' He stole a look at her implacable face. 'Sitting ducks, like I say.'

Her voice was frosty and measured. 'I'm not a perfect hostess; I'm a good hostess. I know who to put on a guest list and who to remove from a guest list.' She trod steadily on down the corridor. 'That's what a good hostess understands – who to add, who to remove.' She sighed. 'There's a little more to it, perhaps, than you may have realised. Or perhaps you have realised. If he did do this, and I'm not saying he did, he didn't do it alone. You'll see that, I'm sure.' She shook her head. 'I have noticed, Sergeant, and you may have spotted this too, that our young kitchen maid Mary has, I'm afraid, rather a chip on her shoulder about the "haves". She'll have set up that little show about Lord Forester, you realise, in a pathetic attempt to destroy the hand that feeds, to somehow imply that, despite being a dirty little ragamuffin, she's better than us. She's the only one who could fit down those funny little corridors with the voice pipes, after all – I'm sure you've already realised that, Sergeant. That's all there is to it. I'm afraid she's rather a tramp.' She smiled. 'And if you'll forgive me, I'll get a little rest. It

could be that you're right about a quiet room and a closed door.'
She let out a deep sigh. 'Perhaps the morning room? I wonder if,
Dottie, you would light the fire? And bring me a pot of tea and
some buttered toast?' She nodded briskly at Dottie.

Frank reached for the door to the butler's pantry. 'A bit of privacy,
Lady Forester. We'll put you in the pantry, rather than the morning room, if you don't mind. It's easy to keep an ear out for you
from here, should you need anything – and this door has a lock. I'll
then separate Lord Forester from the other guests, for their safety
of course. This must be a terrible shock for you. Help will be here
soon. This will all be over soon.' He pushed open the door.

'Awful.' She stood her ground. He pushed the door a little further and stepped in front of it to hold it open, gesturing the way
with his left hand. Lady Forester didn't move.

'Would you mind giving Dottie your pistol, the one that you
keep in your pocket? We had best keep Lord Forester under armed
guard, for the other guests' safety. Don't worry. Help will be here
soon,' he repeated.

She hesitated. Dottie held out her hand. He continued to
hold out his hand towards the butler's pantry – the only downstairs room with no phone and just a small, high window. He
smiled. 'You can help yourself to a cup of tea in here until
Dottie can get you breakfast. If you don't mind, Lady Forester.
I'm sure you'll understand that I'd like to get back to Lord Forester quickly and telephone the station again before any more
time is lost.'

Lady Forester stood her ground. 'Lord Forester. What a terrible shock. Yes, he's an angry man, amoral at times, but would he
do this? I doubt it. He got expelled from school for stealing, did
you know that? You know, perhaps it does all make sense. Perhaps
it does. Devastating. To have one's life whisked away from one.
To go back to being alone, running a house and business without

one's husband. To be free of the joys of wedlock – to be solitary again.'

'Awful. The pistol?'

Lady Forester said nothing. She didn't move for a beat, two. Then she very slowly held out her hand, a small silver pistol in the palm.

'Thank you very much.' Suddenly Lady Forester looked smaller, less steady on her feet. 'Come along. Here we go. This way. You'll find there's a bottle of brandy on the table. A small one might help your nerves. Not a good man, your husband?' said Frank, as Lady Forester took an uncertain step into the butler's pantry. 'You think he may, after all, be capable of such a crime?'

She took another step towards the pantry and then stopped. Her voice suddenly got stronger and more confident again. 'Worse than not good, Sergeant. He is weak, and, like all bullies, the power is a drug to him.' Her voice got a little shriller. A fire was blazing in her eyes. 'And, like all bullies, he assumed his victim would get weaker and weaker, rather than stronger and stronger. Whatever his dessert is for this little mess he's created, be assured it is just.' Her eyes lit up and she stood a little straighter. 'Whatever fate awaits him tonight. Or perhaps another night soon.'

'Perhaps,' he said. 'Please . . .' He gestured towards the butler's pantry again. Lady Forester's eyes flicked towards the telephone handset next to the silver tray on the stand behind them.

'Apologies, Sergeant,' she said. 'I believe I left my glasses in the dining room. I'll just—'

'Dottie will go. Dottie?'

Dottie nodded and walked fast up the corridor, disappearing behind the dining room door.

'Thank you, Sergeant,' Lady Forester said. 'Perhaps I can just have a quiet word with Jessop while we're waiting.' Her eyes flicked straight to the butler's room door. She took a step towards the door. 'You stay here,' she said. 'No need to join me.'

She caught his eyes and he looked back, careful to keep his expression neutral and his posture relaxed. 'I saw Jessop a short while ago,' he said. 'He was fine.'

She nodded 'Of course,' she said. 'I just need to make an arrangement.'

And then Dottie appeared through the dining room door, cheeks slightly flushed. She marched quickly towards them. 'Here, my Lady,' she said, 'I've got your reading glasses.'

Lady Forester stopped in her tracks. 'Why thank you, Dottie. I just need—'

'To arrange for the servants' return?'

'Precisely.'

'All done, my Lady,' she said. 'I spoke to Jessop earlier.'

'Ah.' Lady Forester nodded, hesitated and took a step back towards the butler's pantry door. 'I suppose that's all, then . . .' She stepped over the threshold, took one step, two. Then she looked round and appeared to hesitate. She took a step back towards them.

Frank quickly closed the door and turned the key in the lock.

'Good,' he said. He let out a long breath and Dottie gave him a quick, weary half-smile.

Frank leaned against the smooth wood of the hallway. Dottie leaned on the wall opposite him; the first time he'd seen her look off duty, he realised. 'I'm so tired,' she said, rubbing her hand across her forehead. 'I just want this all to be over. I just want to be alone in my room.'

'Thirty-one doors on the telephone exchange,' he said. 'And that's some sort of signal for Jessop to send a communication. But to whom? And there's something else. Somewhere else I've seen—'

'The advent calendar,' she said, her eyes gleaming. She stepped forward.

'Yes. You're right. It should have—'

'Twenty-four doors, isn't it?' she said. 'Mrs Radcliffe—' she paused, took a deep breath and continued, 'we've only had them at Christmas for a couple of years. But I'm sure they normally stop on Christmas Eve. It's the—'

'Count up to Christmas Day,' he said. 'Yes.' He took it out of his pocket quickly and unfolded it. Thirty doors on the house.

'Here,' she pointed.

Right in the corner of the calendar, not on the main house, but in the distant village there was another door with the number thirty-one in tiny, black brushstrokes. He looked closer. The entire cardboard door was a picture of a cottage. It looked like Frank's own, with a ladder up to the bedroom window. He prised opened the door. There was a cut-out picture of a man asleep in bed. The alarm clock read five o'clock. Next to the bed, a man was standing with a gun.

'That's you,' said Dottie. 'They're going to kill you.' She looked at him quickly. 'Frank,' she said. 'Doesn't that mean they're going to kill you?' She stared at him. 'Frank! And Jessop sent that wire when the signal came through.'

'He did,' he agreed. 'But I'm not there in my cottage now, am I? And I'm forewarned.' But a chill had gone down his back. 'It's good. It's an opportunity to catch more of them, see?' he said. 'Get a little more of the network.'

She nodded but she looked worried. 'If you say so,' she said. 'It doesn't make sense to me. Why have it all there, spelled out? There to be found if someone looked?'

He shrugged. 'People like their little signals and codes. It gets to be like a game to them – like a theatrical piece. People get into criminal activity for all kinds of reasons, but the main one is always power. Feeling strong. Feeling in control.' He glanced at his watch instinctively, without taking in the time. There was somewhere he needed to be, someone he needed to find. He shifted his weight from one foot to the other.

Dottie moved her hand over her hair, tucked it behind her ear, leaned back against the wall. 'I just don't think like a criminal,' she said. 'Maybe I wouldn't be a good detective after all. The sun's going to be up soon,' she added. Out of the window, Frank could see the softening of the black sky, the beginnings of a muted light appearing on the horizon over the black trees and the snow-covered ground.

'Right,' he said. 'Won't be long now till help's here. They'll know to come.' He smiled at her and rubbed his eyes. 'We use signals too, see. If you don't phone in after a night call, they come to get you.'

'It's been a long night,' she said. 'Poor Jessop.'

'Poor Jessop? He killed a man.' He still couldn't get the crushed face out of his mind. Maybe he never would.

'His dreams were crushed. He longed to find his sister, always hoped against hope he'd find she'd not been drowned after all, that he might find her and live a happy life in Ireland with her. And then to find out such awful things about her. To do something like he did to Prince Rudolph, he will have been feeling desperate. He won't be able to live with himself. He's a kind man, a decent man.'

'You see the good in everyone. Let's find him,' he said. And they walked the few steps down the corridor to the butler's room. He held the door open for her.

This time she didn't scream; maybe she'd seen too much now. She just held her hand to her mouth and gasped in horror. Jessop's legs were too high. The feet weren't on the ground. They were swinging too passively, his feet hanging like a wooden doll's below him.

# CHAPTER TWENTY-EIGHT

## THE CLOCK TOWER

They gently laid him down on the cold stone floor. Dottie smoothed his hair and straightened his jacket. Then she took a damp cloth and wiped the corners of his mouth and his cheeks and chin. She straightened his tie and fixed an undone button on his jacket. She looked at Frank enquiringly, helplessly, but he just shook his head. Her head bowed. She sat there for a second or two and then she sat up straighter. Her mouth was set in a straight line. There were no tears in her eyes, though there would be many later. He met her eyes and held them. He didn't need to speak.

'Where are we going?' she said.

He bowed his head slightly at her courage. 'We're going to double check the dining room door is locked and then I'm going to find Mary.' He was about to walk to the door and then he stopped and said, 'You're a good woman. You were a good friend to him. A loyal friend. You weren't to know this would happen. No one could.'

She nodded, but he could see a tiny glimmer of judgement in her eyes. *You could have known,* it seemed to say. Or maybe that was his own judgement. All she said was, 'I'm coming with you.'

'It's not safe,' he said, though what could Mary do, alone? And what would she want to do, now the subjects of her wrath were locked away or dealt with. But he saw the vulnerability beneath Dottie's strength and he wanted to protect her, to show her that someone was looking out for her the way she was looking out for everyone else.

'That didn't stop you before,' she said.

'You were safer with me then.'

'Everyone's locked up now, too.'

'One person isn't,' he said.

'I'm safer with you, then. It's settled.' She pushed the palms of both hands into her lap and stood up, her chin only very slightly trembling. She brushed some hair back from her cheek.

And then there was a loud crash. Dottie jumped and stared at him, open mouthed. And another crash.

He stared at her in horror. 'What . . .?' he said. 'Where . . .?'

'It's coming from—'

They both instinctively glanced upwards. There was a third crash. It sounded like an impossibly enormous weight smashing down into the gravel outside.

'This way,' she said, her breath coming quickly. She led him up the corridor to the corner stairs and up the first flight of stairs. They walked fast. Then they ran. They heard another crash, louder now.

They'd reached the door to the narrow spiral staircase that led to the eyrie suite. He flung it open and ran up the stairs.

'Where? Where am I going? Quick!'

'The clock tower,' she said. 'Be careful. The work's not done. The stones aren't—' She pointed at a wooden door to their left. He sprinted to the door, flung it open and ran. He could see a narrow walkway and a large bell. Mary was outlined against the grey sky, the rising sun behind her. She was as slight as a child with her short hair and straight dress. She was wearing the stockings and heeled shoes he'd seen in her room.

'Mary! What are you doing? Stop. Mary, stop now. Come here.'

Mary had pivoted another of the stone slabs over the edge of the tower. She looked back at him and then she sent it flying to the gravel below. She'd pushed four or five out now, leaving a small gap in front of her.

He took another step towards her. 'Mary,' he said. 'Just stop. Let's talk about it. It's been a long night. You've been brewing this for a while. I know what you get like, Mary. I know how once an idea is in your head you can't let it go. But it's done now. You can stop now. You don't have to do any more damage to these people. It's done. It's all done.'

She lifted up a knife. 'Don't come any closer!' she said. 'I'm warning you, Frank!'

'What are you doing, Mary? This is madness.'

'Of course it is!' she smirked.

'Stop then. So what if they're rich, they're selfish, they're the type to push people aside, tread on them. It's done now. Find better people. Find your own people and forget about these.'

'You were right,' she said. 'They were using me. All of them. Prince Rudolph – I was just a piece of meat to him, wasn't I? Something to sell. One of his girls. I thought it was on my terms, but it never was, was it? I was nothing to him. Not his special girl at all.'

'Why would you want to be his special girl?' The air was ice cold out here, but the dawn was coming. The birds were singing all around them.

'He made me feel good. That a prince would think me worthy of interest. Beautiful, he said I was, and he knew all the best ladies in the world.'

'You are beautiful,' he said, but his words sounded flat and unconvincing.

'Even Lady Forester was using me,' she said. 'I wouldn't have seen that if it weren't for you.'

'Listen—'

'You were right. She just wanted me to do her dirty work. No better than scrubbing the floor, is it, really? Like you said, she'd never take me seriously. I thought I'd be her next in command, that's what they call it, isn't it? A rich lady myself! But you were right, I hate to say it, Frank, but you were right. I was nothing to her. I never would have been. She wouldn't have pulled me up next to her. She'd have kept me pushed down.'

'Mary, it doesn't matter now. You've set them all against each other. They've shown their worst natures and destroyed each other. You achieved what you wanted to achieve. Selfish, cruel people will stop at nothing, will do the very worst.' He looked at her ice-white face. 'So, come down now. Come down and talk to me. Let's sort this out.'

She pivoted another slim slab off the tower and sent it crashing below.

'You're right. I've done it. I've made a show of them. So why not make a show of myself, eh, like I've been doing anyway?' Her eyes were black as a crow's. The early morning sun made a fiery halo from her fine, black hair. The knife was still hanging from her hand, as casually as a tennis racket. The watery sun glinted off it.

'Mary. Come here. Put the knife down and come here. We can sort this out.' He took another step towards her.

She stepped closer to the edge. 'Sort me out with the gallows, Frank?' Her eyes were huge, glittering with a different sun that was shining on a different world that made a different kind of sense.

'You haven't killed anyone.' He said it softly, soothingly.

'James'll be killed won't he, for what he did to Rudolph?' She tilted her head, daring him to disagree.

'James? Jessop, you mean? I don't know,' he lied. 'Nothing's certain yet. The world's a different place to the one it was before. The rules are different. Who knows how it will be seen? We don't know,' he begged her. 'We don't know anything. The war, all that death, all that fear we've lived through. It reset everything, didn't it? We can make different rules, ones we all think are fair.'

She looked at him as though his words were just noises. 'And Mr Gray, for what he did to Professor Webber. I don't care about that, though.' She glared at him. 'He was the same as all of them – rich, sure of himself.'

'Perhaps. Perhaps not.' He thought about Mr Gray's crumpled face. 'It's not as simple as have and have not,' he said. 'Everyone has their struggles.' Perhaps he'd only fully realised that tonight.

She laughed, a laugh that didn't stop when it should have. 'But Lady Forester will be alright, won't she? She didn't do anything herself. She got everyone to do it for her.' Her eyes didn't bear looking at.

'That depends. Come on now, Mary; come down. Put the knife down and come with me.' He could sense Dottie behind him, on the steep staircase. She stayed there, not moving. The low sun lit the white landscape with a peach glow. Frank could hear a motor-car in the distance. The birds were whistling up a fury now. You could see the rocks on the scarpside, poking their faces through the snow.

'Come on, Mary,' he said. 'Trust me. Mary, trust me.'

She was standing in the makeshift doorway she'd created on top of the tower, framed by the orange sky. Her eyes were black with kohl. She smiled at Frank and leaned back.

'Goodbye, Frank,' she said, and she disappeared from view.

Frank ran.

She fell silently. Until a ghastly thud.

He stood on the tower. He couldn't look down.

Already the sky was brightening. They'd be here soon. He felt Dottie's presence behind him, but he didn't turn around.

They'd be here soon.

# EPILOGUE.

## THE COTTAGE.

19 December 1924

Frank kicked off his shoes, lifted the needle onto the gramophone and picked up his glass. The whisky smelled of distant fires and peat. He could hear a brass band playing carols in the village square. He unfolded the newspaper. *Blue-blood murderer found: husband kills wife and mistress.*

It was long dark outside, but from the light of the cottage window he could see the wet village streets, last week's snow turned to sludge from tramping feet and cartwheels and the odd car or bicycle that had risked it. Just a week ago the village had been a mess of police and officials. But already all was quiet again. And all would be quiet for quite a while. His own heart was still sore with horror, bigger gaps had started to appear between the waves.

He took off his tie and lay down on the small sofa, his socked feet overlapping the end by a good foot or so. His eyes were itching with fatigue but there was no winding down after a week like that week, after a night like last night, after a day like today, lying in wait like a piece of cheese in a trap, waiting for Lady Forester's men to come and get him. But he – and Marsh and Riley – had been a step ahead of the game; this time, anyway. He had no chance of sleep for a good couple of hours, maybe more. His feet tapped along to the gramophone music and his middle finger beat time on the side of the sofa. If he were in Manchester, he'd go out for a dance and get the wild feeling out of his system. Maybe he'd be back there before long – quite a coup in a night, and then another one a week later. Atkins was pleased.

The image of Mary falling, black figure against black sky. The thud. Then the silence. Gone so quickly. Gone so willingly. Did she know she'd die? Did she somehow think she'd rise and fly? The glint in her eye, the fever in her cheek. Maybe she could have been saved. Maybe he could have saved her.

He went through all he knew about her, from the first meeting in the club to their evenings together and whispered plans. Where was the place that the story could have been changed; before she'd bought the gun; before she'd got in with Lady Forester? Or was it, could it have been, might it even have been so much more recently – the day before the party, the morning of the party, even? Had there been a point he could have spoken quietly to her and diverted her to another path, or was it all long written in stone by then?

He pictured a young, slight, frightened girl, drifting alone in the cold and dark water for hours, not knowing if help was any-where near, not knowing if she'd freeze to death, starve, die from a lack of water or an excess of it. He thought of the fear and the anger and how there was nowhere for either to go, and how if something foul grows and grows but its container doesn't there is no option but for it to rip the container apart. It was a law of physics, you might say. He tried to rewrite it and put himself in the picture somehow, be on the ship, get on the driftwood with her, float there with her, keep her talking, keep her focused, keep her inside herself. Hold her hand, tell her to mute the anger, calm the fear, just wait and be quiet and be still and try not to worry. That he was there.

But he hadn't been there.

He poured another whisky.

Kate Hulme

He hadn't been there. She was alone. She drifted without him, alone with her thoughts and her terror. She drifted off and in his mind's eye now he watched her, helpless, knowing what would come but unable to stop it – unable to save her.

His mind drifted off too, to another woman and another time, another life senselessly crushed too soon. He sighed, a long, deep, rattling sigh, and allowed himself to properly think of her, his dear, cherished ma, to let his thoughts linger on her without shying away for the first time in a very long time. Perhaps for the first time since she'd gone all those years ago. He thought of her quick laugh, quick mind, quick temper, her mouth quick to kiss, her arms quick to hug. He thought of the huge loss of her voice, her chuckle, her breath. He thought of her smiling face, so alive – always so alive – and he could almost picture her in front of him, looking at him with so much love. He smiled, a sad smile, but a smile nonetheless. He reached out a hand for her, touched the warm hand that wasn't there, and then he let go. He let her walk away into the darkness. He was alone, on his small sofa; she was gone. But it was alright. He was alright.

The sky outside his small window got blacker and blacker. He could see the North Star from here. A sure, steady point. Bright and showing the way, should anyone need it.

It was time to stop living alone. He thought he'd look into getting a dog. Perhaps call it Red. Nothing wrong with a bit of companionship. Nothing wrong at all.

# ACKNOWLEDGEMENTS

Thank you to:

Tony Barry, for getting me out of a plot hole
Melissa Cox
Erika Koljonen
Libby Martin, for a great idea about birds
Lisa Rigg, for the photo
Morgan Springett
Joanna Swainson
Jon Wood

And Maud, Ben and Bert Barry